SHADOWS
OF THE
LOST SUN

SHADOWS OF THE LOST SUN

The Map to Everywhere:
Book 3

by Carrie Ryan & John Parke Davis

Illustrations by Todd Harris

Little, Brown and Company
New York Boston

Copyright © 2017 by Carrie Ryan & John Parke Davis
Illustrations copyright © 2017 by Todd Harris

Cover illustration copyright © 2017 by Todd Harris. Cover copyright © 2017
by Hachette Book Group, Inc.

Little, Brown and Company
Hachette Book Group
1290 Avenue of the Americas, New York, NY 10104
Visit us at lb-kids.com

First Edition: January 2017

Little, Brown and Company is a division of Hachette Book Group, Inc. The Little, Brown name and logo are trademarks of Hachette Book Group, Inc.

The publisher is not responsible for websites (or their content) that are not owned by the publisher.

Library of Congress Cataloging-in-Publication Data

Names: Ryan, Carrie, author. | Davis, John Parke, author. | Harris, Todd, illustrator.
Title: Shadows of the lost sun / Carrie Ryan & John Parke Davis ; iillustrations by Todd Harris.
Description: First edition. | New York : Little, Brown and Company, 2017. | Series: The map to everywhere ; book 3 | Summary: "Marrill and Fin continue their adventures as they race to stop the destruction of the Pirate Stream by a frightening ancient power whose coming was prophesized in The Map to Everywhere"—Provided by publisher.
Identifiers: LCCN 2016022402| ISBN 9780316240888 (hardcover) | ISBN 9780316240871 (ebook) | ISBN 9780316240857 (library edition ebook)
Subjects: | CYAC: Adventure and adventurers—Fiction. | Pirates—Fiction. | Maps—Fiction. | Fantasy. | BISAC: JUVENILE FICTION / Action & Adventure / Pirates. | JUVENILE FICTION / Fantasy & Magic. | JUVENILE FICTION / Social Issues / Friendship.
Classification: LCC PZ7.R9478 Sh 2017 | DDC [Fic]—dc23
LC record available at https://lccn.loc.gov/2016022402

ISBNs: 978-0-316-24088-8 (hardcover), 978-0-316-24087-1 (ebook)

Printed in the United States of America

LSC-C

10 9 8 7 6 5 4 3 2 1

For Sam and Jake, who sat patiently
by our side throughout.
Our memories of you are woven through every word.

Contents

Ship's Log of the Streamrunner *Enterprising Kraken,*

a vessel of peculiar design and origin (privately owned)

Logkeeper: Coll, Ship's Captain

Crew List

- Ship's Wizard Ardent
- Deckhand Remy
- Deckhand Marrill   ^and Stowaway Fin!
                                          —Marrill
- Quartermaster Naysayer
- ~~Wizard Annalessa~~ ☹️

Note: Ship's wizard taking this loss very hard.

^Unreasonably Dangerous
Cargo Manifest

- One (1) Bintheyr Map to Everywhere, with evil wizard Serth <u>and</u> Stream-destroying Lost Sun of Dzannin trapped inside
- One (1) orb filled with concentrated Stream water, capable of granting one wish, at the cost of unleashing an evil living fire and a tide that turns everything to iron
- One (1) Wiverwane, living memory of ancient wizards. Creepy-looking.

Remarks

<u>Squidsday, 5th of Ambletide</u>

Clear skies, light breeze from SSW. Chased by
Iron Ship down massive whirlpool into city outside
of time called Monerva. Destroyed an out-of-control
wish machine, stopped a living fire from conquering
the Pirate Stream, evacuated city in wake of
apocalyptic Iron Tide. Returned through whirlpool
and arrived twelve and a half seconds after first
entering. Day otherwise uneventful.

<u>Fetchday, 6th of Ambletide</u>

Partly cloudy with mild lizardrain, strong breeze
from E. Set course today for the Ashen Flume, the first
on list of destinations provided by Ship's Wizard
Ardent. Ship's wizard convinced the apocalyptic
Meressian Prophecy is still unfolding, and the metal-
clad mariner known as the Master of the Iron Ship
is key. Master now believed to be one of the Wizards
of Meres, ship's wizard's old comrades. <u>Kraken</u> is to
visit each of the remaining members to uncover his
identity.

Personal note: Have decided to promote Remy to first mate, teach her to sail the <u>Kraken</u>. Impressed by her natural ability. Has all the makings of a great captain.

Wickeday, 8th of Ambletide

Ashy sky, ash wind carrying ashclouds from ashward. Arrived at Ashen Flume, found name to be appropriate. Ship's wizard and Deckhand Marrill disembarked, returned unharmed. Landing party reports locating former Wizard of Meres Forthorn Forlorn—turned to iron.

Locals reported major storm blew through just last night. Storm with red lightning. Master clearly survived Monerva and remains a threat. Spirits low.

Settleday, 10th of Ambletide

Crystalline seas, heavy breeze from top down. Course set for next destination on list of Wizards of Meres: The Great Game of Margaham, whatever that means. Decided to take a slightly meandering path. Lovely stretch of dreampuffs off starboard, and the sun is just right. After recent events, crew deserves a break.

CHAPTER 1
A Lazy Day in the Sunshine

"Hey, hold this," Marrill said, passing her sketchbook to a deckhand.

Through the waving stalks of giant dandelions, a lilting melody drifted over the *Enterprising Kraken*, wrapping Marrill in the arms of a lovely daydream. Karny lay belly up in her arms, exposing his soft tummy to the sunlight that wove through the great fluff balls leaning over them. Not far from her, Fin dozed against the railing, arms behind his head, feet kicked up against the side of the forecastle.

On the quarterdeck, Coll let out a playful laugh. Remy guided the ship under his watchful eye, navigating it through green stems that sprouted straight up from the waters of the Pirate Stream. Marrill smiled at how happy her babysitter seemed, even though they were both so far away from home.

"What a perfect day," Marrill murmured.

Even Ardent had come out of his cabin to enjoy the scene. It was good to see his grandfatherly smile again. Ever since they'd left Monerva, the wizard had taken on a haggard look, as if the cheer had drained right out of him. After their discovery of Forthorn Forlorn at the Ashen Flume, Marrill had half feared she might never see him smile again.

"The Soporific Straits," Ardent announced to a sailor behind him. "Or so I name this place. I daresay I have not passed this way before, but I will make a habit of doing it again in the future. Just lovely." He reached out and stroked a hand across a puff ball, sending a cloud of fuzz dancing through the air.

"It's kind of hard to see through this stuff," Remy said, but it was barely a complaint. Coll was teaching her to navigate the ship by feel, after all, and the Ropebone Man and pirats made sure the leaning dandelions didn't tangle with the rigging. The world was peaceful, soft, and pleasant. After everything they'd been through, traveling through the Soporific Straits was like getting a massage straight on the brain.

Marrill knew that this was just a brief detour on their way to the Great Game of Margaham, that soon enough they would be facing untold dangers to unravel the secrets of the Master of the Iron Ship. But right now, the trip could take eternity, and she wouldn't mind one bit.

"I like your sketches," the deckhand said. He held up the pad, showing a drawing of old ships resting on scarred rock in a barren desert. Marrill could barely muster the energy to look over. He was a small man, dark haired and olive skinned like Fin. She hadn't seen him before. But then, the sailors were such an integral part of the ship, she barely noticed them at all.

"Thanks," she mumbled. Rumbly Karny purrs drifted up between her fingertips as she rubbed the ruff of his neck. "That used to be the harbor of the Salt Sand King, back before he burned his whole kingdom to ash. Those ships were his fleet. Can you believe it?"

The deckhand nodded. "Oh, yes. I see his sigil on their hulls now," he said, pointing to the symbol of a dragon beneath the waves of the Wish Machine, carefully drawn on the side of each vessel.

The melody of the straits whispered softly in Marrill's ears. "Yep," she said with a yawn. "Did you know Fin was supposed to be part of his army?"

"Is that right?"

"Turns out." Marrill nodded. That was something else they'd discovered in Monerva. Fin's origins. Why he was so forgettable. "Way back when, the Salt Sand King wished for an unbeatable army and spies who could never be seen. And Fin's people were the spies. Isn't that cool?"

"It sure is," the deckhand said. "Wonder where they are now."

Marrill shrugged. "No idea. The Salt Sand King was trapped in Monerva and never actually saw them. But now that old Salty is out of the picture, we're totally going to help Fin find his family."

She looked over at Fin. He snored ever so slightly, tossing his head in the sunshine. Of course, it would be kind of tricky convincing the crew to help find Fin's people; no one but her even remembered him for more than a few minutes. And with the Master of the Iron Ship out there, Ardent was pretty determined to visit the other Wizards of Meres. But she would make sure they found Fin's mom. No matter what.

It was one of the main reasons she'd stayed on the Stream. She couldn't leave him here alone, to be forgotten again.

Marrill sighed as the wind trailed through her hair, dandelion puffs tickling her cheeks as they drifted past. Thinking about Fin's mom reminded her of her own. She couldn't imagine what it would be like to grow up without her parents. And *that* reminded her of the other reason she'd stayed on the Stream. Back home in her own world, her mom was sick. There had to be something, in all the magic of the Pirate Stream, that could help her.

Fortunately, Marrill still had time to find it. Her mom and dad were still in Boston. They wouldn't be missing her yet. And even if it took a little longer, even if they figured out she was gone again, showing up with the magic to make her mom better would make it all worth it.

Besides, Monerva had shown her that time could be flexible. Maybe she would find a way to go back home before she'd even left.

She closed her eyes and let the melody wash over her, smiling at the sound of Fin's snores. The sun speckled her skin, and the breeze was cool on her cheeks. Just yesterday, it had all been overwhelming: finding Fin's people; curing her mom; knowing that the Master was still out there, playing his role in the Meressian Prophecy to bring about the end of the Stream.

But in the peace of the Soporific Straits, that all seemed doable somehow. Just new adventures to have, new quests to embark on. The worst was behind them. No more living fires. No more Iron Tide chasing them through whirlpools. No more Serth spouting dark prophecies and turning people into weeping slaves.

"You know what would be a good idea?" one of the sailors whispered in her ear. "We should all go check on something. Something *inside*."

Marrill's drowsy mind couldn't tell if she was sleeping or awake. She felt like she needed to check on something... but she couldn't even tell where the thought had come from. She grasped for the first thing that came to mind. "The Map to Everywhere?"

"Sure," the voice whispered. "The Map to Everywhere... You really should check on it... *now.*"

Marrill sat up with a start, looking around. Right behind her, a sailor was strolling away, joining a few others walking the deck, securing the ropes. She shook her head, realizing she'd been dozing.

A thought occurred to her, still clinging from the dream. "Hey, Ardent," she called, lowering Karny to the ground. The cat gave her a withering glare with his one good eye and slunk over to plop down in a sun patch. "I just had the strangest thought—maybe we should check the Map?"

Ardent turned away from some poor sailor he'd caught in a lecture and raised an eyebrow. He seemed to roll the thought around in his head. "Odd you mention it. I was *just* thinking there was something I needed to check on...."

"Me too," Coll added from the quarterdeck. "Remy and I were just talking about it with..." He looked around.

Remy looked around the other way, mimicking the motion. "Someone," she finished.

"Most peculiar," Ardent said. "Well, if we all had the same thought...hmm...it *has* been a while since we checked on the Map. Perhaps we best follow our joint intuition." He spun, lazily kicking aside the hem of his purple robe, and ambled toward his cabin at the rear of the ship. Marrill rose to follow, leaving Fin to snooze in comfort for the time being.

Inside, the wizard's cabin was a wreck. Boxes lay on their sides, one of them oozing a bulbous pink substance. A scary-looking nightmare shield hung crooked over the bed, which was itself heaped with random debris. Nearly every surface was piled with open books and old scrolls filled with Ardent's florid writing.

She picked up the book nearest her, glancing idly at the spine. "*Riddles in the Dark*," she read. Her eyes skipped to the subtitle. "*On Magical Games and Playing to Incinerate.*"

"Oh, not *literally* incinerate," Ardent offered as his fingers entered the combination to a lock only he could see. "Usually. Regardless, all valuable knowledge we will need if we are to best Margaham at his game. Which is, of course, the only way to have a meaningful conversation with the crazy—ah, here we are!"

Ardent turned to them, slapping the Map to Everywhere onto the center of the table. It still surprised Marrill how ordinary the thing could look—just a scrap of old parchment with curling corners. And yet, it held tremendous power. The Map could lead you anywhere you needed to go. And with its Key, you could use it to find anything on the Pirate Stream.

But the Map was more than that. It was a prison created by the Dzane, the first wizards. They made it to hold the Lost Sun of Dzannin, the mythical Star of Destruction, prophesied to destroy the entire Pirate Stream. And now Serth, the Meressian Oracle who'd spoken that Prophecy, was trapped inside it as well.

The last time she'd seen the Map in Monerva, it had been blank. But now lines of ink flowed across its surface, tracing together into the scrawled shape of a bird.

"Rose!" Marrill breathed.

The Compass Rose of the Map to Everywhere flapped to life, beating her scrawled wings as if trying to claw her way off the page. Her beak opened in a soundless screech, filling Marrill with dread.

"Is that...normal?" Remy asked.

Ardent shook his head. "No.... She's trying to warn us of something." He bent over the parchment.

"I don't like this," Coll said. "I don't like any of this. Something isn't right."

Marrill gulped. She could feel it, too. Something was off. A memory tickled the back of her mind but danced away when she tried to grab it. "Do you think it's the Meressian Prophecy?"

Ardent arched an owl-like eyebrow at her. "All the more reason for us to hurry to reach Margaham. Because if it is, something very significant is about to hap—"

Just then, Fin flew into the room at a full run, chest heaving, eyes wide. "We've been boarded!"

"Nice of you to announce it," Coll growled, advancing with one hand on his dagger.

Fin shook his head furiously. "Not by *me*. I'm with Marrill."

Marrill sighed, nodding to reassure the others. As forgettable as Fin was, Coll tried to throw him in the brig at least twice a day. "He's with us," she reminded the captain. "Fin, what's going on?"

"Shhhh!" he hissed. "Look!" He slammed his body up against the side of the doorframe, peeking out at the deck beyond. "They're everywhere!"

As one, they all joined him at the doorway. But as Marrill scanned the deck, she didn't see any invaders. Just sailors, pulling ropes and securing lines.

"Are you all right, young man?" Ardent asked. "There doesn't seem to be anyone out there."

Remy nodded in agreement. Over her shoulder, Coll snorted derisively. Marrill touched Fin lightly on the arm, wondering if perhaps he'd just woken from a bad dream.

But Fin looked at them like they were crazy. "What about all those *people*?" he whispered, pointing from one crewman to the next.

Marrill's brow furrowed. Now that she was forced to focus on them, now that Fin specifically pointed them out, the sailors *were* all behaving quite oddly. They weren't hauling ropes, she realized, so much as tying them to one another in a tangle. Instead of raising and trimming the sails, they'd lowered them. Several clustered together, whispering and motioning toward the cabin. One leaned off the bowsprit, waving a shiny mirror to catch the light.

Signaling to someone, Marrill realized.

Remy leaned in beside her. "What's going on with the deck...hands...?" She trailed off.

Fin caught Marrill's eye. Coll twitched with fear-tinged anger. Ardent stroked his beard furiously. Marrill gulped and dared to say what they were all thinking:

"The *Kraken* doesn't have any deckhands."

CHAPTER 2
A Few Extra Hands

Fin blinked in disbelief. Twenty, maybe even thirty, sailors moved across the deck as if they belonged there. It took a lot of effort to look that effortless. Fin knew—he'd done the same thing a million times himself.

But style wasn't the only thing he had in common with the invaders. They all had olive skin, dark hair, rounded features. Features he recognized from the fragments of his earliest memories, back from the night he first arrived at the Khaznot Quay when he was a child.

They were the features of his mother. The same features he saw every time he looked in a mirror.

These people looked like *him*.

The revelation twirled around in his stomach, fear and awe and hope and confusion all mixed together as one. Heart pounding, he spun to face the rest of the *Kraken* crew. "How long have they been on board?"

Ardent frowned. "How long has who been on board?"

Fin resisted the desire to roll his eyes. "*Them*," he said, flinging an arm toward the sailors.

"Oh." Ardent's forehead pinched. "We seem to have been boarded. When did that happen?" he asked Coll.

"Um," Coll said.

Marrill and Remy glanced at each other, slow embarrassment creeping across their faces.

Fin raised an eyebrow in alarm. "You don't know?"

Remy shrugged. "I remember talking to someone earlier, but...it just didn't seem that significant."

Ardent tugged on his beard. "Powerful magic must be at work here. And yet, I would have sensed *that*. Whatever is causing this, it isn't magical."

Fin sucked in a breath. Ardent had said the same thing to him when trying to explain Fin's own forgettability. That confirmed it. He turned to Marrill, his eyes wide. "Marrill, they're like me! These are my people!"

"A traitor, I knew it!" Ardent snapped. "I mean, I didn't

know it. I don't know *you*. But you seem a treacherous sort, now that I spend some time with you."

"Hush, Ardent," Marrill said. "Fin's our friend. He'd never betray us."

Fin flashed a smile of thanks at her. But as nice as it was to be championed, it didn't answer the many questions bubbling up in his head. His thoughts raced out, stumbling across one another until one made it through. "What are they doing here?"

"I'd like to know the answer to that myself," Coll said, a sharp frown creasing his forehead. He pushed himself from the doorjamb and strode confidently out to the center of the deck. The rest of the *Kraken* crew followed.

"You lot," Coll barked. "Explain yourselves. Now. And don't leave out the part about why I shouldn't just throw every one of you in the brig for boarding my ship without permission."

Ardent cleared his throat and stepped forward, taking charge. "What the good captain is saying is..." He frowned, looking at the newcomers and then back at the crew as though struggling to remember. "Welcome aboard?"

"That's not what I was saying at all," Coll corrected.

"It wasn't?" Ardent asked.

"I..." Coll's mouth hung open a moment. And then he closed it, scowling. "Maybe?"

"You were asking them to explain themselves," Fin

reminded them. Ardent and Coll both looked at him, the usual fog of forgetfulness clouding their expressions.

Fin threw up his hands in exasperation. "You, with the braid," he called, pointing at a thin rail of a man who'd been flashing his mirror from the bow. "Yes, you. Don't duck away. I can see you. Still see you. Still see you."

The thin man straightened and crossed his arms. But it wasn't he who answered. A girl stepped out from behind him, her long dark hair framing her wispy features.

Fin recognized her instantly.

He'd only run into her once before. Or rather, *she* had run into *him*, fleeing from guards in the musty, squishy streets of Belolow City. But he was sure it was her. After all, before today, she was the only person he'd ever met who was like him. Running into her had given him hope that he wasn't alone. That there were others like him, others who might hold the answer to finding his mom.

This girl may have been forgettable, but he couldn't possibly forget her.

She beamed at him. "Brother Fade," she said, stepping toward him. "It *is* you!"

Fin narrowed his eyes at her cheerful greeting. They hadn't exactly parted on great terms; she'd framed him for her own crimes and fled the city. And then there was the small matter of the silver bracelet he'd swiped off her wrist in the process. Which she of course hadn't noticed, what with Fin being a master of thievery.

Then again, her presence on the *Kraken* strongly indicated she *had* picked up on it at some point.

At his side, Marrill leaned close. "You know this girl?"

"Of course he does," the girl chirped.

Fin crossed his arms, trying to appear nonchalant, as though his heart wasn't beating like a herd of giraffalisks. Whether she was here for the bracelet or not, *she was here.* A million questions raced through his head, but he swallowed them all. Knowing how desperate he was for answers would only give her the upper hand.

"You owe me a Puff-Decoy," he told her. "I had to use my last one getting away from those guards who were after you." The girl threw her head back and laughed. Fin felt a smile of his own twitching at his lips. "So what brings you to the *Kraken*?" he asked her. "Uninvited, I might add."

Her expression sobered. "We came for something, Brother. Something very important to us."

Ardent stepped forward. "Lovely!" he announced. "A negotiation it is. Coll, fetch my ransoming hat. Marrill, brew up some bargaining tea." He cupped one hand over his mouth. "Make it strong," he whispered.

All the sailors laughed together. "Oh no, friends," said the thin man with the braid. "*We* don't make bargains."

Ardent sighed. "Thieves then, is it? Very well. Make that my ransom-*taking* hat." He narrowed his eyes menacingly. "And cancel the tea."

"Guys?" Next to them, Remy tugged at Coll's arm. "Did the music here always have drums?"

Fin paused, listening. Sure enough, a steady drumbeat danced through the melody of the straits. Something about the rhythm was familiar to him. It made his mouth go dry and his gut clench. His heart seemed to fall into the same pattern, the beats short and fast.

Marrill pointed off the port side. "I think it's coming from that direction."

Fin spun just as the dandelion stalks bent aside in the distance. The prow of a great ship hove into view, fluff scattering on the breeze in its wake. She was bigger than the *Kraken*, broad and ribbed and rigged for battle. Fin couldn't see the mark emblazoned on her side, but he didn't need to. He already knew it was there.

A dragon beneath a wave-filled circle. The same sign he'd seen on the girl's ship back in Belolow. The same sign he'd seen in Monerva. The sign of his people.

The sigil of the Salt Sand King.

"We've got company!" Coll shouted. Without hesitating, the captain sprinted for the quarterdeck. "Ropebone, pirats, full sail!" he bellowed as he spun the wheel to put the oncoming ship behind them.

The ship's rigging sprang to motion all by itself. But just as quickly as they started moving, the ropes snapped to a screeching stop. Everywhere Fin looked, the lines had been tied together, tangled into elaborate knots, secured in the wrong places.

So this was what these "sailors" had been up to, he realized. They'd crippled the *Kraken* so this new ship could overtake her.

Fin spun toward the forgettable girl. She smirked at him, an eyebrow raised. "Sorry, Brother," she said with a shrug. "But we can't let you leave. Not until *they* arrive."

Fin's eyes darted to the knotted lines, tugging and testing themselves. The boarders had tied the *Kraken* up good. Good enough to disable just about any ship.

But then, they weren't on just *any* ship.

"Oh, looks like no one told you bloods," Fin said with a laugh. All around them, ropes slithered to life, untying themselves in a flurry. Sudden confusion danced across the girl's features. "A few knots are no match for the *Enterprising Kraken*."

Pirats galloped across the deck and through the rigging, unsecuring and resecuring lines. The boarders jumped after them, trying to keep the ship under control, but it was too late. Behind Fin, Ardent raised his hands and, with them, the main sails.

Dandelion seeds filled the air as the *Kraken* jumped to life, crashing through the stalks of fluff. Fin snatched one, twirling it between his fingers as he swaggered toward the forgettable girl. He pointed it back at the menacing vessel chasing them. "Bad breath of breeze on that one, jog. Seems we're going to miss your connection after all."

The oncoming ship was already losing ground. It was fast, no doubt. Just not *Kraken* fast. The girl's smirk faltered. She didn't seem to know what to say.

"New plan, brethren. Retreat and regroup!" the thin man with the braid called, waving his hand in a circular motion. The fake crewmen swarmed to one side of the ship. Two of them swung a coiled rope ladder over the railing to a small getaway boat lashed against the hull below.

The girl stepped back, moving to join her compatriots. "Time to go," she said, waving Fin after her. "Come on, Brother!"

Fin blinked. She was looking at him like she expected him to join her. "Come on? I don't even *know* you. I'm not going anywhere."

She tilted her head to the side as though trying to fit a new piece of information into an existing puzzle. "But...I can't just leave you. Not after we've been looking for you all this time."

It wasn't easy to render Fin speechless. But the forgettable girl had succeeded in robbing him of coherent thought once again. He opened his mouth and closed it twice before finally getting out, "For me?"

She blinked. "Of course. Don't you get it, Brother? We came here for you. Your whole family has been looking for you for years!"

Fin's legs seemed to have suddenly been replaced with

jelly. "I have a...family?" His heart tripped unsteadily. The words sounded foreign in his ears.

"Come on, Sister Fade," the last of the crewmen yelled, slipping over the side. "We'll find another way on another day."

"Hold up!" the girl cried back. She grabbed Fin's hand. "Of course you do! Didn't you know? Didn't your mom tell you who you are? Didn't she tell you about the Rise and the Fade?"

Fin could barely even shake his head. "My mom left me at the Khaznot Quay when I was four. I've been searching for her ever since."

Her eyes widened in confusion and then concern. "Oh, Brother Fade," she said, placing her other hand on top of his. "The Khaznot Quay? That's where you've been all this time?"

There was a shout from below. "Time to go!" called the man with the braid, waving for her to hurry.

"Wait!" Fin protested. She couldn't leave. There was so much he didn't know. So much he wanted to ask her. "What did you mean, 'all this time'? Who are you, really? Where do you...I...*we* come from?"

"Come back with us," the girl urged, tugging him toward the ladder. "We can answer everything."

Fin's heart jumped. He'd been searching for answers for so long. And here they were, just a few steps away. He glanced across the deck of the *Kraken*.

Coll and Remy stood on the quarterdeck, one holding the wheel as the other called out orders. Ardent stood behind them, his long white beard and the tip of his cap flapping wildly in the wind. "Faster, faster!" he called, like a kid on a playground. Marrill was laughing, chasing Karny across the deck as he leapt and batted at the floating white tufts filling the air.

With the forgettable interlopers forgotten and the pursuing ship now hopelessly behind, they seemed to be genuinely having fun. No one was missing him. He could easily slip away.

Then Fin snapped back to his senses. Marrill had given up her chance to go home to her family after they'd defeated the Salt Sand King, just to help Fin find his mom. And she still needed to help her own mom. He couldn't abandon her.

"I can't." Fin's voice broke. He swallowed. The thought welled up inside him before he even had time to think it over. "But...why can't you stay here?"

"Me? Stay here? I..." The girl looked back to her people. Below, the tiny getaway boat crashed against the *Kraken*'s hull as it bounced along in the larger ship's wake. The girl bit her lip, face scrunched up in concentration.

As suave as Fin wanted to be, it all dropped away in that moment. He'd been searching for his mom his entire life. He didn't know much about this girl and her people. He didn't know whether he could even really trust her. But she was like him. The only person he had ever met like him. And she knew where he came from, how he got here; she had come *for him*.

"P-please?" he stammered.

"Last chance, Sister Fade!" the braided man called from below.

"Well…" She bit her lip again. "I did let you get away once. When I ran into you at Belolow—I didn't even realize who you were until I was back on the ship and we'd sailed away. So…I guess I owe it to you not to let that happen again." She nodded, as if convincing herself. Then her lips spread into a huge grin. "Okay, I'm staying!"

She turned and called over the side of the ship, "I'm staying, brethren! Tell the Rise I'll keep him safe!" She immediately tugged free the ladder, letting it drop toward the getaway boat below. The rope exploded into a riot of skipping stones as it splashed into the raw magic that was the waters of the Stream.

The girl turned back to him. The smile on her face was excited and nervous all at once. Fin knew exactly how she felt.

"Make a wish," Marrill said, coming up beside them. She held out a big dandelion puff in front of him.

He couldn't help laughing. "Shouldn't we be done with wishing after what happened in Monerva?"

She giggled. "No, silly. It's what you do with dandelions where I'm from. You make a wish and then blow the seeds into the air. If you manage to scatter them all, then your wish comes true."

Fin glanced at the white bit of fluff and then over at the girl. A girl like him. The key to his past. To who he was.

He was pretty sure his wishes were already coming true.

CHAPTER 3
Our New Friend, What's-Her-Name

The *Kraken* sliced through waves, the drumming trailing off as they left the menacing ship far behind. Marrill cupped the dandelion in her hands and closed her eyes tight. *I wish my mom weren't sick and my parents could be here on the Stream with me,* she thought, before blowing and watching the bits of fluff float away on the breeze.

If you'd asked Marrill six months ago if she believed such a wish could come true, she'd have laughed. But that was before she'd met Ardent and set sail on the *Enterprising Kraken*. Before she'd learned that magic was real. Now, even the impossible seemed within reach. Just the other day she'd been holding a real live wish in her hand, in the form of the orb from the Syphon of Monerva. Sure, using that particular wish would rain down living fire and creeping metal on the Stream. But still—if she could find an orb that granted wishes, she could find something else equally as powerful. If she stayed on the Stream long enough, Marrill *would* figure out a way to fix her mom.

She allowed herself another moment of indulging the daydream before pushing the thoughts aside and turning back toward Fin. She blinked in surprise to find a girl leaning against the railing beside him. She looked to be about their age, with dark hair and olive skin.

"Hi, I'm Marrill," she said, giving the girl a small wave.

"Check it out, Marrill!" Fin said with a grin. "This is the girl I told you about, the one I met in Belolow who's like me! She's going to stay with us and tell me all about where I came from and help me find my mom!"

It took a moment for the words to sink in. But as soon as she realized what they meant, Marrill jumped in the air and clapped. She couldn't believe it. The mysterious forgettable girl had been their only lead and now here she was, just appearing out of thin air. "Fin, that's amazing!"

"Fin?" the girl asked, staring at her weirdly. "What's Fin?"

"That's his name, of course," Marrill said. "What's yours?"

The girl turned and tilted her head, seeming not to understand. "I...my people...we don't really have names. I'm just Sister Fade, like all my other sisters."

"Ohhhh," Fin said. "That's why you call me Brother."

Marrill waved her hand. There was no way this girl could stick around without a name. "Well, that's ridiculous. Let me think." She put her hand on her chin and squinted. "Fin is Fin because that's what was written on your file at the orphanage, right?"

"Orphan Preserve," Fin corrected. "And yeah. *FNU LNU*. First Name Unknown, Last Name Unknown."

"FN. Fin. And she's like you, only a girl...a forgettable girl...*F*...*G*?" Marrill snapped her fingers as it came to her. "That's it. Fig! We'll call you Fig!"

"Fig," the girl repeated softly. Her lips curled into a smile, and she looked away, almost as if she was embarrassed. "I... like it. Thank you. I'll remember that. Even if you won't."

"What are you talking about?" Marrill laughed. How could she possibly forget *this* news?

Just then, Ardent strolled toward them, a sheaf of papers in one hand. "Ah, there you are, Marrill. Now that we're good and under way, we really should discuss Margaham's Game. We will have to play to even *speak* to Margaham about anything of substance, and there is significant strategy involved, so..."

"Ardent!" Marrill started, turning to introduce the newly christened Fig. "This is—"

Ardent waved his free hand. "Yes, it's a bit annoying, I agree. But I suppose every wizard is entitled to his eccentricities. Better an elaborate game than a moat of skinnerwogs. Now if you'll take a look at this diagram from the last time I visited..." He shoved the papers toward her.

Marrill rolled her eyes with a sigh. "No, Ardent, listen...Wait, why are these stars dancing on a wedding cake?" She squinted at the drawing, if it could be called that. Ardent had done it himself; that much was clear. And with his drawing ability, that was the *only* thing that was clear.

The wizard snatched it back quickly. "Those 'stars,' as you call them, are people. And that's not a wedding cake, it's the many levels of the game. You see, they stack up on top of each other, like..." He frowned. "Well, maybe it is like a wedding cake. *Hmph.* Anyway."

Marrill opened her mouth to say...something. She frowned. She'd just been about to tell him something important. She was sure of it. But somehow, the thought seemed to slip away from her. "Oh...kay..."

Fin coughed beside her. Marrill glanced over, to find him standing next to some girl she didn't recognize. He nodded to the girl. "Marrill? Remember Fig?"

Marrill squinted at the girl. She did look vaguely familiar...and yet, Marrill had absolutely no idea who she was. Still, Fin seemed so expectant that she automatically mumbled, "Sure. We met...uh..." She trailed off, hoping the girl would fill in the blank.

Fig cocked an eyebrow, clearly amused. "Three minutes ago."

Marrill's eyeballs bulged. No way they'd just met.

"Told you she wouldn't remember," the girl snickered, nudging Fin. "That's the whole point."

"The point of what?" Ardent inquired, inserting himself into the conversation.

The girl grinned. "Exactly."

"Exactly how?" Ardent asked.

Fin let out a sigh. "Exactly how you've already forgotten about the fake deckhands and how they signaled that *ship* that was just *chasing* us. Anyone even wonder who that was?"

Ardent absently tucked his papers into a pocket in his robe. "Well, given the sigil on the side, the nature of our recent jaunt to Monerva, and the, um... *cargo* we're carrying, I assume they're the army of the Salt Sand King."

Marrill's head snapped to him automatically. "Wait, what?" She couldn't believe he'd kept that to himself! "The army of the Salt Sand King is after us? Why didn't you say something?"

Ardent shrugged. "Well, I don't recall you asking. Also, they're supposed to be an army of unstoppable soldiers. It's not like we were going to do anything *other* than run away from them. Besides, we're in the middle of a terribly important mission. If we allowed ourselves to get distracted every time some army decided to chase us..." He waved a hand dismissively.

"They're called the Rise," the new girl chimed in. "And they *are* unbeatable, just like the legend says. No one can hurt them; no one can stop them. They don't lose at anything."

Marrill frowned. Who *was* this girl? Where had she come from? And why didn't Fin seem to care there was a stranger on board?

Ardent peered at the girl...and at Fin. " I don't believe I've met our guests," he said.

Understanding hit Marrill like a soccer ball to the gut. Ardent looked at Fin and the girl the exact same way. He didn't remember *either* of them. Just like Marrill didn't remember the girl. And yet Fin did.

The girl was forgettable. Marrill pressed her fingers against her temple, wondering if this was even the first time she'd been through this with the girl. Had they met before? Carried on conversations?

"You're forgettable," Marrill said, confirming her suspicion. "Like Fin. Which means...we've probably already met, haven't we?"

The girl smiled at her and winked. "We're called the Fade. The spies who can't be seen. And yes, we have met. You just named me, actually. I'm Fig." She said the name carefully, as though still getting used to it.

"Huh." Marrill found it disconcerting; she had absolutely no recollection of Fig, no matter how hard she searched for something familiar about her. But then, if she really was forgettable like Fin, there wouldn't be. Marrill had remembered Fin at first because he'd seemed so lost, just like the injured animals she always loved so much back in her world. She'd cared too much about lost things to forget him.

And sure, there'd been a brief period in Monerva when she'd started to forget him, but that had only been temporary. Now, she remembered him because he was her friend— she remembered *him*.

But this girl wasn't her friend, and she definitely didn't seem lost or in need of special care. Fig was confident, which meant Marrill would keep forgetting her. It was an intensely uncomfortable revelation.

"We can remember the Rise, though?" Marrill asked just to confirm her understanding.

"Yep. They're the other, more memorable half of the Fade."

Ardent clapped his hands. "Excellent. Well, that solves that. The Rise are unbeatable soldiers we *can* remember; the Fade are unseeable spies we can't. Now, who are the two of you again? Because I'm afraid you've picked a bad time to visit. We're on a terribly important mission, you see, and I've just learned we're being chased by some very dangerous people called the Rise."

"Don't worry about it," Fig said with a wink.

Ardent crossed his arms. "I'm afraid we can't let the subject drop there, young lady. I've learned over my many years as a wizard that when people tell you not to worry about something, it means there is definitely something worth worrying about."

He tucked his hands behind his back in his storytelling stance. "One time that stands out particularly, I was trolling through the Question That Shall Not Be Asked—don't ask—when Calixto the Magister told me, 'Look, it's nothing to worry about, but I'm pretty sure I once burned down a small village somewhere near here.' So, naturally, I said, 'What village around here is made from something flammable?' And he said, 'Well, none of them *now*'..."

As Ardent droned on, Marrill tried to catch Fin's eye to share a laugh. But he was deep in discussion with a girl she'd never seen before. As subtly as possible, Marrill slid a step closer, wondering what they could be talking about so intently.

"...the Crest of the Rise," the girl was saying. "She's the leader of the army."

"Do you think she might know where my mom is?" Fin asked.

Marrill's eyes widened with surprise. They were discussing Fin's mom! She held her breath, waiting to hear the girl's answer.

"Well," the girl began. "Maybe—"

Just then, Ardent's story reached a crescendo. "Which went *exactly* how you'd expect!" he declared. "Didn't see that twist coming, did you, Marrill? Because neither did Calixto." He settled his hands on his hips triumphantly.

For the first time ever, Marrill wished the wizard's story

had been longer. "Uh...yeah." She scrambled to come up with a question that would keep him talking. "So, Calixto the Magister—isn't he one of the Wizards of Meres?"

"Oh yes," Ardent said.

She fished for something else to add. "So...he could be the Master of the Iron Ship?"

Ardent tapped his fingernails against his teeth in thought. "Interesting theory. Hmm, I suppose he *could* be.... Calixto did have a penchant for tyranny. Unfortunately, Calixto did not survive that night at Meres when Serth drank Stream water." He paused. "Unfortunately for him, anyway. I suppose there were a great number of people in his magisterium who were pretty happy about it. Oh, which brings me back to that burning village!"

Marrill tuned him out and turned back to ask Fin about the lead he'd gotten on his mom. But when she did, a girl she'd never seen before was placing a hand on her friend's arm, laughing.

"Excuse me!" Marrill chirped, grabbing Fin by his other arm and pulling him away. Keeping her eyes pinned on the interloper, Marrill asked, "Um, Fin? Who is that?"

"That's Fig. She's one of my people." His expression fell. "You really don't remember her?"

Marrill shook her head. She was pretty sure she'd never seen the girl before in her life. "Should I?"

"I guess I kind of hoped, since you remember me..." But his voice trailed off.

And then Ardent clapped his hands. "So you see," he intoned, finishing his lecture, "I was correct as always. Just like I'm right in this instance." He paused in his musing and looked around. "I've already forgotten what I'm right about."

His eyes fell on Fin and the girl, and he brightened. "Oh, hello. You must be Marrill's friends. Please pardon my rudeness for not introducing myself earlier. I am the great wizard Ardent," he said with a bow. "Perhaps you've heard of me?"

Understanding hit Marrill like a soccer ball to the gut. Ardent looked at both Fin and the girl the exact same way. He didn't remember *either* of them. The same way Marrill didn't remember the girl. And yet Fin did.

The girl was forgettable. Marrill pressed her fingers against her temple, wondering if this was even the first time she'd been through this with the girl. Had they met before? Carried on conversations?

Why did this entire revelation feel so familiar?

"Of course I've heard of you," the girl said, elbowing Fin with a roll of her eyes. He stifled an awkward laugh, and she cleared her throat before asking, "So, where are we headed anyway? Because we could always turn around. Go back to see the Rise and the Crest...." Marrill caught the girl stealing a wink at Fin, but she didn't have the slightest clue what it meant.

Ardent shook his head vigorously. "Oh, goodness no. You may not be aware, but those people back there are an unstoppable army aligned with our newest old foe, the Salt Sand King. Besides, we are on a mission of the utmost importance."

"Oh?" the girl said.

"Indeed," Ardent continued. "We have to play a game!" He paused. Even he seemed taken aback by the statement. "It's a very serious game," he added. "The fate of the Stream is at stake."

"Sure," the girl said. "Well…where do you play this game? And how long until we get there?"

"Technically the game itself is a place," Ardent corrected her. "An island, to be precise. You'll see when we arrive. Margaham is a master of transformation and of illusion. It's what makes him so much fun." He turned to the quarterdeck. "Coll—how long will it take to reach the Great Game?"

Coll glanced at where his knotted rope tattoo wound its way around his bare ankle. Marrill still found it weird that the tattoo not only moved but acted as a compass, helping the captain navigate the Pirate Stream.

"Probably be a day or so. We're taking a shortcut through the Ravingorge." He leaned toward Remy. "Lots of odd winds and sharp teeth, which will be good practice for your tacking."

"Teeth?" Remy seemed uncertain.

Coll lifted a shoulder. "More like fangs, really."

The new girl glanced back toward the clouds of dandelion

fluff disappearing on the horizon behind them and nodded. "Margaham's Game. One day. Got it."

Marrill frowned. "Got what?"

The girl waved a hand with a self-satisfied smile. "Nothing important." She then linked arms with Fin. "How about a tour of my new home, Brother Fade?"

With a furrowed brow, Marrill watched the new deckhand escort Fin belowdecks. *Coll must have picked her up in Monerva,* she thought. Then her thoughts slid away, and the girl slipped out of her mind entirely.

CHAPTER 4
This One's a Scream

That night, Fin awoke to screaming. He bolted upright. The *Kraken* rocked roughly from side to side. Through the shrieks, he could hear a rumbling churn, a sound like a stomach gurgling all around them.

"Must be in the Ravingorge," he mumbled to himself. Though no one had ever mentioned the Ravingorge *screaming*. He slid from his bunk, snatching his thief's bag and skysailing jacket, and headed to the door.

Before he could even get his bearings in the dim hallway, Marrill's cabin door burst open across from him. Her head popped out, eyes white and wide in the darkness. Her cat, Karnelius, glowered from the crook of her arm.

"What *is* that?" she whispered.

The shrieks were high pitched and growing louder. "Sounds like it's coming from above." Fin started for the stairs. "Come on."

Marrill took a hesitant step after him. "Do you think that's a good idea?"

Fin paused. They *were* charging into the darkness toward the source of mysterious screams, after all. "Nope. Do you?"

Marrill let out a sigh and settled Karny over her shoulder. "Nope. Let's go."

They raced each other up the spiral staircase. Fin burst through the hatch first, Marrill and her cat just a step behind. But as soon as he struck the cool night air, Fin's stomach turned. The stench hit him like mildewed rotten eggs bathed in week-old mustard.

Marrill blanched, nose wrinkling. "Ugh." Karnelius squirmed in her arms, clearly unhappy to have been dragged into the stink. "What *is* this place?"

Fin looked around. The Stream had narrowed into a river once more, but this sure wasn't the Ravingorge—the lack of teeth made that obvious. Stonework banks penned in the river on either side, broken only by muddy side channels and high, arching bridges. Gothic buildings loomed on the banks like fat spiders, their stained-glass eyes lit with candles as they watched the night for prey.

But what defined this place most was the gas. Bubbles of it popped and belched everywhere, illuminating the darkness in an odd, wavering assortment of ill-scented hues. The *Kraken* shook from side to side as the Stream practically boiled beneath it. This, Fin realized, was what made the weird churn-and-chug noises he'd heard earlier. The stink had a familiar tang to it, one he recognized from the trading docks back at the Khaznot Quay.

"We're in Listerd Light Alley," he choked over the shrieks that continued piercing the night. "Has to be. Nothing smells like Listerd gas."

Nose still wrinkled in disgust, Marrill pointed toward the rear of the ship and the source of the screaming: Ardent's cabin. The door hung open, the wailing sound spilling out along with an oozing flood of gelatinous goop.

Ardent stumbled out beside it in a daze, dark stains of sludge sticking his robe to his skin. He flicked his hand, and a wad of goo flew through the air. The wailing increased to a howl as it landed just at Fin's feet. He looked down at the glob. The *goo* was screaming, he realized.

Just then Coll and Remy joined them on the deck.

"Ohthankgoodnessyou'reokay," Remy breathed, clapping a hand on Marrill's shoulder. "You too, Plus One," the babysitter added, dropping her other hand on Fin's arm.

Fin smiled. Remy didn't really remember him, so much as she remembered that there was another kid besides Marrill she needed to look out for. But that was still more than most anyone else in his life had ever remembered him, and he was thankful for it nonetheless.

Coll, meanwhile, cringed, pulling a curved blade from his belt. His eyes swept the deck, looking for trouble. "What's going on?" he shouted over the whirlwind of noise.

Ardent twitched his fingers as he waved toward the sludge. It fizzled and crackled, the screaming turning torturous. Then all at once, goop and noise evaporated, vanishing in a puff of steam. A few stubborn streaks of the stuff still clung to Ardent's robe and Coll's boots, emitting tinny mews of angst.

"My alarm," Ardent said, scowling. His eyes scanned the buildings around them as more and more candles flickered to life in dark windows. Crooked shapes like broken dolls cast their silhouettes out into the night.

Turning, the wizard stalked back into his cabin, Coll close on his heels. Marrill and Remy scrambled to follow.

"What's going on, Brother—Fin?" Fig asked, coming up behind him. She yawned as Fin looked at her. Clearly, she was still half asleep; she hadn't even had time to put on shoes.

"Wizard alarm, screaming gel, the usual," Fin told her. "Where did you get off to?"

She shrugged. "Found a nice pile of blankets in one of the cabins downstairs. Had to snuggle up to a really grumpy four-armed monster to get any covers, though. Called me a 'squirt larva' and grunted something about hibernating."

Fin shook his head. He'd wondered where the Naysayer had been all this time. Though frankly, the ship was much more pleasant without him. Even with the screaming, come to think of it.

"You may want to double-check you still have everything you went to sleep with," Fin warned her. "The Naysayer can be a bit...sticky-fingered."

Fig cocked an eyebrow. "Now what kind of Fade would I be if I let someone else get the drop on me?"

"Fair enough." Fin laughed. The more time he spent with Fig, the more he realized how much they had in common. He really *was* Fade, he guessed. It seemed weird...almost like belonging. He felt himself blushing at the thought, so he pushed it away and tilted his head toward the stern. "Let's go see what this screaming is all about."

They reached Ardent's cabin to find the wizard surveying the scene. The place was a wreck, junk everywhere. "Wow, they really tossed the place," Remy said, toeing a broken vase. The vase let out a curse, and Remy scooted away.

Ardent glanced around. "Hmm, no, this is pretty much what it looked like when I went to bed."

Coll sheathed his blade and crossed his arms. "Then why the annoying alarm?"

Ardent beamed, moving toward a stack of ornately carved chests under the windows. "I thought it quite clever myself. I filled the chest with enhanced and enchanted unending supersonic screaming gel. Loud as anything and always one second away from a panic attack. Best part is, it's quite sticky, making it easier to catch the thief. Hard to run and hide when you're covered in screams."

Ardent crossed his fingers across the top of one of the chests, knocked twice on the side, and let out a whistle. The lid flipped open, revealing a star-shaped crystal just inside—the Key to the Map to Everywhere.

"I use it to protect my most valuable and/or dangerous possessions," the wizard continued. He waved at a trio of clear cubes laid out neatly just behind the Key, each nestled on a velvet cushion. The first held a collection of small objects Fin had never seen before: a stone that looked like it was made from a boiling storm, what appeared to be a ball with the label SOUL OF IMALUPHUS KHAN—DO NOT BOUNCE, and a glass figurine that bowed to each of them in greeting. Fin nodded back unconsciously.

The second cube had something far more familiar floating inside: the wish orb, nearly filled with concentrated Pirate Stream water, which could grant all but the absolute most extreme of wishes. And if the Master of the Iron Ship had managed to fill it completely when they were back in Monerva, even *those* wishes would have been possible.

Fin gave a silent thanks that he and Marrill had showed up in time to stop it.

It was the third cube, though, that caused Marrill to

let out a strangled squeak. "My Wiverwane!" She dropped Karny to the floor, ignoring his howled protest, and raced toward the cube, where a black spot of a creature cowered in the corner. It looked like a bat and a spider all in one, or more like a pair of hands joined together at the wrist. Long spindly finger-legs drummed against the side of its enclosure.

Marrill's eyes narrowed as her hands clutched into fists. Fin could see the shock and anger twining across her face. Frankly, he'd never been a fan of the creepy creatures, but Marrill had been partial to them, especially this one. Which made sense, since it *had* kind of saved their lives.

"Marrill, it's all right," Fin started.

She shook her head violently, cutting him off. "It is *not* all right. The poor thing's cramped and scared." She spun toward Ardent. "How could you keep it in there like that?"

Surprised, Ardent twittered his fingers. "Marrill, the Wiverwane is not some pet. It is the memories of the Dzane made flesh, the recollections of the first wizards going all the way back to the birth of the Stream. Perhaps beyond. I have already seen…disturbing things by touching this little creature. That kind of knowledge, unleashed willy-nilly, could cause grave consequences."

"But it's a living creature!" Marrill protested. "And it's not dangerous; it's sweet."

"Marrill…" Remy interjected. "It *does* cause people to fall into, uh, memory-comas, or whatever, when they touch it. Maybe he's right?"

Marrill crossed her arms, undeterred. "No. I carried it all through the catacombs of Monerva, and it didn't do a thing to hurt anyone. It *helped* me."

Ardent cocked his head to one side. "Well, that's debatable, certainly." The two stared at each other for an awkward moment. Fin shot a glance at Fig. She was staring at the big wooden chest, brow furrowed as she scanned its mysterious contents.

Wait a second, Fin thought, putting two and two together. The wish orb was the key to releasing the Salt Sand King… and someone had tried to steal it. On the very same day one of the Salt Sand King's army of spies had joined their crew.

He didn't know what felt worse: being deceived, or having fallen for it.

Fin grabbed Fig's arm, yanking her toward the doorway. "It was you, wasn't it? You tried to take the orb." His chin quivered, feeling hurt and betrayed and angry and confused all at once.

"What? Brother, what do you mean?"

Fin wasn't about to be tricked twice. "Don't play dumb," he growled. "You tried to steal the wish orb to free your king. You said your people came on board to find *me*. But that was a lie, wasn't it? You used me, and you were here for that orb all along."

Fig looked offended. She was good, Fin had to give her that. "No. It *was* you. Brother, really! I don't even know anything about that orb—"

He cut her off with a stroke of his hand. "Where are your shoes?" Her eyes slowly dropped to her bare feet, then off to the side. Clearly, she hadn't anticipated that tell. "Well? Did you throw your shoes overboard, or are they belowdecks somewhere screaming their little hearts out?"

Fig blew a hair out of her face in frustration. Fin glared at her, waiting for her to cave.

"Overboard," she finally huffed. "One of them turned into a really beautiful songbird. The other one ate it." She paused. "But it wasn't a lie!" she protested. "We really *did* come for you."

"Then why all the sneaking around the ship?" he pressed. "Why didn't you just grab me when you had the chance?"

"We're Fade. That's not our style—we're more for subtlety and subterfuge. Besides, the bigger a scene we cause, the more noticeable we become, and the longer it takes people to forget us."

"And I'm sure that's the only reason," he said drily.

"Okay fine." She rolled her eyes. "We also thought we'd take a look around for anything that might be, you know, *useful*. And unguarded. But I really didn't know about the orb until your wizard mentioned something about having cargo that the Rise would want. And even then, I just wanted to find it and figure out what it was."

Fin's stomach sank at the confirmation of her deception. "And steal it for them."

She looked down and away. "You don't understand,"

she said. "If it's something they want, the Rise *will* get it. They're unstoppable. We can't resist them, Brother. We can only help them; it's for the best, really."

Fin shook his head sadly. "If they're so unstoppable, how come *we* got away from them?"

"Yeah, well." She shrugged. "I'm not really sure what happened there, either. That's why we were so thrown when your ship started outracing them.... That's never really happened before."

Fin snorted. Fig was clearly untrustworthy. Still, it did make some strange sense. And he had to admit, if what she said was true, breaking into Ardent's cabin like that was exactly the type of thing *he* would have done.

"It's not really betrayal," Fig argued. "You're one of us, Fin. You're Fade. You should be on our side. You should *want* to help the Rise recover that orb."

As one, they looked back inside, past where Marrill and Ardent were still debating the fate of the Wiverwane. Beside the skittery creature, the orb sat glowing, like a fallen star caught on a pillow.

One wish, Fin thought, and the path to Monerva would reopen, setting free the Salt Sand King to torch every world he touched. And opening that path would *also* unleash the deadly Iron Tide, which they had just barely halted before their escape. That was why no one could use the orb; that was why wishes were better left unspoken. It would be an apocalyptic race to the finish, the fire and iron competing to see which could do the most damage to the Stream the quickest. After that happened, they might *want* the Lost Sun of Dzannin to escape from the Map to Everywhere, just to clean up the mess.

He wondered what Fig would think if she *did* know all of that. But then, he didn't plan on telling her. At this point, the less she knew, the better. "I guess I have to turn you in." He looked out at the angles and arches of Listerd Light Alley. In the belch of a Listerd bubble, something long and ungainly moved. "Shame you didn't betray us in friendlier territory."

Fig waved her hands. "Brother, wait! I know I over-reached. I'm sorry. What can I say? I'm an achiever." She smiled at him mischievously. "But we can still both get what we want. The Rise will be plenty happy if I help you find your mother and bring the two of you back to the fold. And in return, I promise not to try to get that orb."

Fin scoffed. But still he hesitated. He'd learned more about who he was and where he'd come from today than he had in his entire life. And even if he wasn't so sure he *wanted* to be one of the Fade, Fig made him feel like there was a place in the Stream where he fit in. Not to mention she was the only lead he had toward finding his mother. How could he turn that opportunity down?

Besides, clearly Ardent's security was top-notch. The best thief on the Stream would be hard-pressed to steal the orb from the wizard. And since Fin *was* the best thief on the Stream, they didn't have to worry about that.

He let out a long breath, wondering if he was going to

regret his decision. But he didn't really see a choice. "Deal," he said at last. "Though one more caper and you're off. I don't care *where* we are."

Fig seemed surprised by his answer. She covered it with a grin, though it wasn't as bright as usual. "Thank you, Brother Fade." She sounded almost genuine.

Uneasy truce struck, Fin and Fig slipped back inside the cabin, just as Ardent's expression softened into familiar lines of a gentle smile. "Of course, Marrill. You're right; a living creature needs the best care we can provide for it. At the same time, we must be mindful of its dangers. Perhaps together we can come up with better accommodations for the Wiverwane."

"Thank you!" Marrill threw herself into the wizard's arms. Fin felt a lump in his throat. Watching Ardent and Marrill was like watching a grandfather and granddaughter. It wasn't very thiefly, but he couldn't help but be touched by it.

When Marrill pulled back, Ardent placed a hand on the third cube. It didn't open so much as dissolve through his fingers. Freed, the Wiverwane flapped furiously, its one broken appendage still making flight a struggle.

It had almost made it to Marrill's shoulder when a low growl rose from Ardent's desk. Karnelius scrambled across the wooden surface, kicking stray papers to the side and upending bowls of various colored stones as he launched himself toward the Wiverwane.

"Karny, no!" Marrill cried. She grabbed for the Wiverwane. Fin saw what was about to happen and leapt forward just in time to catch her. Because the moment her palm brushed against the Wiverwane, her skin rippled like water, and she collapsed.

A memory coma. Wiverwanes did that—filling the heads of anyone who touched them with someone else's memories, leaving them dazed.

"Marrill!" Remy shouted, taking her from Fin. "Coll, help me get her up!"

"I knew this was a bad idea!" Ardent grunted, tiptoeing toward the Wiverwane. The Wiverwane, however, wasn't fooled. It bolted out the door and flew toward the port railing. Karnelius jumped to follow.

Everything that happened next seemed to go in slow motion.

"The cat!" Fig yelled.

Fin twisted, just in time to see Karnelius coiled on the stairs to the quarterdeck. And then

he

pounced.

The Wiverwane flapped its broken wing, managing to float up just an inch above the railing.

"Catch them!" Marrill screamed, coming out of her stupor and pushing to her feet.

Fin lunged, trying to intervene. But he was too late. Cat and creature collided. Legs and claws scrabbled against the railing. And just like that,

they were gone.

CHAPTER 5
Into the Drink

K arny, no!" Marrill screamed. Her heart lodged in
her throat as her cat sailed through the air, collided
with the Wiverwane, and scrambled for purchase
on the railing before momentum carried them overboard.

With a yowl of outrage and surprise, Karny plummeted
toward the glowing waters of the Pirate Stream. Overhead
the tackle squealed. Lines flew from the rigging, trying to
snatch the pair midfall.

For a moment, Marrill's pulse seemed to beat in slow motion.

Ropebone got there in time, she told herself.

It was okay. Karny was safe.

But then she heard the splash. A band tightened around her lungs. "Noooo!" she wailed as she raced to the railing, Fin chasing after her. In the windows of Listerd Light Alley, twisted shapes moved in a cruel mockery of the anguish sweeping through her.

We're still in the alley. Not out on the open Stream. The water is brackish, she told herself. *Karny is fine.* But she could already see that the Stream had taken them outward again. The Listerd gas bubbled less. The waters of the Stream glowed golden with magic.

Deadly magic.

"Beast overboard!" Coll hollered, racing out of Ardent's cabin toward the ship's wheel. "Heave to!"

Despite their dislike for the cat in question, the pirats scampered dutifully along the yards, hauling up the mainsail and bracing the mainmast square as Coll turned the ship perpendicular to the wind.

Marrill pushed herself out over the railing, farther than she would normally dare. Her eyes scanned the surface frantically, desperate for any sign of Karny or the Wiverwane. With one hand, she swiped away tears to keep her vision from blurring.

But what was she looking for? What would Karny be now? *Aflightofowls-atelephonepole-aburstofyellow.* Her heart pounded. Her mind, unfettered, raced through horrid possibilities. *Thetasteofmarshmallows-anoperamelody-afeelinglikeyou're lostandsofarfromhomeandyouletdowntheonlythingthatlovesyou.*

And then, like a miracle, she heard it. A feeble yowl.

Far below, right at the waterline, something clung to the netting strung along the *Kraken*'s hull. In the dark, the glow of the Stream wasn't enough for her to see what was there. But she knew immediately the yowl was Karnelius. But was he *still* Karnelius?

-acatfish-amancat-acaticorn-anoctokitty-acatcallonlyacall nothingleftbutacall-

"I think I see him!" Fin threw a leg over the railing, ready to climb down. Marrill was half over with him when firm hands hauled them both back.

"The creature's far too close to the water," Ardent warned. "Allow me." The wizard pinched at the air and lifted his arm. Karnelius rose toward the deck, as though plucked from the Stream by an invisible hand.

A moment later, a limp Karnelius swung over the railing, dangling in midair by the scruff of his neck. He was drenched, his fur plastered against his skinny frame, making him appear far smaller and more vulnerable than usual. Water dripped from him, forming a glowing puddle on the deck.

"Still a cat! That's good news," Ardent announced happily. He frowned. "If odd."

"Karny!" Marrill scrambled toward the poor, soaked creature, falling to all fours when she neared. Just before she reached him, however, her head slammed into an invisible wall. She looked up to find Ardent holding his palm toward her, stopping her.

"Careful." He nodded toward the quickly growing puddle of raw magic. "The deck is made of dullwood. You are not. The magic will dissipate shortly, mingling with the air until it is no longer lethal. But not yet."

Marrill took a deep breath and clutched her hands to her chest to keep from grabbing her cat. "Is...is he okay?" she asked in a trembling voice.

In response, Karnelius twisted against the invisible hand holding him and let out an angry hiss. He swiped at the air, claws bared. All of a sudden, Ardent let out an "ouch!" and the cat dropped to the deck, landing gracefully in a crouch.

Marrill extended her fingers toward him. "It's okay, Karny," she cooed. "You're safe now."

His one eye flashed. Each twitch of his tail sent droplets of water arcing across the deck. A low grumble sounded from his chest.

And then he began to speak.

I, the Dawn Wizard, being of inscrutable mind and inexplicable body, do hereby bequeath the following to those who will follow:

Marrill froze. She was sure she couldn't be seeing—or hearing—this. But one glance at the others told her that she wasn't alone—they'd all heard Karny speak, too. Remy's eyes were wide, Fin's mouth open in shock.

"What just happ—" he started to ask.

Ardent cut a hand through the air. "Let the cat finish, young man I don't recognize."

First and foremost, to those who would play the Game of Prophecy, I leave a stratagem. You will find it buried in the lines of this very will, should you have the will to find it.

They all held their breath, staring at Karnelius, waiting for him to say more. The cat shook his head and snuffled. Then he let out a sneeze so enormous it made his fur stand on end—his suddenly dry fur, Marrill realized, as though the force of the sneeze had flung every last drop from his body.

Then he sat, lifted a paw, and began to lick it. Grooming himself as though nothing had happened.

With trembling fingers, Marrill reached for her cat, pulling him into her arms. She didn't care if any residual magic clung to his fur, didn't care what it might do to her. All she cared about was holding Karny and keeping him safe. He settled against her shoulder and bonked her chin with his forehead. Perfectly normal once again. Or at least as normal as he'd ever been.

Fin was the one to break the shocked silence. "Well,

that's a thing that just happened." He scratched his head. "So... does anyone actually know what that was?"

Ardent considered the cat with a puzzled expression. "Extraordinary," he breathed. "I've never seen anything like it."

"The surviving a dunk in the Stream or the talking cat bit?" Fin asked.

Ardent shook his head. "Either." He tugged on his beard as he studied the cat.

Suddenly, Marrill straightened. She'd been so worried about Karny that she'd forgotten he wasn't alone. "Where's the Wiverwane?" she asked. She spun, scanning the deck. "What happened to it?"

Fin, Remy, and a deckhand raced to the side of the ship, peering over. Ardent stood stock-still, brow furrowed.

Marrill's stomach felt like it was turning inside out. If something happened to the Wiverwane, she was responsible. She'd been the one to demand it be set free, after all. And it was her cat that had chased it.

"I don't see it!" Fin called, running down to the back of the ship.

"Nothing over here," said whoever had gone to the front.

Marrill caught Remy's eye. Her babysitter shook her head sadly. "Wh-wh-where is it?" Marrill stammered. "It has to still be here. It has to be!"

Coll's strong hand dropped onto her shoulder. "I'm sorry, Marrill."

But Ardent raised a finger. "Hold off on being sorry, I'm

having a theory." He chewed a stray hair from his long beard absently. "Oh yes. Hmm. Yes. Oh, that makes...yes...I think...I believe...the Wiverwane *is* still here, after all!"

Marrill wasn't the only one confused. Her frown echoed those of her crewmates. "It is? Where?"

"You're holding it."

Marrill's eyes dropped down to her cat. He looked back at her. He seemed unamused. "Karny?"

"The Wiverwanes were a product of the Dawn Wizard, one of the more powerful Dzane," Ardent explained. "And as we have well established in the past, what the Dzane have made, only the Dzane can destroy. A dunking in the Pirate Stream certainly wouldn't *destroy* something like a Wiverwane. But it could...interfere with certain aspects of it."

He began pacing furiously, a habit he often adopted when thinking. "The Wiverwane was living memory, that we know. And the Pirate Stream couldn't change that aspect, no. But it could change its form. Make it...more pure. After all, what's a memory without a place to live, a body to hold it? Why, that power could actually be fueled by the magic, making its owner impervious to—"

Coll cleared his throat. "Human, Ardent. We speak human on this ship. Not wizard."

"Ah, yes. Apologies." The wizard spun on one heel, kicking aside the hem of his robe. He looked Marrill dead in the eye. "Simply put, the memories that were the Wiverwane are now living inside your cat."

Marrill looked at Karny again. He purred lightly. His one eye winked, but she couldn't for the life of her say it was anything more than normal cattitude. "You mean like my cat ate it?"

"Well, not so much consumption as absorption. That's my theory at least," Ardent offered.

That didn't sound much better. "So... how do we get it out?"

Ardent shrugged. "Difficult to say. At least without further study." He held out his hands. "May I?"

Marrill bit her lip. After what had just happened, she didn't want to let go of Karnelius anytime soon. But if Ardent could help, she had to let him try. Reluctantly, she handed Karny over.

Ardent's expression shifted from one of anticipation to disappointment as he carefully collected the cat. "So the Wiverwane memories no longer transfer when you touch the creature, then." He pressed his lips together, holding the cat at eye level and considering him. "This puts a dent in our mission to uncover the identity of the Master of the Iron Ship."

Remy crossed her arms, frowning in confusion. "How's that now?"

"The Wiverwane carried memories of the Dawn Wizard. I've been sifting through them ever since our return from Monerva—barely enough to scratch the surface—but I have seen some most interesting things. It seems the Dawn

Wizard crossed paths with the Master more than once." Ardent winced as Karny's claws raked across his wrist. Marrill reached for her cat and Ardent handed him over gratefully.

"But…" Marrill said, pondering this. "If the Master is one of your old friends…"

"Then how could he have also met the Dawn Wizard, who died long before I was even born? Excellent question!" He rubbed his beard. "I have no idea. Which is the point. There are still a number of gaps in my knowledge, which I had hoped the Wiverwane might fill, and this development makes that a touch tricky. Still, if what we heard was part of the Dawn Wizard's will, perhaps there is a way yet."

He clapped his hands with excitement. "Not to mention the incredible opportunities for research! Imagine Zambfant the Great's consternation when it turns out *I've* discovered the Stream's first recorded instance of feline testation! Oh, I wish I could tell Annalessa about this.…"

The wizard looked away. Marrill felt her heart squeeze at the sorrow in his voice. He forced a smile, though, and started toward his cabin, already lost in thought as he mumbled about the research he intended to conduct on the matter.

"You okay?" Fin asked, coming to stand beside her.

She gave him a wan smile. "Yeah, I think so. I guess this means both Karny and the Wiverwane are okay. But…" She clutched her cat tighter. "What if I messed up our chance to figure out who the Master is?"

"Hey, it's not your fault those two beasts decided to have a high-dive competition," Fin reassured her.

She wished she believed him. "If I hadn't forced Ardent to set the Wiverwane free—"

Fin cut her off with a laugh. "When has anyone forced Ardent to do anything?" He leaned his shoulder against hers. "Besides, the part of you that cares about the Wiverwane is the same part of you that remembers who I am."

She covered a blush by rolling her eyes. "I remember you because you're my friend."

"Then, as your friend, I'm telling you not to worry. Ardent seems pretty convinced the Master is one of the Wizards of Meres, which means all we have to do is go down the list until we figure out who it is. Easy peasy."

"Teeth ahoy!" a girl called from the bow. Marrill looked up. Ahead of them, the Stream funneled into what appeared to be the lower jaw of a massive beast. Enormous, pointy teeth jutted up from the water, hemmed in on either side by slick red walls that looked like the inside of a mouth.

But there was no upper jaw; she was sure of it because stars still shone down from above, as far away as she could see. And the teeth, as jagged and dangerous as they looked, were way too large to pose a danger; the *Kraken* could easily sail right between them.

"It's the Ravingorge, everyone," Coll said, his voice calm. "Remy, take the wheel, and don't worry: If you mess up, the swallowing will keep us moving downstream. Marrill, you and your cat should probably get belowdecks. It can get a little…gross in here."

"At least we won't mind the smell after Listerd Light Alley," Fin joked, nudging Marrill with his elbow as he started toward the hatch. He glanced around. "Eeeeew. Saliva-covered stomach walls." He shuddered before ducking inside.

Marrill followed after him. But on the threshold, she froze. Someone moved in the shadows off to her right. A slight figure—a deckhand, Marrill noted with relief—darted through a patch of light and pulled some sort of creature from her pocket. She held it up to her mouth, as though whispering to it, then tossed it up into the night air.

The creature spun, long iridescent wings unspooling from its body. With a soft buzzing sound, its wings began to beat, almost as fast as a hummingbird's. After a moment of hovering, the thing darted into the blackness, disappearing instantly.

As she ducked through the hatch, Marrill made a mental note to introduce herself to the girl in the morning. Maybe she'd even have the chance to see the glorious winged creature up close.

"Sleep well, everyone!" Ardent cried from the door of

his cabin. "When we reach the end of the gorge, the Great Game of Margaham will have already begun."

And with that, any thoughts of the new deckhand and her bird were completely forgotten. Marrill squeezed her now-enchanted cat close, her mind swirling with curiosity about what kind of games the Stream had in store.

CHAPTER 6
Margaham's Game

When Fin stepped on deck the next morning, Coll was pointing to where the angry red walls of the Ravingorge sloped downward, dropping into the calm of a broad, rippling bay. "Exit ahead," the captain pronounced.

A low mist obscured the land beyond; all Fin could see were the triangles of mountains, the green of deep forests, the outlined towers of some mysterious city.

"Oh, thank heavens," Remy said. Her hair stuck out at

odd angles, plastered in place with what looked like dried saliva. Apparently, the Ravingorge had not been kind to the *Kraken*'s student driver.

As the mist lifted, Fin studied the shore ahead. Something about it was weird, he realized. Nothing was changing. Nothing at all. The *Kraken* was moving, which meant that even if the land was completely frozen, his *perspective* should have been shifting. But it wasn't. It was like they were moving toward a flat painting.

Now that he thought of it, the whole panorama seemed *exactly* like a painting. The outlines were two-dimensional. The smudges of color were *too* smudged. He snapped his gaze down to the waters of the bay. They weren't just calm; they were motionless. Even the ripples were frozen in place.

They *weren't* ripples, he realized. They were just lines *drawn* there to look like ripples. The *Kraken* was about to sail straight onto fake water!

"Coll!" Fin yelled to the quarterdeck. "Full stop, full stop!"

But it was too late. A second later, a great screeching squeal tore the air as the *Kraken* crashed onto the painted water of the false bay. The deck shuddered, throwing Fin to his knees. His teeth rattled in his head. Remy screamed. Coll let out a bellow as he toppled down the stairs.

The *Kraken* listed to one side as momentum carried it forward, slowly grinding to a halt. A second later, the door to Ardent's cabin burst open.

"What in the name of the Thirty-Four and Seven

Thunders!" the wizard shouted. His purple cap hung to one side of his head as he strode out onto the still deck. "Oh," he said, stopping. "We're here. Well, that would have been nice to know forty-five seconds ago."

Coll rolled over and groaned. "You *knew* this would happen."

Ardent sniffed and straightened his cap. "Well, I *thought* we had a competent captain who knew how to park on cardboard, so no, I didn't think this would happen."

"Hey!" Remy protested. "I'm still learning how to drive this thing, so lay off!" She turned back to the wheel, gripping it tightly.

Fin stumbled to the tilted railing. What should have been golden waves beneath them were marred with furrows of torn brown paper. He could see clearly now that the new "land" ahead of them was just a painted backdrop. Behind them, the water pouring out of the Ravingorge merged seamlessly with the flat expanse: liquid one second, painted surface the next.

He couldn't help but laugh. "Margaham's Game is literally a game," he said with wonder.

"Well, of course it is," Ardent declared. "I mean, it's—"

"Right in the name," Remy finished.

"Exactly. Because the Stream—"

"Touches all waters. Even the ones that aren't technically waters." She sounded exhausted. "I hate this place. I hate that I'm starting to understand this place."

The hatch opened, and Marrill struggled out of it, Karny in her arms. "What in—"

Fin shook his head. "Catch you up later."

She stopped, looking around. "Oh, it's *literally* a game...."

"And now you're caught up." Fin had to admit, it did make a stupid sort of sense.

Remy scanned their destination. "You're sure this is the only way to talk to Margaham and find out what he knows about the Master? To play his game?"

Ardent nodded. "It can be terribly frustrating when all you want to do is drop by for tea, but Margaham insists that the only way to gain entrance to his castle is via his game." He lowered his voice. "I think he has a hard time finding people to play against otherwise."

"Wizards are weird," Fin mumbled under his breath. But he didn't plan on letting that stop him. He'd been looking forward to the game. "So, how do we play?"

Ardent clapped. "Excellent question, my good random street urchin! Let's take a look at the board." He strode to the bow of the ship, where a circular board and pewter pieces had been set atop a small wooden table. Fin had never seen either the game or the table before. In fact, he was quite certain they hadn't been there a moment ago.

"Now then," Ardent said, leaning over the board. It was a series of concentric rings, nestled inside one another. Each ring was unique in its own way: One was divided into checkerboard squares; another flickered with arcane symbols; still another had been painted to look like the rampart of a castle wall. The circle in the center rose up into the carved shape of a miniature castle, the middle of it completely flat and smooth.

"Is that the board?" Marrill asked. "I guess I can see how it looks like your wedding cake sketch." She tilted her head to the side. "Kinda."

Ardent cleared his throat. "Yes, well. Let's see what pieces we got this time.... Knight, Blackguard...ooh, Lion Tamer!"

Fig appeared by Fin's side, rubbing her arm. "Are the wake-up calls usually so...abrupt?" she asked, stifling a yawn.

"Morning, snoozy," he told her. "Good job not stealing the ship's wheel during the night. And you're in luck. Apparently we've reached Margaham's Game, and you're just in time to learn how to play."

"Oh," she said. "Yay." She stepped back as though intending to sneak away. Fin smirked and tugged her forward so she could see.

A flash of confusion crossed Ardent's face as he took the two of them in, but he just shrugged. "Ah. Well, the more the merrier, I guess," he said, snapping his fingers to call for a chair.

Ardent sat, kicking aside the hem of his robe, and cracked his knuckles. "Okay, the goal of the game is simple," he explained. "One player, which is always Margaham, is the defender. His Wizard will be placed here." He tapped the smooth center of the castle. "All the other players are attackers, who compete with one another as well as the defender. Of course, the only attacker this time is us, so our goal is simply to move our pieces through the rings to the center and capture the defender's Wizard."

He picked up one of the pewter figurines and held it up. "Of course, each of our pieces is unique and has its own movement and abilities. The Lion Tamer moves like so"—he clacked the piece quickly across the board in a Z-shape— "and the Knight like so." This time, he moved the piece in an inverted L around the outer ring, then in the opposite direction.

He turned to them with a sharply raised eyebrow. "Now, the Knight can destroy any obstacle ahead of it and shield any other player from harm. But it can only move *around* a circle, and never up to the next circle, unless another piece helps it. The Lion Tamer, meanwhile, can send out its lion to find secret paths between circles, which it can use to advance or go back and retrieve the Knight."

Fin smiled. He'd never really played a board game before. At least not with other people. It was kind of hard when he kept getting his turn skipped because no one remembered he existed. He wondered if the same was true for Fig or if the Fade even played games.

He picked up the last of the pieces and studied it. It depicted a shadowy figure, crouched and masked. *Very thiefy*, he noted with a smile. "What about this one? How does it move, and what does it do?"

Ardent took it from him and twirled it around in his fingers. "The Blackguard's move *is* its power. It can go in any direction, taking any path it finds, so long as no one sees it moving."

Neat, Fin thought. That was totally his piece.

"That's totally my piece," Fig said under her breath.

Fin's jaw dropped. "I thought you didn't want to play."

She lifted a shoulder. "Maybe I will if I get to play someone cool."

"Hmph," Fin grumbled, crossing his arms.

"Now, there's one thing we must all remember before we begin," Ardent continued. "Margaham created this game to satisfy anyone who might come to play it. Thrill-seekers have played to find the ultimate entertainment; kings have used it to battle to the death. Because of that, there is only one central rule, and you must never forget it: The more seriously you take the game, the more deadly it becomes."

There was a beat of silence as they took in this information. Fig was the one to break it. "What do we get if we win?"

Ardent winked. "Whatever we seek! We shall state that ahead of time, and if our opponent can give it, the game will begin."

"What will our opponent be playing for?" Marrill asked.

"We have no idea. Only that it's something we have."

Fin met Marrill's eyes. Her expression mirrored his own

discomfort. They had some pretty valuable cargo on board. He shot a glance toward Fig. Good thing the Rise weren't playing this game, he thought.

"Are you sure that's a good idea?" Marrill asked Ardent.

He waved a hand. "I've played against Margaham more times than I can remember, and his wager is always the same. If he wins—which he won't—he'll want me to admit he was right about disproportionate intertime transpositioning—which, of course, he wasn't. No real risk. Besides, if that's what it takes to uncover the Master's identity, I'm willing to sacrifice."

Fin felt the need to point out the obvious. "But if we think Margaham might be the Master, then won't his stakes be higher?"

Ardent lifted an eyebrow in Fin's direction. "Since you're obviously new to the crew, I won't hold your ignorance against you. But understand, I am one of the most powerful wizards on the Stream—far more powerful than Margaham. I do not intend to lose."

Ardent plucked a card from out of thin air and scribbled something across its surface. "Our stakes," he announced, slipping it into a crisp white envelope before Fin could see what he'd written.

"Now let's begin, shall we?" With a swift motion, Ardent tapped the flat space in the center of the castle. In the moment Fin blinked, a round metal piece appeared. It was a wizard, no doubt; the robes were a dead giveaway, though its hat looked far more like a jester's than like Ardent's floppy cap.

"Welcome, players!" said a reedy voice coming from the game piece, though it was just as motionless as the others. "Welcome to my Great Game. It is I, the Inevitable Margaham!"

"And I am the great wizard Ardent," Ardent called in response. "Come to play your game."

There was a pause before the pewter wizard answered. "You should not have come here, old friend."

"He was always one for dramatics," Ardent whispered behind his hand.

"Obviously," Fig said drolly, scanning their surroundings.

Ardent raised his voice. "Margaham, listen—we've come on a mission seeking the identity of the Master of the Iron Ship. What do you know of him?"

"As I told Annalessa," the game piece answered, "you may find some answers here. But they may be answers to questions you should never have asked in the first place."

"Annalessa?" Ardent stood abruptly, knocking against the game table and causing the pieces to rattle. Any trace of humor drained from his face. His eyes turned cold, serious. "She was here? When?"

"Those are not questions you should be asking," Margaham responded. "You should turn back now." His voice escalated, growing more insistent. "Leave, and be safe; find some kind of happiness in ignorance. Trust me—" His voice cut out abruptly.

This did nothing to dampen Ardent's ire. The whole board—the whole table—seemed to shake with his anger now. He snatched the envelope from the game board and tore it open, yanking the card free. He scratched out what he'd written earlier and furiously scribbled something new. "I will have my answers!" he shouted, holding the envelope aloft.

Suddenly Fin had a very bad feeling.

There was a pause. "Ardent the Cold." Margaham sounded almost resigned. Even a little sad. "Who can't leave the past behind."

"Maybe we should listen to him," Fin suggested. "He doesn't seem to be the Master. Let's move on to the next name on the list." But it was like he'd never even spoken. As soon as Margaham mentioned Annalessa, the stakes of the game had changed. Ardent had been searching for her for years—if he had a chance to learn what happened to her, he was going to take it, and there was nothing any of them could say to stop him.

Fin couldn't blame him for that. There wasn't much he wouldn't do to find his own mom, after all. If there was one thing that linked Fin and Ardent, it was their continued search for someone they loved.

"We will play your game," Ardent insisted, waving the envelope. "And these are my stakes."

Margaham's pewter piece let out a sigh. "Very well. Welcome, player one." And with that, the envelope clutched in Ardent's hand disappeared in a snap of light.

Ardent resumed his seat before the board and took a deep breath. Then he raised one of his pieces into the air. "Game on," he said grimly.

Almost instantly, the world seemed to explode in noise and motion. Around the *Kraken*, the painted water changed color. In front of the ship, dark lines raced across the flat bay, resolving into the circles of the game board.

But unlike the flat game board on the table before Ardent, the rings in the bay began to twist and turn against one another. Margaham's castle rose, pulling the rest of the board up after it so that it turned into a vertical, terraced spire.

It looked like a massive tiered cake, each layer peppered with its own obstacles and spinning in different directions at different speeds. It towered before them like a mountain, the castle perched on the very apex. Squinting, Fin could just barely make out the outline of Margaham inside.

"Okay, *that* looks a lot more like your sketches," Marrill conceded to Ardent. "Only a bit more—"

She didn't have a chance to finish the sentence because at that moment the *Kraken* shuddered, her deck tilting. A massive stone hand thrust up from the bay, clutching the ship and lifting her into the air.

Fin raced to the railing to get a better look. Through the fingers of the statue, the golden waters of the Pirate Stream poured down in a torrent.

"What's happening?" Marrill yelled. Fin shook his head. He glanced back to Ardent. The wizard's jaw was clenched, his eyes intense.

He was taking it seriously, Fin realized. His gut

clenched. The wizard himself had warned them not to. "Ardent, don't take it—"

"KNIGHT, GO!" Ardent shouted, slamming one of the pieces onto the board.

And the next thing Fin knew, he stood on the bottom layer of the game. The giant stone hand clutching the *Kraken* towered above him. "Shanks spinning!" he cried, darting away from the flow of golden water still running off the ship. One step, two—

And then he stepped into nothingness. He twisted backward as he fell, landing against the ground with a harsh smack that took his breath away. Fin rolled, staring at where he'd nearly fallen.

He was lying on the checkerboard pattern of the outermost ring of the game. But the square he'd just stepped on was missing; below it, the magic waters of the Pirate Stream glimmered, threatening. If he hadn't controlled his fall, he could have been turned into a winding country lane or a common domestic pinch wren.

Understanding dawned. *He* was the game piece. The game was real. The board was real. Which meant the danger was real as well.

He took a deep breath and forced himself to focus. He didn't see anyone else around, which meant his move probably wasn't over yet. He popped to his feet and was about to start toward the next tier when he remembered what Ardent had said. *Knight, go.*

Fin closed his eyes and struggled to remember the rules. The Knight moved in an L pattern. He toed the square before him carefully. It vanished at his touch.

He gulped. "Okay, I'm the Knight, then." He skittered sideways four squares and stopped, holding his breath.

"End of movement!" Margaham's voice cried from far above.

Fin let out a sigh of relief.

"LION TAMER, GO!" Ardent yelled.

With no warning, Marrill popped into existence in front of him, the orange fuzz of her cat balled up in her arms. "What the—oh, hi, Karny," she said.

"Marrill," Fin said, grabbing her. "Be careful. We're the pieces! We have to move like the pieces!"

Her brow furrowed. "What do you mean, 'we're the pieces'?" She looked down. Then back up. Their eyes met. "We're on the game board," she said. "We're the pieces!"

Fin nodded. "Right. I'm the Knight. I'm pretty sure you're the Lion Tamer, which means you have to move in a Z...."

Just then, his eyes locked on Fig, creeping across the squares nearby. As soon as he saw her, the square she was about to step on vanished, dropping away to the Stream below. "Fig, watch out!"

She froze, staring back at him, her mouth twisted with fury. "Brother! I'm the Blackguard! I can't move if you see me!"

Of course she'd ended up as the Blackguard. "Sorry. Didn't mean to mess up your move."

"End of player one's turn!" Margaham announced.

Fin let out a long breath. They'd made it through one round pretty easily. Maybe this wasn't so bad after all. He rubbed his hands together, studying the board and planning his next move. "Okay, so it should be my turn again. I think maybe this time we should try to—"

He was cut off by the boom of Margaham's voice announcing, "Welcome, new player!"

"New player?" Fin glanced uneasily toward Marrill. "I thought we were playing against Margaham."

Marrill chewed her lip. "Ardent *did* say there could be more than one attacker...."

"Maybe another player will liven things up a bit?" Fin offered. "Make the game more fun?" The reassurance sounded hollow even to him.

"Somehow I don't think so," Marrill said, pointing into the distance.

Past the great arm, past the rain of magic falling from the *Kraken*, a ship raced down the last torrent from the Ravingorge. Fin recognized it instantly. The broad bow, the square sails. He didn't even need to see the side of it to know the Salt Sand King's sigil would be etched there.

The other half of his people were coming. The unstoppable army, who existed for one reason: to conquer all of the Pirate Stream.

The Rise had joined the Great Game.

CHAPTER 7
(Un)Friendly Competition

As the warship bore down on them, Marrill could see the expert sailors moving like clockwork through her rigging. Along her bow, rows of honed warriors stood at stiff-backed attention. The gleam of their daggers didn't make it seem too likely they'd come for a tea party.

Once the ship grew close enough, another giant stone hand thrust from the Stream, lifting her into the air as its twin had done with the *Kraken*. The two stone arms rotated around the board, coming to rest on opposite sides so that the ships faced each other like competitors across a table.

"Welcome, player, to my Great Game!" Margaham's voice boomed.

A lone figure strode confidently toward the bow of the warship, but with the angle and distance, Marrill could barely make it out. From the outline, she could tell it was a woman. From the stance, she could tell it was a warrior.

"I am the Crest of the Rise. I speak the will of our people." The woman's voice echoed, clear and loud and calm even across the distance. "Here are our stakes," she said, holding a crisp white envelope aloft. "We will play the game, and we will not be beaten."

There was a soft buzzing and a flash of light. The envelope in the woman's hand disappeared, and three figures appeared on the opposite side of the giant tiered game board. They were too far away to see clearly, but they moved with a confidence that Marrill completely lacked.

"Looks like the Rise have their pieces." She gulped. "But why are they here? How did they find us?"

Fin said nothing. Instead he spun, skewering a young girl standing several tiles away with a glare. "Yeah, *Fig*, how *did* they find us?" Marrill was surprised by the vehemence in his voice, especially to a total stranger.

The girl held up her hands defensively. "Wait—it's not what you think."

Fin crossed his arms. "I think you found a way to tell the Rise where we were going so they could ambush us here."

The girl swallowed. "Okay, so maybe it is *a little* what you think."

He shook his head sadly. "And I'm going to guess you told them all about the wish orb, too, so now they're here to take it?" The girl opened her mouth to protest, but Fin cut her off with a sweep of his hand. "But you feel like you kept your promise to me because you didn't *personally* try to steal the orb?"

"Okay," the girl admitted sheepishly. "Maybe it's *entirely* what you think."

"Whoa, whoa, whoa," Marrill said, interjecting. "What do you mean?"

"The wish orb, Marrill," Fin explained. "The Rise know about it now. Fig told them, and they've come to take it and free the Salt Sand King."

Marrill inhaled sharply. Of course! What else would a leaderless army want but to free their king? "We can't let that happen."

"You're right," Fin said. "Which is why we totally have to win." He actually grinned at that.

"No, Fin," Marrill said, grabbing his arm. "This is serious. We *can't* play against them if the orb's at stake! We have to drop out of the game." She drew a breath, about to shout that they conceded when Fin clapped a hand over her mouth.

"There's no dropping out," he told her. "They've already

joined the game. The orb's *already* at stake.... We'll just be giving up our chance to save it."

He had a point. Marrill bit her lip, trying to figure a way out of their predicament. This was bad. They were stuck on a giant, magical game board, playing by rules they barely understood, with a good dip in the Stream waiting for literally any misstep. And now they had an opponent who was, by definition, unbeatable.

Suddenly, the game seemed more serious than ever.

"We just need to win," Fin said matter-of-factly.

"Thank you, Captain Obvious," Marrill grumbled.

"I prefer Colonel Obvious," Fin replied, waggling his eyebrows.

"Lion Tamer, go!" Ardent cried from the bow of the *Kraken*, far overhead.

"Great," Marrill muttered. "Just great."

She had no option but to keep playing. With a quick back-and-forth of her finger, she mapped out a course that would take her up to the twelve-foot wall leading to the next layer of the game. But when she reached it, the flat surface towering before her offered no purchase, no way to climb. She pressed one palm against it. The stone was cold and unyielding, an odd contrast with Karny's warm fluff pressing against her other palm.

A thought jogged through her head. *Karny.* If she was the Lion Tamer, he was her lion. And wasn't it in her power to have him find secret paths between rings?

Marrill held her cat up like a rag doll, looking him eye-to-one-good-eye. "Okay, Karn. It's all on you. Do your thing!"

She set him on the ground at her feet. He strolled lazily over to the next square, and promptly dropped right through it.

"Karny!" Marrill shrieked.

The cat struck the surface of the Pirate Stream with a splash, then shot into the air like a rocket, straight up the wall of the next ring. His feet left a trail of fire zigzagging back and forth up the vertical surface. When he reached the top, he sat and stared down at her, like he was the Cheshire cat.

To the King of Salt and Sand, I leave a wish ungranted, an ambition unfulfilled, an army leaderless, and an orb of gold, its waters as pure and true as the headwaters of the Stream itself.

"Shanks," Fin called from behind her. "Karny's still Stream proof! Are we going to get another line of the Dawn Wizard's will every time he gets doused?"

Marrill shook her head. She didn't exactly intend to let her cat *get* doused with Stream water again. But she had to admit, she was curious.

Amazingly, after Karny's blazing trail died down, it left behind perfect footholds Marrill used to scrabble up after him.

When she reached the top she found Karny cleaning himself leisurely, apparently completely reverted to normal catness.

"All right," Marrill said to herself. "That's one ring down. Just..." She stopped and counted. There seemed to be several more layers to the game here than when it was flat, she realized. "...a bunch more to go," she murmured.

She turned and surveyed the tier ahead. Her stomach dropped. The game board squares on this level were decorated with pictures of the elements: flames, lightning, water, and wind. Past the maze of elements, the next ring was suspended in the air above, spinning slowly, with two glass staircases supporting it on either side.

The upside was that there wasn't another wall to climb. The downside, however, was that the Rise were already almost to their staircase. The other team was winning. By a lot.

"Hey," Fin called from below. "A little help down here?"

With a defeated sigh, Marrill peered back over the side. Fin was scrabbling at the wall, slipping and sliding each time he tried to use the handholds. For a second, she didn't get it. Fin was an awesome climber. Maybe the best ever. How could she climb those handholds and he couldn't?

Then she remembered the rules of the game. The Knight couldn't move between rings without help.

"Oh, right." Dropping to her belly, she reached as far down as she could. Fin stretched toward her, and the moment their hands touched, he practically flew up the wall to land beside her.

"That was spiff," he said. His smile faltered, however, when he caught sight of the Rise and how much farther ahead they were. "They're beating the pants off us," he said, sounding incredulous.

"Thank you once again, *Colonel* Obvious," Marrill mumbled.

Fin fisted his hands. "We'll see about that. I'm not finished with my move just yet." He stepped toward the next square, and the flames painted on it exploded into real ones.

Fin jumped back, straight onto a square painted with the lightning bolt. Marrill grabbed him, pulling him out of danger just as a blast of real lightning arced through the air. "I guess that's what Ardent meant about the game growing more dangerous the more seriously we take it," she pointed out.

Fin threw up his arms. "How are we supposed to *not* take this seriously when it's threatening to kill us every second?" He slumped, his expression sour. "This game is the worst. I'd rather play Drop Things into the Pirate Stream and Guess What They'll Turn Into any day. A pepper shaker turning into a kraken is less dangerous than this, and way more fun. At least if we give up, we can do that while we wait for the Salt Sand King to burn the world down."

Give up…have fun… A lightbulb went off in Marrill's head.

"That's it!" she cried. "That's what we need to do: Give up and have fun!"

Fin arched an eyebrow. "For real?"

Marrill jumped up and down. "Totally! Fin, we've been taking this super seriously, and in the end we're going to lose anyway because the Rise are unbeatable, right?"

He nodded. "Sure looks that way."

"So if we're going to lose no matter what, we might as well have a good time doing it!" Marrill poked him on the arm. "We've been in crazier places and ended up laughing. This is *actually* a game! Let's play it."

She scooped up Karnelius and jumped onto a tile marked with water. "Race you to the staircase!" she called as a tidal wave lifted her, carrying her sideways across the squares.

"You're on!" Fin leapt onto a wind square and popped his skysails, swooping in an L-shape. "Heat makes wind go farther!" he yelled, touching one foot downward to tap a fire square. The flames blazed to life, lifting him up to sail past her.

"Oh-ho-ho-ho no!" Marrill yelled, jumping for lightning. The charge shot her around the board, only stopping when she rolled off onto a water square. Electricity surged through her, rattling in her teeth and setting her cat's hair on end. "Bad move," she whispered to herself. "Bad, bad move."

Somewhere nearby, she heard another girl laughing. "You guys!" the girl called. "The lightning tingles!"

They zigzagged and L-walked and slid across the tier, joking and jibing each other the entire way. Finally Marrill found herself at the foot of the staircase, with Fin only a few squares away. She was about to dash up it when she remembered he couldn't move between tiers without help.

"Gibbering Grove!" she called. That was all she needed to say for him to understand. He leapt onto her back, and she raced up the stairs, laughing (and puffing) the entire way.

Even though she didn't know the girl at the top of the stairs, she bum-rushed straight into her, collapsing them all into a snorting, laughing pile. "This game is so much more fun when you're having fun," Marrill said, struggling to control her giggling as Karny pulled himself free, flashing them a dour look.

She rolled to her feet, taking a moment to steady herself as the tier spun beneath them. They were almost level with the ships now; indeed, the Rise warship was coming up fast. As she took in her surroundings, she realized something was missing. Or rather, some*one* was missing.

She laughed, incredulous. "You're never going to believe this, Fin, but we're actually beating the Rise! They're still on the second tier!"

When Fin didn't respond, she turned. "Did you hear me? We're winning...." But the words died in her mouth. Fin stood behind her, seemingly anchored in place, eyes wide with shock.

Alarm fluttered in Marrill's chest. "Fin?" she asked. "You okay?"

Slowly, Fin raised one hand, groping blindly through the empty air. As though he were trying to reach the Rise warship looming closer as their tier spun. "Marrill," he whispered, "that's . . . that's . . ."

Marrill peered past him, following his gaze. For the first time she could see the Crest of the Rise clearly. A woman with dark eyes and olive skin stood razor-straight with one foot on the base of the ship's bowsprit as though she were standing on the neck of her foes. Her fingertips rested on the game board by her side. Not a trace of passion or compassion crossed her face. Deftly, she raised one of her pieces.

Fin glanced back at Marrill. Awe and fear and desperation mingled in his eyes. His outreached hand curled into a pointing finger.

"Marrill," he breathed, "that's my mother."

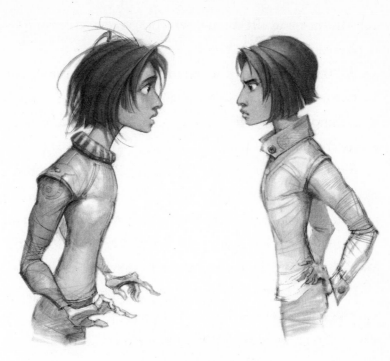

CHAPTER 8
Meet the Family

H er dark eyes weren't as gentle as they were in his memory. Her voice was sharper, too, but now that he saw her, he recognized it. He wondered how he could ever have *not* recognized it. After all, in his head he'd heard her speak the same words a thousand times:

No matter what happens, so long as that star is still shining, someone will always be out here thinking of you.

Fin's heart clenched so tight he thought it might implode on itself. He'd never thought this day would come.

All these years he'd spent searching and wondering.

All the times he'd almost given up.

All those nights he'd ached to feel her arms around him.

His mother had come for him at last.

Behind him, Marrill let out a tight breath. "*That* woman is your mom?"

Fin nodded. "I remember her, Marrill! I saw her when I used the Map to Everywhere after we first beat Serth, before you went home." Back then, Fin had taken the Map without anyone knowing, when everyone believed he'd destroyed the Key. "She was standing on the prow of a ship just like that one."

If Marrill said anything in reply, he didn't hear her. He was too busy studying his mother's face, tracing every line of it as the game board rotated them closer. He'd imagined this moment a million times, wondering what he would say to her. But the words got tangled in his head, and his tongue felt frozen to the roof of his mouth. In the end he could only manage to squeak, "Mom?"

Her eyes regarded him coolly—the same eyes that had glittered beneath the sky of the Khaznot Quay in the only memory of her he had. He waited for her to say something, anything. But her gaze slid past him, as though he were no one.

Fin staggered back, his insides collapsing. She didn't even see him. No, it was worse—he was used to not being seen. She saw him. She knew who he was. She just didn't seem to *care*.

A hand grabbed his, holding him in place. "Lemme go," he grunted, struggling to break free. He wanted to run away. He wanted to be alone. He wanted to go home, but he wasn't even sure where that was anymore. The Parsnickles' attic where they thought he was a ghost? His cabin on the *Kraken* where they constantly forgot him?

Marrill tightened her grip. "It's not your turn," she reminded him. "Moving now could be deadly."

"I don't care," he argued, fighting to pull away.

She clamped her hands on his shoulders, refusing to let him budge. "Well, I do. We're in this together, Fin, from the beginning until the end."

Their tier continued to rotate, dragging them farther away from the Rise warship. His mother was almost out of sight when Fin saw her slam her next piece against the game board, her sharp voice calling, "Vell, go!"

As Fin watched, the smallest of the three Rise players began his move across the board. He didn't bother to zig or zag or move in the shape of an L, or anything like that. Obstacles popped up before him: fire, lightning, water, wind. But they didn't slow him. In fact, they didn't seem to even touch him.

He simply barreled straight forward, heading directly for the other staircase leading to Fin, Marrill, and Fig. Fin had never seen anything like it.

"How's he doing that?" Marrill breathed.

"He's Rise," Fig answered from her spot behind them.

"They're the army unbeatable. No blades will cut them; no magic will harm them."

"But—" Marrill's protest cut off when the Rise player reached the stairs and vaulted up them. At the top, a three-legged stone statue wielding a triple-sided scythe waited for him. The kid didn't pause or hesitate; he simply leapt onto the statue's back and vaulted over it, spinning a somersault through the air straight toward them.

The player landed smartly in a ball before Fin and rose with a flourish.

Fin gasped.

Because he was looking in a mirror.

This, Fin knew, was the boy he'd seen in the Map to Everywhere, standing next to his mother. At the time, he'd thought the boy might be his brother. But in person, it was more than that. He didn't just look *similar* to Fin. The boy looked *exactly* like Fin. If they were brothers, they were twins.

There were some differences, of course. Fin's hair was shaggier, his face dirtier, his frame a bit more wiry. And they held themselves differently, too. If Fin was an alley cat, at any moment half swaggering and half ready to run, this *other* Fin was a lean, young tom, all effortless power that didn't need to strut to be seen.

The boy's eyes traipsed over Fin. "My Fade. We've been looking for you for a long time."

"Wh-who…" Fin's voice cracked. "Who are you?"

"And more specifically," Marrill said, stepping forward, "why do you look exactly like Fin?"

"I am Vell." The boy lifted his chin. "Your Rise." He ignored Marrill, speaking only to Fin. "And I don't look like you. *You* look like *me*. Because you *are* me, to the extent you are anything."

Fin frowned. "What?"

"The Rise are strength, power, resolve," the boy said. A look of disdain crossed his features. "When we are born, we cut the weakness out of ourselves so that only our true selves remain. That weakness coalesces into the form of the thing that once gave it purpose and meaning."

He stabbed a finger at Fin. "*You* are what was removed—my Fade. I am the *real* you. The memorable part. The noticeable part. The thing that commands attention. You slip in and out of memory, in and out of notice, because in truth, you really aren't a person *at all*."

The words hit Fin like a wall. He looked to Fig, hoping she would tell him this was all a cruel joke. But she just nodded sadly.

It was true.

Fin's lungs became heavy; his legs grew weak. He really *was* no one. Literally not a person. Worse, he was all the bad bits: the gristle and fat that gets tossed to the dogs when the butcher carves the meat. A sudden sick feeling growled in the pit of his stomach; he felt light-headed.

Marrill shoved her fists against her hips. "No one talks

to my friend that way!" she shouted. "Fin is someone! He is a real person! And he's memorable to *me*." At her feet, Karny hissed in agreement.

Vell shrugged. "Fade sometimes are to those who have a particular attachment to a certain kind of weakness. A weakness for a weakness, if you will."

Marrill paused, finger held high in midresponse. "I— was that an insult or a compliment?"

The boy dismissed her with a wave of his hand. "A statement of fact. But you indulge his weakness, when what is proper is to *use* it."

"People aren't meant to be *used*," Marrill spat.

Vell's grin turned brutal and sharp. "Fade aren't people."

Marrill sucked in a breath, her face reddening with rage. But before she could say anything, she was cut off by Fig clearing her throat.

"It's your turn, Fin," she said softly.

Vell rounded on her. "You call him Fin now? Like Fade deserve names?" He snorted, as though the very notion was ridiculous.

Fig instantly curled in on herself, her shoulders slumping as she murmured an apology and dropped her eyes. Gone was the cocky tilt of her chin, the confident smirk, the perpetually crooked eyebrow. In the face of Vell's ire, she'd turned into someone totally different.

Someone who believed she didn't matter. Fin knew the feeling well—he'd felt that way much of his life.

"Vell!" the Crest shouted. "Quit toying with them and finish the game. The Salt Sand King is waiting!"

Vell nodded coolly. Turning, he dismissed Fig with a wave of his hand. "You're their piece for the game, Sister Fade. Hurry to the top, and try not to die." He spun sharply on his heel. "It would so pain your true self to have to remove you again."

With that, he took off across the game board, joining the other two Rise players as they advanced toward the next tier. Fin's team had lost its lead.

"Knight, go!" He heard Ardent bellowing in the distance. His gut roiling with new revelations, Fin glanced toward Fig and Marrill, wondering what to do. Marrill clutched Karny to her chest and stared back at him, chewing her bottom lip as her eyes clouded with concern. Fig still kept her focus on the ground.

And just like that, Fin decided it didn't matter. Suddenly, whatever he was feeling, whatever thoughts he was having, he didn't need to deal with them right now. He could just bite them back and focus on the *game*.

He forced a smile. "You two don't look like you're having any fun at all."

Marrill started to protest, but he placed a hand on her shoulder. He clapped his other hand on Fig's shoulder, pulling her into the huddle. Marrill quietly introduced herself.

"Look, we're kids," Fin said. "For once, let's act like it. Because you know what I care about more than anything else? Playing a game with my two friends and having fun. Now who's with me?"

The girls looked uncomfortable for a long moment. Then slowly, Marrill smiled. "Done and done," she said. "Just try to keep up!"

She took off, zigzagging across the ring, then tossed Karny through the air. He landed on his feet, darted across the open space, and sat casually on a tile. The tile lifted into the air, ropes trailing off it.

"Swing time!" Fig announced. "Nobody look at me!"

Over the next twenty minutes, they laughed, shouted, played, and cavorted their way across the face of the Great Game. Fin squared off against a towering, evil-looking knight. He ducked, he dived, he reached up and tweaked its nose. Marrill clapped as Karnelius discovered a tunnel slide that they all piled into. They laughed as it spun them around in loops, somehow taking them up instead of down.

Finally, they stumbled onto the second-to-last tier, the castle towering high above. They were in a forest of towering trees, with leaves that shone in a cacophony of bright colors. Karny dashed into the branches, raining candy-tasting fruit down on Marrill as she zigzagged in circles through spun-sugar underbrush.

Fin stopped to have a casual conversation with a selkie that was interrupted by Fig calling out, "I'm the queeeeeen!" as she hung, giggling, off the side of the castle in the middle of the forest.

She'd made it to the end!

Marrill balled her hands on her hips. "Oh, no you don't," she said, with mock severity. "Wait for me!" Grabbing Karny, she rushed forward, and a zig and a zag later, a glass tile raised into the air, shooting her straight up next to Fig.

Fin moved in a straight line, the length of the L taking him to the edge of the next tier. But he couldn't move up on his own—he would have to wait for Fig or Marrill's next turn.

Fin glanced across the gap in the middle of the tier. On the other side, Vell and his comrades were chopping their way grimly through their own side of the forest, but for them it was a tangle of traps and adversaries. Invincible as they were, they were still getting bogged down just forcing their way through.

The Rise were taking the game too seriously, Fin realized, and the game had found a way to punish them for it. Even so, their next move would take them to the castle. If Fin didn't make it up right now, it would be too late.

He took a deep breath. "Get ready!" he called to Marrill and Fig.

With his last move, the crook of his L, Fin leapt straight into the air. Fig stretched out as far as she could, but the timing was off; she couldn't quite reach him. He yanked hard on the strings of his skysails, feeling them billow out, supporting him. Just long enough for Fig's hand to touch his.

At the brush of her fingertips, a sudden gust of wind

billowed him straight over the wall to land on the edge of Margaham's castle.

Marrill grabbed him in a hug. "We did it! We actually did it!" she shouted, bouncing up and down with joy. "You know what this means? The wish orb is safe!"

"I can't believe it," Fig said, incredulous. "We won. Against the Rise. But we can't beat the Rise. The Rise can't *be* beaten."

A wide smile broke across Fin's face. "Well, sure looks like they can!" He stared down at where the Rise stood with eyes wide and jaws slack, as though they, like Fig, couldn't believe what was happening.

He had to admit, it felt good to be a winner.

Just then Margaham's voice bellowed through the air, blowing the feeling to pieces.

"The game is ended. YOU LOSE!"

CHAPTER 9
No One Said the Game Was Fair

Marrill's heart clenched. They'd lost? How? She stomped toward the castle and pushed her way inside. "But we made it here first!"

Margaham waited for them in a small chamber, a dark outline against the sunlight streaming in from outside. Beside him stood a pedestal with three white envelopes resting on top. "The rules have been rewritten. Now, the *defender* wins when player one's team reaches the castle."

"But that's how *we're* supposed to win," Marrill argued.

"The win condition has changed." The wizard's voice echoed from bronze piping that covered the ceiling.

Marrill couldn't believe what she was hearing. "What? That's cheating! How were we supposed to know? That's not fair!"

"No one said my game was fair."

She was about to keep arguing when Fin tugged on her sleeve. "Look," he said under his breath, pointing at where the piping carrying Margaham's voice converged on a single point next to a stool.

But it wasn't Margaham sitting on the stool, speaking into the pipes. It was a brown-and-yellow frog.

Marrill's eyes widened. "A speakfrog," she whispered. Speakfrogs were the tape recorders of the Pirate Stream. They took messages and repeated them in the same voice that dictated them in the first place.

Marrill's anger turned swiftly to unease as the frog opened its mouth and Margaham's voice echoed forth: "There, that's everything you wanted me to say. Congratulations, you've rigged the game."

She turned to face Margaham himself, who still stood wreathed in deep shadows by the window. Her heart tripped inside her chest as she stepped closer. Close enough to see the hard edges. Close enough to know that the darkness covering him didn't just come from the shadows. Close enough to realize that the man before her wasn't made of flesh and blood. At least, not anymore.

The Inevitable Margaham had been turned to iron. Just like Forthorn Forlorn back at the Ashen Flume, he'd been frozen in place, petrified. As if he'd been taken by the Iron Tide.

Like the entire Pirate Stream would be if the Master of the Iron Ship had his way.

"Blisterwinds," Fin breathed beside her.

The frog continued speaking, running through his script. "I doubt they even have what you want. Am I done now? What will you...Wait, what are you doing? What's happening? My legs are so cold. I can't move! Waaai—"

The echo of Margaham's voice lingered for a long moment. The frog let out a *ribbit* and yawned.

The Great Game of Margaham was finished.

Marrill's throat dropped into her gut. "If we weren't playing against Margaham, then who were we playing against?" she croaked. "Who won?"

But even as she said it, she didn't need to see the shadow fall across the doorway to know. She didn't need to see the blank visage, the black iron, the thick beard and blue eyes that were the only signs of humanity. Metal-clad fingers sliced through the air as the Master of the Iron Ship curled and uncurled his hand.

Marrill's insides froze. Even after all they had seen, up to and including Margaham petrified in iron, she almost hadn't believed it could be true. After all, they'd blasted the Master with the rays of the Lost Sun of Dzannin back in Monerva. He'd fallen into the pit of Stream water collected beneath the Wish Machine. He should have been dead.

But here he was, cold and cruel, standing before them.

Outside, red lightning crashed across the suddenly dark sky. The Master reached out one sharp-edged finger, pointing past them to the pedestal containing the three crisp white envelopes, one for each of the players.

Marrill's chest squeezed tight. She plucked the one that had *Defender* scrawled across the front of it, ran her thumb under the flap, and pulled free the card inside.

Her eyes went wide and blood drained from her cheeks. It was worse than she'd thought. "Oh no," she whispered.

"What?" Fin pressed. "What did the Master play for?"

She flipped the card so the others could see. "The Bintheyr Map to Everywhere," she told them, her voice cracking, "complete with its Key."

As soon as she uttered the words, there was a loud pop, and the other two envelopes disappeared from the pedestal. In their place sat a rolled piece of parchment and a carved crystal sun.

The Map to Everywhere, and its Key.

Dread filled her heart. In Monerva, the Master had shown himself to be Serth's lieutenant. Which meant he was likely there to finish Serth's quest to destroy the Stream. Which meant...

"He's going to open the Gate!" she shouted. Without

thinking, she lunged, hoping to snatch the items before the Master could. But it was like there was some sort of force field around them. A jolt of something hot and tingly zapped her fingers, throwing her back.

The Master looked at her. His metal mask was a sheer wall, blank and pitiless. Through the narrow slit, his ice-blue eyes were as cold as the metal surrounding them.

Every muscle in her body quivered. "Who are you?" she whispered.

As always, he remained silent. He raised one hand back toward the entrance, just in time to catch a blast of energy that surged in at him.

"You're good, I'll give you that," Ardent said. Ropebone's lines untwined from around his ankles and retreated. "Thought I had the jump on you there." He strode in casually, flames burning around his knuckles. "You can remove the mask now, Margaham. I'll admit to being surprised you're the Master, though I guess the discovery was inevitable. You must have spent the past century training quite diligently in order to match my skills."

Marrill cleared her throat. "Um, Ardent?" She pointed toward the metal statue in the corner. His eyes shifted, taking in his iron-coated friend. A look of regret crossed his features, and he sighed.

He turned back to the Master. "Ah. Not Margaham. Well, that does at least explain the skill level." He squinted as he considered his opponent. "Very well, keep your secrets, then. We're narrowing it down, aren't we? Serth, Annalessa, Forthorn, Calixto, and now Margaham crossed off.... That only leaves two Wizards of Meres to choose from."

Marrill's eyes darted back and forth between them. Slowly, they circled each other. At any moment, a wizard's duel would break out. She was pretty sure this little castle wouldn't be enough to contain the devastation.

"Tanea Hollow-Blood?" Ardent mused. He studied the other wizard thoughtfully. "I admit, you're not really built like a woman. But then, Tanea *did* have a magnificent beard."

He snapped his fingers. "Alexter Strate! Of course!" The Master stopped. Ardent stopped with him, a smug smile on his face. They'd rotated 180 degrees so that Ardent was now closest to the Map. "I should have known. You always were the *third* most powerful of us. Behind myself and Serth, of course. Close tie with Annalessa." A sly smile played on Ardent's features. "How does that rhyme go?"

Out of nowhere, Margaham's voice spoke again, coming from the speakfrog in the corner.

The eight, cursed eight, who spat at fate,
First was Serth, and the rest came late.
Ardent the Cold was the right hand so bold,
He gathered the Stream with Alexter Strate.
Calixto and Margaham and Tanea filled them up,
The font formed by Forthorn, by Annalessa, the cup.

Marrill shook her head. *Ardent the Cold?* It was the same thing Margaham—or his frog—had called Ardent before the game had even begun. Clearly, they hadn't known Ardent too well. *Cold* was the last way she would describe him.

All of a sudden, the Master lunged. Ardent dodged easily, sending back a volley of energy. The Master staggered, but he hadn't been after Ardent. He'd been after a young girl reaching for the Map.

With a swipe of the Master's arm, she flew through the air, smashing against the wall. "Fig!" Fin cried. But before he could move, before Marrill could ask how he even knew the girl, before anyone could stop him, the Master snatched the Map and Key from the pedestal.

He held them aloft in his gauntlet-clad hands.

"No!" Marrill screamed.

"Alexter, Tanea, whoever you are, listen to reason!" Ardent begged. "You must not open the Gate!"

But the Master didn't hesitate. He moved the Key toward the Map. Magic crackled through the chamber.

The hairs on the back of Marrill's neck danced. Through the windows and the door, dark clouds choked the sky. Red lightning played through them like the energy of a Tesla coil. The energy of the end of the world.

It was too late. They'd failed.

After everything they'd been through.

After all the times they'd defeated Serth.

It didn't matter.

The Master had won.

Serth had won.

Marrill's mouth filled with the sharp taste of iron as red lightning crashed around them. Above his head the Master touched the Key against the Map.

The Lost Sun of Dzannin began to dawn.

CHAPTER 10
Not Who You Were Expecting

Fin felt like razor blades were slicing his stomach as the Master of the Iron Ship touched the Key to the Map. Behind his steel faceplate, the Master's eyes were a still mask of hard-edged determination.

"Stop this!" Ardent boomed. The air erupted in shrieks of agony as he let loose an onslaught of magic. Fire, lightning, dark energies Fin couldn't even name, ripped through the room. But they did nothing to slow or stop the Master.

And then Fin realized the shrieks weren't coming from

Ardent's fingertips but from somewhere else. The pitch grew higher, almost painful. The surface of the Map buckled and strained as the Key pressed against it. It opened, folding around itself and stretching higher, wider, into the shape of a door, the Key now a knob stuck in its center.

Ink ran down the page like the bars of a cage. Fin could see the dark sketch of a figure behind them, and the furious flapping of a maddened bird.

Though the Map was still flat and two-dimensional, the figure reached out a hand. The surface of the parchment rippled and warped. The air around it seemed to hiss and burn. Long, sketched fingers broke through in three dimensions and gripped the knob, pulling at it from somewhere within.

The Gate to the Lost Sun of Dzannin burst open with a ferocious boom that sent shock waves rippling out from it. The blast hit Fin with a physical force, propelling him backward. Light seared out from the glowing doorway. Time seemed to slow as it grew somehow brighter, hotter. Fin had no choice but to close his eyes.

When he opened them again, a shadow stood against the blinding light. Fin's insides went cold.

Beside him, Marrill stiffened. "Serth," she choked.

"Wh-what's going on?" Fig asked in a trembling voice.

The figure stepped forward, the glow continuing to pulse and coalesce around him and into him. His cloak began to take on color, its once dark cloth now a shining silver, the white starbursts now turned to black holes that seemed to devour light. His face was polished alabaster, inlaid with lines of sharp obsidian that had once been traces of his tears.

The shining figure held out his arms in a gesture of gracious offering. Energy didn't so much emanate from him as it *was* him. It seemed like the very floor vibrated beneath his feet, the atoms of the stone spinning faster and with more force.

"I have arisen," Serth said, in a voice that sounded nothing like him. Every time they'd met before, the Meressian Oracle had been stooped, his voice cracked and trembling. Now it was firm, commanding, and confident.

A screeching caw ripped through the room, defying the hum of power. A blur of scribbled feather tore free from the Gate. It burst past Serth's shining form in a frenzy of inky wings and soared through the air, banking and swooping in the tight chamber.

"Rose?" Fin gasped as she shot past him. The Compass Rose of the Map to Everywhere soared high to the ceiling. Serth's head turned slowly, watching her. He raised a hand, and cold light seared the air, slashing a gash through the castle walls.

"Rose!" Marrill shrieked. The bird dodged and weaved expertly, evading the bright death that followed her. She wheeled around the room once, let out a loud cry, and dove.

Fin stumbled back as the bird streaked past them, straight toward the exit. Fig jumped aside. Ardent ducked. Rose reached the doorway, nothing between her and freedom.

Just then, the Master stepped into her path. An iron

cage snapped shut in his hands. Rose beat her wings against the bars, screeching and cawing. The Master held her high, regarding her impassively through the blank metal mask. And then he turned and left.

Fin spun toward Ardent, expecting him to do something. But the wizard no longer seemed interested in the Master. Instead his gaze was focused on the figure that stood in the threshold of the Gate. "Serth!" he cried, stepping in front of the silver-robed figure. He held up his hands in a peace offering. "It's Ardent. Your friend. Please, come to reason. It's not too late."

The radiant Oracle strode forward. Behind him, the light died away. The Map turned back to ink and paper, falling empty to the ground. Now the glow filling the room came only from the man himself.

"It is done." The Oracle's new voice was calm but powerful. Fin could feel it buzzing in his teeth, setting his very soul on edge. *"I have taken a new vessel. I have arisen."*

Ardent stopped short, then let out a long, slow exhale. His shoulders stooped. He looked more frail than ever before.

"You're not Serth," he whispered.

The thing wearing Serth's body barely looked at them. His face was an empty mask, devoid of sorrow, devoid of joy. Nor was there sympathy or anything that could be called human. It was like looking straight at the cruel sun, bright and heartless and bare.

"I am the last child given life and form by the first wizards," he said. **"I am the end of possibility, and the possibility of end. I am the prisoner of the Bintheyr Map to Everywhere, the horrible truth that the Stream was created to conceal."**

Fin swallowed, remembering when Ardent had first told them about the Meressian Prophecy and its awful origin. In the days before the Stream was made, back when everything was raw potential, the Dzane crafted new worlds with their whims, and everything was possible. Even the end of possibility.

A hundred thousand stars shone on a hundred thousand different creations. But only one star shone on destruction.

That star had been locked away in the Bintheyr Map to Everywhere, bound by the boundless power of the Pirate Stream. But now it had broken free and arisen once more.

"You're the Lost Sun of Dzannin," Marrill breathed.

Fin closed his eyes. Was it really possible? Could the man who was once Serth have *become* the Lost Sun?

"That is the name that the first wizards gave me, for I am the child that they called wayward," Serth's body spoke. Cracks grew out through the stone beneath his feet.

Ardent scowled, recovering some of his familiar defiance. "Call yourself what you will, be it man or star or both at once, for all I care. I will not let you destroy the Stream."

The Lost Sun cocked his head to the side, eyes sweeping across the man who'd long ago been Serth's closest friend. There was no compassion in his gaze, no evidence of their former bond. *"You have no say in the matter."*

He then spread his hands wide. Power flexed and bowed within him. For a moment it seemed that perhaps his human form would be too weak to contain such energy. Tiny fissures erupted across his skin, letting through cracks of light.

He raised his arms to the side. *"The end begins."*

"Serth!" Ardent called, lunging toward him.

But he was too late. The creature who had once been Serth dropped his hands. The ground below him began to buckle. Fin grabbed Marrill and stumbled back as the floor of the castle gave way.

Except there was something off about the way it crumbled. Fin had grown up in a ramshackle city on the steep slopes of Khaznot Mountain; he'd seen his fair share of buildings lose stability and collapse. Usually they fell in on themselves, crumbling into a pile of rubble.

That wasn't what happened to Margaham's castle. The floor didn't just fall away; it disintegrated. Everything about it simply ceased to exist. And below it, there was nothing. Just a great, gaping chasm.

But that wasn't right, either. Because a chasm had a bottom. It had walls. And this had none of those things. It had nothing.

It *was* nothing.

And as they watched, the void grew in diameter, pulling everything around it into that nothingness.

Ardent stood his ground, placing his hands together, palms facing the void. His face was a scowl of concentration as energy radiated around him. "The Stream is infinite!" Ardent called to his former friend. "You can never hope to destroy it all!"

The Lost Sun stepped slowly forward, the world falling away in the wake of each footstep. *"I am not hope. I am certainty. And though I may walk across an endless river, I know the wellspring from which it flows. The pure headwaters of the Stream beckon. My essence will pour forth into them, touching all possibilities at once. And when it does, this chaos will end. These possibilities will end. All of them. Forever."*

Ardent shook his head fiercely. "We don't have to be what we're told," he shot back. "You can choose to stop this. Your Prophecy is only one possibility in an endless sea of others."

"You misunderstand," the shining wizard told him. *"I am the fulfillment of your Prophecy. I am that one possibility made real. I am the end of choice. I am finality. I cannot stop, and I cannot be stopped."* He continued his advance, the world dissolving into an ever-widening void behind him.

"*This is not malice*," the Lost Sun said as he neared Ardent. "*It is simply necessity. All must end. You, too, have a role to play in my design.*"

For a moment, Ardent refused to cede. Fin held his breath, waiting for what would happen next. Then the old man took a slow step back.

"What do we do?" Marrill squeaked in Fin's ear.

Fin hung his head. He wanted to smile, to come up with something witty, to give her a hope to hold on to. But at this point, for once, he didn't see a way out of their predicament. Serth had been powerful enough on his own. With the power of the Lost Sun—*being* the Lost Sun—he seemed unstoppable. If even Ardent couldn't stand before him, Fin wasn't sure what they had left to hope for, except maybe to survive the next few moments.

"Run?" he said at last.

Marrill nodded vigorously. "Agreed." Together they raced for the door. Fin paused to yank Fig to her feet and shove her forward. Marrill made it out of the castle and sprinted across the game board, not even hesitating before leaping to the next level. Fig followed close behind.

Fin bolted after them, bringing up the rear. But he had barely made it a few steps onto the lower tier when a hand grabbed his wrist, yanking him to the side. It was Vell, his face a mask of anger.

Even with all that had happened, Fin couldn't resist

rubbing in the Rise's loss. "So sorry you couldn't join us on the winning square. You nearly missed the end of the world."

"The orb," Vell demanded. "Where is it?"

Fin patted his pockets with his free hand. "'Fraid I don't have it on me."

"Vell, bring your Fade and come!" their mother shouted over the roar. "We sail!"

From the opposite direction Marrill called, "Fin, hurry!"

"The Crest summons us." Vell tugged Fin in the direction of the Rise warship. Fin glanced at his mother standing on the bow, waiting. So much about her was familiar. And at the same time, nothing about her was familiar at all.

At that moment, understanding hit so hard it left him light-headed. This woman looked like his mother in the same way that Vell looked like Fin. Because she was Rise. But the woman Fin remembered was like Fin. Fade.

The Crest wasn't Fin's mother. Her *Fade* was.

Fin dug in his heels and ripped free of Vell's grasp. "I don't think so, jog. Now's not a good time for a family reunion. Especially when you're *not* my family."

He didn't wait for Vell to respond. He sprinted across the game board, leaping to the next tier without hesitation.

Marrill was waiting for him below, and she grabbed his hand. "We've got to get out of here!" Together they ran for the *Kraken*.

Fin risked one last glance over his shoulder. Ardent still faced the Lost Sun, bombarding him with energy and power that sizzled the air. But the old wizard was no match against the living star-made-human. The Lost Sun walked forward without slowing, forcing Ardent to retreat toward the *Kraken*.

Across the board, Vell had reached the Rise warship and stood by the bow, glaring at Fin. "The Rise can be delayed!" he shouted. "But *never* beaten. We will not stop until we have both you and the orb back in our control!"

Fin shook his head, wondering why the orb even mattered to them anymore. There were way more important things to worry about now that the Lost Sun had risen.

The *Kraken* jumped to life as the stone hand holding her shook and shattered. Fin braced for splashdown, while behind them, Margaham's Game crumbled into nothing.

And still the Lost Sun strode forward, as though all the Stream awaited him.

CHAPTER 11
Game Over

A s they fled Margaham's Game, Marrill stood with the rest of the crew at the railing of the *Kraken*'s stern, watching the Lost Sun continue his slow march onward. When he reached the edge of the massive game board, he didn't even pause before stepping onto the Stream, walking across its surface as though it were solid.

Destruction flowed in his wake, the world crumbling behind him with each step. *Crumble* wasn't the right word, she told herself. It was more like the entire Stream was pouring into the void the Lost Sun had created in a torrent, a massive waterfall, straight into oblivion.

Even as she watched, the void grew larger, expanding outward in all directions, slowly devouring the Stream. This was their worst-case scenario. This is what the crew had been trying to prevent ever since they'd first run into Serth in the Gibbering Grove, so long ago. The rise of the Lost Sun. The destruction of the Pirate Stream. And it was even more terrible than she'd imagined it could be.

"What happens to it all?" Marrill asked in a small voice, unable to look away from the creeping emptiness.

Ardent sat at a table behind her, hunched over the Map to Everywhere and examining it closely. He didn't even look up when he answered her. "It is destroyed. Utterly."

The rumor vines at the ship's stern echoed his words softly, as though even the plants understood the solemnity of the situation.

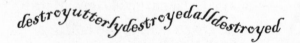

destroyutterlydestroyedalldestroyed

The thought of so many worlds—of so many possibilities—destroyed struck terror in Marrill's heart. She didn't understand why anyone would want to cause such a thing. "But why would the Master do that? Why unleash the Lost Sun and destroy the Stream?"

Ardent lifted a shoulder. "To finish what Serth began, I

imagine. The Master seems to have been operating as Serth's second in command after all."

That didn't make Marrill feel any better. "Will there be a way to fix it? I mean, once we figure out how to stop him?"

Ardent took a deep breath and let it out slowly, considering her question. "No," he finally said. "I'm afraid that everything the Lost Sun touches will be gone forever."

A gruff voice nearby grumbled. "You guys ever noticed that every world you visit ends up broken or destroyed? I'm just saying. Folks should really cross you off their invite list." The Naysayer lumbered toward his fishing lines, tugging on each one to check for a fresh catch before settling into his chair. Karny immediately jumped into his lap, nestling in the crook of one of his arms and purring contentedly.

Marrill didn't want to consider the truth of his words. "But we *can* stop him, right? Before he gets to Meres and destroys everything?"

This time Ardent did look up. He slumped back in his chair. "I don't know."

The rumor vines took up the sentiment:

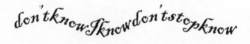

Marrill blinked. Since when did Ardent not have the answers?

"Well, all we have to do is figure out how to get the Lost Sun back into the Map again, right?" she asked, gesturing toward the table. "And the Dzane did it before, so there's got to be a way...."

"And maybe it would work again if there wasn't something wrong with the Map." Ardent lifted it between them, and that's when Marrill noticed the hole in the center of the parchment.

The rumor vines continued to echo what was now obvious:

mapiswrongsomethingwrongmapwork

Marrill frowned and caught Fin's eye. He seemed as surprised as she did. She moved closer to get a better look at the Map. "Isn't that where Margaham's Game was?" she asked, tracing her finger around the edge of the hole.

"It is." Ardent stood and began to pace. "The Map is the embodiment of the Stream itself. The void created by the Lost Sun is growing, and with every step, the Lost Sun is opening up more of it. If I had to hazard a guess, and it seems that I do, my hypothesis would be that the deterioration of the Map will mirror precisely the destruction caused by the Lost Sun."

"So," Remy interjected, "more and more of the Map will be destroyed as the Lost Sun destroys more and more of the Stream?"

"You could put it that way," Ardent grumbled. "If you don't like precision. Or extraneous quantities of verbiage."

The rumor vines tried to take that one up, but it just ended in a tangle of random words.

Marrill stared at the Map, her eyes tracing all the worlds swimming across its surface. All the places she'd never get to visit. All the places that would disappear unless they stopped the Lost Sun. Including, eventually, her own world.

"But maybe the Map will still work," she offered. "Maybe the hole doesn't matter."

Ardent let out a sigh. "I've already tried." To demonstrate, he gripped the crystal Key and held it against the surface of the Map. Nothing happened.

"What about using the wish orb?" a deckhand Marrill didn't recognize proposed. "Couldn't you just wish this all away?"

Ardent shook his head. "I wish." When no one laughed at his halfhearted joke, he cleared his throat. "The wish orb is powerful. It contains perhaps the purest, most concentrated water on the Stream, outside the Font of Monerva itself."

He tapped his fingers against the railing, thinking it through. "My guess is that partially filled, it could possibly contain the power of the Lost Sun for a short period of time, but not stop it. Not for long. And using the wish orb would unleash the Salt Sand King and the Iron Tide, which would, of course, certainly only serve to make matters worse. You'd have three entities vying to destroy the Stream rather than just one."

"Right," Fin said, glaring at the deckhand. "So no using the wish orb. In fact, maybe we should keep it in a very, *very* secure location."

"Okay, the Map and wish orb are out," Remy said. "How long do we have to figure out another solution?"

"Until the Lost Sun arrives at Meres and pours his power into the Font, I should think," Ardent said.

Remy rolled her eyes. "Right, I know that." She looked to Coll. "But how long until that happens?"

The captain shrugged. "Depends on how fast he's moving."

Ardent stared toward the horizon. "Walking speed."

"Seriously?" Remy scoffed. "Dude's the most powerful entity that exists, and he's going to walk all the way to Meres? You'd think he would magic up a boat at least."

"The Lost Sun does not create," Ardent said. "Plus, I imagine that's exactly why he feels no need to rush. Because he *is* the most powerful entity on the Stream. He's confident nothing can stop him. Besides," he added with a chuckle, "it wouldn't be easy to sail a ship when every step you take destroys the world. The whole thing would keep sinking out from underneath you. Unless of course—"

"Well, less than a week," Coll said, cutting Ardent off. He stood by the table, his fingers stretched across the Map, connecting Meres to the hole. "That's how long we have."

Everyone fell silent, lost in thought. Marrill slumped against one of the masts, staring up into the sky, hoping for inspiration to strike. High in the rigging, a trio of pirats scampered across the yard. Squeaking among themselves, two of them maneuvered a scrap of cloth into place over a tear in the sail as the third dangled from his back feet, using a tiny needle and thread to sew it into place.

For a moment Marrill wished she could trade places with

the creatures whose only concern at the moment involved fixing the sail rather than fixing the world.

She blinked. That was it! She pushed from the mast excitedly. "What if we repair the Map?" she asked. "If we fix the hole in the Map, we can use it to retrap the Lost Sun, just like the Dzane trapped him in the first place. Right?"

Ardent snorted. "Well, certainly. But you can't just *fix* the Map to Everywhere."

Marrill put her hands on her hips. "Why not?"

"Well, because it's *Dzane* made. It's not like you can stitch a patch on that hole and call it a day!"

"Why not?" Marrill repeated.

Ardent flapped his hands through the air in exasperation. "Because…well…because you can't! I mean, the power you would need to pull it off—"

"So the great wizard Ardent isn't wizard enough to fix it?" Fin poked. Marrill smiled at him.

Ardent opened his mouth, then closed it. "I'm not saying—"

Coll cleared his throat, a mischievous smile on his lips. "Come on, Ardent. I've seen you do things no other wizard could ever do. Are you *really* telling us you're not wizard enough to patch a map?"

Ardent's nose twitched. One eyebrow popped up. Marrill could see the pride wrestling with the thoughts behind his eyes. "Okay, yes, I think I could possibly manage it." Marrill grinned, giddiness bubbling through her. "BUT!" he said, raising one finger. "We would need the very same ingredients that the Dawn Wizard used to create the Map in the first place. Anyone know where to find those?"

Coll's eyes dropped to the deck. Fin looked around, like he wasn't sure who Ardent was talking to.

Marrill's smile drooped a little. But hope still flowed through her. So long as there was a chance, she couldn't give up. "What do we need?"

Ardent stepped close, giving her his grandfatherly smile. He was doing his best to look earnest, but Marrill could tell he was humoring her. "Well, we would need the right parchment, of course. And ink. We'd then have to take it all to the Font of Meres, before the Lost Sun gets there, and use the headwaters to redraw the secrets of the Stream straight onto our new Map."

Fin rubbed his hands together. "Then what are we waiting for? Let's swing by the Khaznot Quay and snag some supplies—they've got everything you need if you know where to look. Then it's off to Meres and *bam*—crisis averted." He took the Map from Marrill and started examining it for the shortest route to the Khaznot Quay.

"Not so fast, my random stowaway," Ardent said. "We can't just grab *any* old scrap of cloth and staining liquid. We would need parchment capable of expanding and shrinking and twisting and growing and containing all the possibilities of the Stream, which are endless. And frankly, I've never heard of anything like that, other than the material of the Map itself."

Marrill bit her lip. It couldn't be hopeless, she told herself, not now that they'd figured out a solution.

"Perhaps if I still had access to the Dawn Wizard's memories, I could use them to find the answers we're searching for. But now that the Wiverwane has been subsumed by your cat, the knowledge is lost to us." He waved a hand at Karnelius, who yawned loudly before falling back into a nap.

"No it isn't," Fin said.

Ardent glanced at him. "And you are...?"

"A friend with a good idea," Fin told him.

"I'll be the judge of that," Ardent said, crooking an eyebrow. "The idea bit being good, I mean. It's really beyond my purview to pass judgment on what kind of friend you'd make, as obviously everyone puts a different priority on disparate traits when it comes to choosing people to become acquainted—"

Coll cleared his throat, cutting Ardent off. "You were saying?" he asked Fin, eyeing the boy with suspicion.

"The Dawn Wizard's knowledge isn't lost. It's just in a different form. We still have his last will. What if it has the information we're looking for?"

Marrill plucked her cat from the Naysayer, ignoring protests from both of them. "You think my cat knows how to save the Pirate Stream?"

"I think the Dawn Wizard knew where to go shopping for the ingredients for his Map," Fin explained. "And I think your cat is the closest we're going to get to the Dawn Wizard himself."

Ardent clapped his hands together. "Coll, your new

deckhand is quite clever." Kicking aside the hem of his purple robe, he turned and pointed a finger in the air. "Pirats! Bring me my dullwood pail. We've got a cat to dunk."

A cheer went up around the ship. The many multilegged rodents chirped excitedly, apparently quite thrilled about the prospect of a Karnelius dunking booth.

Marrill sighed. She knew Ardent and Fin were right. But that didn't mean she liked it. When the pirats returned with the pail of Pirate Stream water, she pressed her face against her cat's neck and whispered, "Sorry about this, Karny."

Karnelius, for his part, would have none of it. As soon as she began to lower him toward the water, he employed the same tactic he used to evade his cat carrier. He thrust out his legs, bracing his paws against the lip of the bucket. The battle was on.

No matter how hard she pushed, no matter how many of them worked to pry his paws free, they got him no closer to the waiting water. He struggled and squirmed, becoming a whirling devil of fur and claw, twisting angrily until he managed to upend the pail. Everyone scrambled back from the slosh of magical water, except for Ardent, who was oblivious, as usual.

Karny landed on his feet in full puff mode, his ears pinned back and teeth bared. The rumor vines took up the cat's protest, their echoes growing louder until the entire back of the ship sounded like it was under attack by hordes of angry snakes.

Slowly, Marrill crouched, reaching for her cat. But the

moment she got close, the cat took off. He sprinted toward the hatch leading belowdecks but banked away when Fin jumped in front of him. He leapt for a mast, but the pirats chittered at him, forcing him back to the deck.

"Aww, now look what ya done," the Naysayer grumbled. "He's all scared. Come here, fella. Uncle Nono will protect you."

Karny dug his claws into the deck and executed a sharp turn, heading for his protector's arms. But just as he leapt toward the purplish lizard's outstretched hands, Remy stepped from behind a bulkhead and tossed an entire pail of Stream water at the cat.

There was no escaping the surprise ambush. The wash of golden water was a direct hit, splashing Karnelius midjump. The cat hung in the air a moment before dropping to the deck and landing on his feet with a sodden splat.

Everyone looked to Remy in wide-eyed surprise, and she shrugged. "You learn a few tricks when you've got seven younger brothers and sisters who all went through a phase of hating baths."

The dripping cat at the babysitter's feet narrowed his eyes and twitched his tail angrily before opening his mouth and beginning to speak.

To the Council of Whispers, I leave the Face
of the Map to Everywhere. I would advise
them to share it well and use it cautiously, lest
suspicion and jealousy take root in their hearts.

"The Map to Everywhere!" Remy said.

Fin puffed his chest, looking self-satisfied. "So Karny *does* know something about the Map!"

Marrill grabbed his arm. There was something about this will that didn't sit right with her. After all, things hadn't exactly gone well for the Council of Whispers. They'd grown so attached to using the Face of the Map to spy on others and gossip that they'd grown roots, literally, becoming the heart of the babbling jungle known as the Gibbering Grove.

"I don't know," she said. "Are we sure we can trust it?"

"Do we have a choice?" Fin fired back.

Remy gave a wry smile. "Well," she said, "at least we know the Dawn Wizard's will has *some* information on the Map. And unless you guys have another lead on how to fix it…" She raised up her dullwood pail.

Marrill poked out her lip in defeat. *Poor Karny.* "Back to wetting down the cat," she said with a sigh.

⊹ ⊹ ⊹

Quite a while later, Marrill sat on the edge of the forecastle, legs dangling in the air, thumb rubbing over the growing ragged hole in the Map to Everywhere. Next to her, a sopping and extremely unamused Karnelius droned out an endless list of the Dawn Wizard's bizarre bequests. So far there hadn't been anything more about the Map, but she still wasn't willing to give up.

To Tealeaf the Stinging Fairy, whom I slighted
by omitting from the Book of Wondrous
Beings, I leave a thimbleful of apologies,
distilled from the very first apology ever made,
by my brother Kab-Who-Dreams to a rather
small stone that he had tripped over in the days
before the Stream was born.

Karny sniffled and then let out an enormous self-drying
sneeze. Again. The recitation cut off, and the cat went back
to grooming himself. Marrill groaned. "Whose turn is it?"
she asked.

Remy lay in a nearby hammock, idly flipping through a
book on advanced sailing warfare tactics. "Not it," she said,
placing a finger against her nose without glancing up. Coll
leaned against one of the masts nearby. He also had a finger
against his nose. Even Ardent, who'd been scribbling notes
in a tattered journal, had a finger against his nose.

Marrill quickly pressed her finger against her own nose
and looked to Fin. He lay on his back beside her, eyes closed
as he basked in the warmth of the sun. Marrill's eyes narrowed. Was it just her or was he clearly trying to pretend he
was asleep?

She nudged him. "I went last time. This round's on you."

Fin groaned and sat up. "Your cat hates me."

"He hates *all* of us right now."

Near the stern, the Naysayer cleared his throat with a wet, guttural *harrumph*. "Speak for yourselves."

speakforyourselvesyourselvesspeakforspeakyourselves

Marrill rolled her eyes. "So you're his favorite right now. I'm sure he'll be quite pleased to curl up with you while the *Kraken* is dragged down into the pit of nothingness the Lost Sun has so graciously created."

The Naysayer looked up from tending his rumor vines to shoot her a sour look. "Don't gotta be rude."

She knew it was bad when the Naysayer was giving her lessons on comportment. She sighed and shoved the dull-wood water cannon to Fin. At least the new contraption Ardent had whipped up allowed them a bit more distance than the pail did. "You wanna save the Stream? Douse the cat and make it quick."

"Fine," he said, pushing to his feet. "But you get to run interference this time when Ardent refuses to heal my wounds and decides to throw me in the brig for being a stowaway. Again."

Marrill tried to keep from smiling. It wouldn't be so funny if Fin hadn't turned seeing how fast he could break through the brig's new singing lock into his own personal challenge. "Done," she readily agreed.

Next to Fin a deckhand laughed. "That's what you get

for being memorable, Brother Fade—people remember it's your turn." He shot her a glare, which only made her laugh harder.

As sweetly as possible, Fin clicked his tongue against the roof of his mouth, calling for Karny. But the cat was more than wise to them by this point and had already taken off across the ship. At least they'd figured out early to lock the hatches to the decks below. The first time he'd escaped he led them in a chase that lasted at least an hour.

Marrill went back to studying the ragged hole in the Map to Everywhere, ignoring Karny's hissing and Fin's swallowed grunts as he chased after the cat.

Ten minutes later she heard Fin shout, "Got him!" And then the familiar sounds of her cat's voice filled the air:

To the Shell Weavers of Oneira, I leave a bolt of ribbon spun straight from the fabric of dreams. Hold it dear, for from this material did I craft the great Bintheyr Map to Everywhere.

Since when had her cat's voice become familiar to her? Marrill shook her head, marveling at how easily she'd grown comfortable with the craziness of the Pirate Stream.

But then she realized what she'd just heard, and she bolted upright. "Did I just hear that right?" she asked. Fin nodded, grinning widely.

Triumphant, Marrill spun to face Ardent. The wizard

blinked, still staring at the cat. Then he let out a laugh. "The Shell Weavers of Oneira—brilliant! And this will give us an opportunity to cross another wizard from Meres off our list. Just so happens that Tanea Hollow-Blood's Dream Garden connects directly with the Shell Shoals."

He stood, thrusting a finger into the air. "Coll, tell your first mate up there to set us a course for Oneira."

Marrill threw up her arms in joy. She'd known there had to be a way if they just didn't give up. "We're going to the Shell Weavers!" she cried. "Whoever they are."

"We'd better make it fast," Coll interrupted, his voice somber. He'd plucked the Map from Marrill's fingers and pointed, holding it out for all of them to see.

Just on the edge of the expanding hole torn through the middle of the Map, just on the brink of the Lost Sun's growing devastation, sat a little round dot. Next to it, in letters already crinkling, were the words SHELL SHOALS OF ONEIRA.

CHAPTER 12
Dream Shells

While Remy set a course for the Shell Shoals of Oneira and Marrill took her cat downstairs to find him some treats, Fin pulled Fig aside. Finally he had a chance to confront her without anyone noticing.

"You're the reason the Rise found us at Margaham's Game," he said bluntly, crossing his arms. "You spied on us."

She lifted her chin, holding her ground. "I told you I'd help you find your mom."

Fin's eyes narrowed. "You wanted to help the Rise steal the orb."

She glanced away and shrugged. "If I'd wanted to steal the orb, I would have."

"That's exactly what I'd say if *I* was trying to steal the orb." He shook his head. "You know I can't trust you."

She winced. "I know."

That she accepted it so easily surprised Fin. He'd expected her to deny it. To try to convince him to give her another chance.

"I'm guessing you came back to the *Kraken* to finish your mission?"

She shifted, clearly uncomfortable. "That's not the whole reason."

He lifted an eyebrow.

She sighed. "I stayed behind to protect you, by order of Vell and the Crest."

He burst out laughing. "Protect me?" The excuse was so absurd he couldn't believe she thought he'd buy it. "Why would *they* care if anything happened to me?"

She looked at him, frowning. "You really don't know how this works, do you?" He remained silent, waiting for her to explain. She blew out a breath. "The Rise and the Fade are...connected."

"I picked up on that."

"No, I mean..." She seemed to struggle for words. "We are their *literal* weakness. We're the reason they're unbeatable. Because they have no weakness so long as we exist separately."

Fin struggled to understand. "So if something happens to me..."

"If you die, Vell becomes vulnerable," she told him. "All that weakness goes back into him. He can then be beaten, or even killed."

"Oh."

Suddenly, the emotions Fin had been pushing away since learning about Vell and his mother, all the pain he'd bitten down since he first learned he was no one, rushed in at once. His deepest fear was true. He really was no one. He was just a vessel for someone else's weakness.

He dropped his chin to his chest, trying to swallow back the emptiness that threatened to overwhelm him. "You're here to make sure nothing happens to me so Vell stays safe."

When Fig said nothing, he took that as confirmation. But then she sighed and leaned against the railing beside him. He could just barely feel her arm brushing against his. "What's it like to have a friend?"

He blinked, surprised by the question. "Why do you ask?"

She lifted a shoulder. "I've just never really had one before."

Fin almost choked. "You have an entire army of friends," he pointed out. "You know, the ones that boarded the *Kraken* with you? And then came after us at Margaham's Game?"

"Just because they can remember me doesn't mean they're my friends."

"What about your Rise?"

She let out a soft chuckle. "Think you could ever be friends with Vell?"

Fin barked out a laugh. "Point taken." He then turned, facing her. "One thing to know about friends: They look out for each other. And that's what I plan to do with my friends on the *Kraken*. Even if that means protecting them from you."

She nodded. "I can't stop the Rise," she told him. "They won't stop chasing you. It's not just about the orb anymore, Fin. It's about you and Vell. And what the Rise want, they will take."

⊹⊹ ⊹ ⊹⊹

Two days later, just when Fin thought they'd taken a wrong turn, just when he thought there was nothing to see, he blinked, and the Shell Shoals of Oneira appeared before him as if they'd been there from the moment of his birth and ever after.

The shoals spread out before them in a low tumble of coral. In places, it rose up to damp plateaus that defied the water; in others it struggled with each wave, and Fin could scarcely tell where land ended and seafloor began.

The *Kraken* slid through a channel that seemed carved just for them, then ground to a halt. Marrill joined Fin as they surveyed their destination. The coral swept around them in the semicircle of an atoll; it reminded Fin a little too much of standing on one of the rings of Margaham's Game, and he shuddered. But that was the end of the comparison; the water in the central lagoon was blue and clear; the coral itself was a maze of sharp and smooth, high and low, rough and pitted.

Tide pools collected all across the pocked surface of the atoll, and from the *Kraken*'s height Fin could see straight down into many of them. In the shallowest, miniature mermen raced iridescent minnows. In the deepest, spiny sea bishops held court in drip-sand cathedrals while spider-limbed lobsters tended their seaweed gardens nearby. A tiny boat bobbed unmanned in one; beneath it, a lumpy inside-out fish played dominoes with a sleek griffin-ray.

The afternoon sun felt warm on his skin; the salt breeze gentle and inviting. Fin glanced toward the wall of black emptiness, chewing its way toward them along the horizon. This was just the edge of the void, expanding outward from the trail of the Lost Sun as he walked on toward Meres. Fin could only imagine what would happen when the Lost Sun reached his destination.

Fin shook the thought from his head and forced himself to remember that the end of the world might be creeping closer, but it hadn't made it here just yet. He should enjoy the place while he still could.

The bang of the *Kraken*'s gangplank shook him out of his reverie. "Shall we?" Ardent asked, motioning to the ship at large.

"I'm in!" Remy shouted, racing across the deck to join them. "I totally deserve a beach vacation." She winked at Fin and Marrill. "Coll can watch the ship to make sure we don't get swallowed up by the end of the universe while we're sunbathing."

"Hold on there a moment, sailor," Coll said, crooking a finger in the collar of her shirt and yanking her back. "Captains stay with their ships."

"That's why *you're* staying behind," she pointed out.

A smile played around Coll's lips. "And why you're staying with me."

"But the Dream Garden..." Remy protested.

"Funny you should mention Tanea Hollow-Blood's Dream Garden," Ardent said, brightening. "While the main entrance is far, far away at Tanea's house, it actually connects *straight* to the Shell Shoals. Tanea was quite adept at pushing the bounds of Stream travel. It was she who first hypothesized the transmotary vortex, if you can believe it!"

"I cannot," Remy said flatly. "Perhaps it's better I stay with the ship after all," she mumbled, dragging her feet as she joined Coll on the quarterdeck. "At least that way we can leave the engines idling and be ready to take off at a moment's notice."

"Engines?" Coll asked, forehead creased in confusion.

Remy sighed, and Fin stifled a smile, but it faltered when he caught sight of Fig sneaking her way to the gangplank. "You too, ensign," he said, catching hold of her sleeve. "You're also staying with the ship."

"But I'm supposed to be looking out for you," she protested.

He nodded toward Ardent. "That's what the wizard's for."

She lifted an eyebrow. "You'd trust me more on board than with you?"

"Yes," he answered without hesitation. He didn't want to spend his entire time ashore looking over his shoulder for her. Besides, even if she wanted, there was no way she was getting that orb. Fin had spent quite a bit of time trying to poke holes in Ardent's security, and it was impossible. He was quite confident that if the Master Thief of the Khaznot Quay couldn't nick the wish orb, neither could Fig.

Her face fell. "That Dream Garden did seem pretty cool," she complained.

"Fin, let's go!" Marrill called, waving for him to join her.

He patted Fig's shoulder. "I'll make sure to tell you all about it."

He jogged across the ship toward Marrill. "Ready to save the world again?" he asked, waggling his eyebrows.

She giggled and looped an arm through his. "As always!" And together they galloped down the gangplank and jumped to the ground beside Ardent. As soon as his feet touched the coral, Fin had to reel backward to avoid crashing into a man who he would have sworn hadn't been standing there a second ago.

"Slow your journey, little fella," the man said. Fin took

a second look at him; the man wasn't human, definitely. He was slouched over a little too far, his face a bit too much like a snout. His skin was wrinkled, and at the same time a touch too smooth. "Welcome, strangers," he said. "Name's Yurl. I keep the Library of Dreams."

Fin looked around. "What library?"

"Oh," Yurl said. "You hadn't seen it yet. Sorry 'bout that." He jerked one long thumb back at the empty lagoon behind him.

Fin looked, knowing full well nothing was there but water. So he was more than a little surprised to find the gigantic tower of coral reaching up from the heart of the lagoon like a massive, branching tree. Overhead, seabirds wheeled in an ever-circling flock. Fin was sure he hadn't heard their cries just a moment ago, but now they filled the air.

"Is it just me or does stuff keep coming out of nowhere?" Marrill whispered.

Yurl answered before Fin could. "Yeah, stuff keeps coming out of nowhere. It's the kind of thing that happens here. It's kind of like this place is a dream place, or something like that?" He shrugged. "I never really followed the reasoning, but hey, I'm just a figment of your collective imaginations."

"Wait, you're not real?" Marrill asked.

Yurl giggled. It was oddly high pitched. "Uh, *no*. Just a projection of the Shell Weavers, like most of this place. Man, you guys really *are* new."

Fin studied Yurl, the man who wasn't there. He *seemed*

real. He seemed like a person. Did he have thoughts and feelings, like Fin did? Or was he all hollow on the inside, just an illusion set up so well that they couldn't tell there was nothing behind those golden gray eyes?

"It's okay, Yurl," Fin said at last. "I'm not real, either." A part of him braced to feel those words tug at his insides. After all, the biggest fear in his life was that he was nobody, and now here he was, stating it as a fact. But oddly, it didn't bother him. Somehow, acknowledging the truth he'd feared for so long just wasn't as bad as being afraid of it had been.

"Right on," Yurl said. He reached over and gave Fin a very real-feeling high five. "Welcome, figment brother. Reality is stupid. You and I know."

Fin blushed despite himself. It seemed so weird, to be okay with being nobody.

Yurl turned to the others. "So, you *realies*," he said with a wink at Fin. "Come to make a donation, or just looking for a dream that suits ya?"

Ardent stepped forward. "We're here searching for the last bolt of dream ribbon, given to the Shell Weavers by the Dawn Wizard in the days of yore, so that we may repair the Map to Everywhere and save the Pirate Stream from the growing void created by the Lost Sun of Dzannin before he reaches the Font of Meres and undoes all of creation!"

Yurl stared at him for a second. "All right. So...I'll just mark you down for a browse, then." He waved his hand toward the base of the great coral spire behind him.

Fin noticed the holes in its pocked surface seemed just big enough for people to fit in comfortably. "How 'bout I put you guys up in shell number three and let you work all that out amongst yourselves. Sound good?"

Yurl escorted them across the beach to the base of the coral tree, giving a well-rehearsed speech as they went. "Thank you for visiting the Library of Dreams, folks. The Library is one of the Pirate Stream's greatest institutions. For millennia, the Shell Weavers have collected dreams from all over the Stream—and some say, even beyond. You never know what you'll find in a dream."

As they drew near, Fin could see inside the pores on the surface of the coral tree. Each one, he realized, was its own little shell, all stuck together to form the larger whole. All of them were white, though some shone bright like ivory and others were dull as horn.

"Here you go," Yurl said as they reached the base of the coral tree. One of the shells opened up before them, revealing an entrance to its own little pod. "The chambers are a bit tight here, but I think you can squeeze in. Hope you don't mind."

"Oh no, that makes sense, certainly," Ardent said, shuffling past Yurl into the nearest chamber, which was dull and yellowish like horn. Marrill gave Fin a worried look, but followed the wizard in. Fin shrugged and jammed himself in next to her. They wriggled around to fit in the space. Though it was tight, Fin was surprised to find that the inside of the shell was actually quite comfortable.

"So, how does this work?" Marrill asked once they were settled.

Yurl smiled a friendly smile. "Once the dreamer's all good and snuggled up, the shell closes and you doze off before you know it. From that moment on, the Shell Weavers' whole collection is open to you. And of course, if you want to have your *own* dream, a Weaver will come straight to you and gather it up to add to the Library."

"Spiff," Fin yawned. "When do we start?"

Yurl stepped back. As he did, his body seemed to fade away. The opening where he was standing was now closed, a ribbed wall of ivory shell sealing them in. Yurl's voice trailed away, until it was nothing more than an echo.

"You already did...."

CHAPTER 13
Weaving Darkness

M arrill loved the taste of it, but all the fudge made it terribly difficult to do a good backstroke. "You know, Mr. Penguin," she said, "we've got a lot of eating to do if we're ever going to clear up this hallway."

"Quite so," Mr. Penguin ballyhooed. "Quite so!"

And all of this made perfect sense to her, in the way that dreams did.

Marrill closed her eyes, licking at her chocolaty lips. It was awfully easy to get distracted and forget she was actually here to find something. Something very important. She rolled her mind. *Ardent*. Right. She needed to find Ardent.

"I need to find Ardent," she said out loud.

Mr. Penguin *harrumph*ed in his way, sending out a geyser of bubbles from his pipe. "Let me see…Ardent… mmm, yes…*magical* sort of chap, that one?"

Marrill kicked herself upright, treading fudge excitedly. "That's the one!"

Mr. Penguin rocked himself off his easy chair, slopping through the chocolate sauce over to a window that was really a painting. He pulled it off the wall and turned it toward Marrill. It was an odd picture, even by dream standards: a little sea anemone, with monocle and top hat balanced on its tendrils, standing before a long, papery tunnel. "Try this one," Mr. Penguin ruminated. "It's one the gentleman you seek deposited previously, if I'm not mistaken."

Marrill breaststroked her way to him. "Thanks," she said, savoring the last bit of chocolate on her tongue. She stared at the painting, unsure what to do with it. As she did, the anemone spread out its tentacles in a broad, radiant fan of color. The paper hallway behind him stretched forward in three dimensions…

…and she was standing on the balcony of a high tower, out above a mushroom forest. Great gothic arches loomed against snowcapped mountains overhead, and a gentle breeze tousled her hair.

She turned at the sound of glasses tinkling. There, at a

table on the balcony, sat Ardent. Before him were stacks of bizarre delights: glasses full of mist, bowls of candy that glittered like diamonds, a braised shank of something that had claws. To one side, a cow with human hands played a soft melody on a harp. And at the other end of the table, dressed elegantly in a jade-colored gown, sat the wizard Annalessa.

Marrill squealed with delight, leaping to give Annalessa a huge hug. "You found her!" she cried to Ardent. "She's here!"

Annalessa's laughter was the tinkling of bells—literally. "Oh, Ardent. Did you not tell her you were coming to see me?" She looked down at Marrill. Annalessa's eyes flashed with mirth. "I'm just a dream, dear. Left here long ago by that old man." She cocked her head to the wizard.

Ardent blushed. He held up his hands guiltily. "I'm sorry for sneaking away from you, Marrill. It would only have been for a moment, and you did seem quite enraptured by that erudite penguin and his fondue problem."

Marrill shrugged. She really had enjoyed swimming in chocolate. "So, what is this place?" she asked.

"Ah," Ardent said. "Yes. This is a dream I had long ago. I have only visited the Library once, but I left this here as my donation. It was such a significant thing, this dream, and I could scarcely keep myself from revisiting it today."

He motioned out over the balcony at the fungus forest below. "You see, everything here is a symbol for something else. The mushrooms represent the decay of the Wizards of

Meres; the tower is the impenetrability of my arrogance; and as you can see, Annalessa has brought me here, above one and outside the other." Annalessa smiled demurely.

The bovine harpist struck a lovely chord. Ardent stared at it, lifting a finger to his lips. "Not really sure about the cow, though."

"Okay," Marrill said. The thought of seeing the inside of Ardent's mind made her more than a little uneasy. "Weren't we looking for something, though?"

Ardent stood up slowly. "Indeed. The dream ribbon. I fear we will have to make our way to the Shell Weavers themselves to uncover that one. We simply have to find Tanea Hollow-Blood and—"

"Ardent, watch out!" Annalessa yelled. Marrill jumped back. Yellow fire spurted from Annalessa's hands, scorching the harping cow.

"What in the—"

The cow lurched forward, wreathed in flame, and standing on its back legs like a man. The firelight glinted off the edge of a butcher's knife glued improbably to one hoof. Its eyes glowed red as coals. With a mighty *moo*, it threw up its knife-wielding hoof and charged straight at them.

Marrill leapt aside. The assassin hurtled past her, swiping the air where she'd been standing. A second later, its momentum carried the creature off the balcony, a long *MOOOOOOOOOOOOOOOOOO* following it all the way to the ground.

Panic and adrenaline pumped through Marrill's veins. "What did *that* symbolize?"

Ardent's forehead wrinkled in confusion. "That's never happened before. It wasn't a part of my dream." He glanced at Annalessa, and Marrill could see real fear in his eyes.

"Nightmares," Annalessa said. "It may be the entire Library is infested."

Ardent drew a deep breath. "Which can only mean the void is drawing closer," he declared solemnly. "It must almost be upon us."

"We have to find the Shell Weavers and get the dream ribbon," Marrill reminded him. "Before it's too late!"

Annalessa traded a look with Ardent. "The nightmares," she told him. "You'll have to draw them away."

He nodded and then stepped forward. "Take care of her," he told Annalessa. Then he reached out and trailed his fingers through the air by her face, as if afraid touching her might cause her to disappear. "And take care of yourself."

Annalessa laughed. "I'm just a dream, silly old man."

"But you're *my* dream," Ardent told her.

She smiled at him. Then, without a word, Annalessa picked up a bowl full of soup from the table and spun toward Marrill. "This way, fast," she said, thrusting the bowl into her hands.

Marrill nearly protested, but looking for reason, she realized, was not the way to go when dreaming. She stared down into the bowl.

The soup was brown, the color of a paper grocery bag. A bubble rose up in the middle of it, then popped. A coiled mass of tentacles bobbed up where the bubble had been.

"Eeewww," Marrill managed. Then the tentacles twitched and fanned out in radiant colors, just like the helpful anemone from the painting earlier. The soup swirled, and Marrill felt like she was falling down into a long, papery hallway.

When she looked up, Marrill found herself hanging upside down like a bat from the ceiling of a cave. The floor below was a field of flowers, but not like any flowers she'd ever seen. More like multicolored fans, again reminding her of the anemones.

"Hey, where did you come from?" a voice nearby asked. She turned to find Fin standing next to her. Or rather, hanging next to her. He was upside down as well.

"Fin!" she cried, throwing her arms around him. "You're okay!"

He hugged her back. "Yeah, this place is weird."

She released him and stared down at the sea of fans beneath them. "Any idea where we are?"

Fin shook his head. "None."

Marrill took a cautious step, waving her arms for fear of losing her balance. As she did, little particles danced through the air around her hands, swirling gently. The air, she realized, wasn't air at all. It was water. They were submerged completely, though it was no trouble to breathe or speak.

She turned, searching for a familiar purple cap. "Where's Ardent?" she asked.

"I haven't seen him since we got here." He scratched his head. "Unless he was the one wearing the basilizard mask earlier?"

Marrill shrugged. "Maybe?"

Fin strolled along next to her, shuffling his feet against the ceiling and causing phosphorescent bits of silt to drift down around them. "Any luck finding the bolt of dream ribbon?"

She shook her head, feeling defeated. "I haven't even found the Shell Weavers."

Fin stopped. "But I thought…" He looked down at the field of fans covering the seafloor below. "Isn't that what those are?"

Marrill blinked. "Wait," she said. "The anemones *are* the Shell Weavers? I thought the Shell Weavers were people!"

"I guess not," Fin offered.

She tilted her head. "How did you figure it out?"

He opened his mouth to answer, but nothing came out. He frowned. "Dream logic? You know how sometimes there are things in your dreams that you just *know* even if you can't explain?"

"Kinda like how we figured out that cow was evil earlier." She frowned. "Though maybe that was obvious because of the knife."

Fin stared at her skeptically. "Um, okay. Sure. Probably."

"It made sense at the time." She waved a hand at the sea fans. "So all we have to do is explain the situation to the

Shell Weavers and ask them to help." She bent her knees, getting ready to push off the ceiling so she could get closer to the creatures.

Fin grabbed her wrist, holding her in place. "Except they won't understand you. I tried earlier, and it seems like they only speak in dreams."

Marrill closed her eyes and took a deep breath of water. So she couldn't explain their predicament to the Shell Weavers, couldn't ask them for help. How, then, could she convince them to give her the ribbon?

She thought and thought. Throughout her life, Marrill had always had a special place in her heart for animals. She knew them, and liked them, better than most *people*. You just had to understand their language, that was all. You just had to come to them on their own terms.

She tried to remember everything she knew about this place, listing it in her head. The Library of Dreams. Collected from all across the Stream. People came here, like Ardent, to make a deposit.... She let out a deep sigh, swirling barely visible plankton in front of her eyes.

That was when it came to her. *Deposit.* She'd thought about it like dropping something off at the bank or returning a book to the library. But *deposit* had another meaning, too. It could mean layers of accumulation, like sediment dropped out of water—or calcium laid down by coral. And wasn't this whole place a coral reef?

"How did I miss that?" she muttered out loud.

"Miss what?" Fin asked, confused.

"These aren't anemones," she explained. "They're coral polyps. They build their reef out of deposits made from dreams." She laughed, still struck at how obvious it was. "Yurl even explained it to us, right from the beginning!"

Fin still frowned. "Uh, sure. How about I just take your word on that?"

She nodded. "And if we want to make a deposit, the Shell Weavers will come collect it. All we have to do is dream our own dreams." She paused, tapping her finger against her chin as she thought it through. "But it has to be something the Shell Weavers will respond to. Something to make the poor agitated creatures feel safe, despite all the nightmares flooding the world."

Fin gulped. "Nightmares?"

"Because of the void," Marrill explained. "It's getting super close, and Ardent said that's causing them."

Fin looked around. "Are we safe here?"

Marrill shrugged. "Ardent's supposed to be distracting the nightmares. He should let us know if things start getting too dangerous."

"But—"

Marrill grabbed his hand, squeezing. "Don't worry. Just dream of something happy and safe." She closed her eyes, already knowing exactly what she planned to dream about.

Drowsiness settled around her. "I'm going to see my mom again."

CHAPTER 14
The One Where You're Falling

Fin stared at the twinkling lights of the Khaznot Quay. A warm breeze blew across the bay, bringing with it familiar scents and sounds: pirates haggling deals on the docks, butterbeast roasting in the market, winds howling down from Nosebleed Heights. The little boat he stood in rocked softly, the wash of waves like the hush of a lullaby.

He sighed, content.

Marrill had told him to dream of something happy and safe, and this was as happy and safe as he could remember—the night his mother had brought him to the Quay.

A familiar hand landed on his shoulder. He knew what would happen next, and he tried to slow the memory down, to savor it. His mother would point up into the night sky, to the brightest star in the heavens, and tell him, "No matter what happens, so long as that star is still there shining, someone out here will always be thinking of you."

He held his breath, waiting. But when she lifted her finger and he tilted his head back, he found only emptiness above. The sky was thick and black, almost viscous.

Not a single star shone in the darkness.

He twisted, trying to turn and look up into his mother's eyes, but she held him fast. Her hand was almost painful on his shoulder. The waves grew choppier, tossing the little boat violently from side to side.

"Where's my star?" he asked, the question edged in panic.

His mother's voice came out cold, hard. "I guess this means you've been forgotten."

Drums began to sound, the beat matching the tempo of his heart. Growing louder. Stronger. More familiar. Dread began to pool in his gut.

"Mom—"

The woman behind him laughed. It was a cruel sound, sharp edged and biting. And he knew then that the woman holding him fast wasn't his mother. She was the Crest of the

Rise. "I told you I would come for you," she hissed in his ear. "Because you belong with us."

Fin struggled to break free, but it was impossible. Large, dark shapes heaved around him in the darkness. Warships with the sigil of the Salt Sand King blazing to life on their hulls, the dragon-under-waves symbol outlined in fire.

They were coming for him. Bearing down on his tiny boat. Above him the sky broke apart, shattering in a spiderweb of red lightning. At the head of the Rise armada, a ship burst from the water, her metal hull cutting through the waves like glass.

The figure on the bow wore the familiar armor, but something was different about him. He was smaller, narrower. As he neared, he tore the iron mask from his face, and Fin saw himself.

It was Vell. It had to be. Clad in the Master's armor, captaining his ship. Except the boy's hair was shaggy like Fin's. His cheeks a bit rounder than Vell's, and the way he held himself looser. Fin's thief's bag hung from his hip.

"Sorry, jog," the boy in iron said as he called for ramming speed. The armada—led by the metal ship—bore down on Fin's little boat, only heartbeats away from crushing it into driftwood.

Fin had no choice but to dive overboard, remembering too late that he didn't know how to swim. The brackish water closed over his head, pressing tight around him. He flailed and kicked but nothing worked. He just sank deeper, his lungs burning.

Breathe, a soft voice whispered in his head. He shook his

head, panic shooting through him like lightning. *Breathe*, the voice said again, more insistent.

He didn't have an option. He fought as hard as he could, but eventually his mouth opened and he sucked in a gasp of water. He felt it fill his lungs, thick and cold. He waited for the choking sensation, for the coughing to overtake him, but nothing happened.

He could breathe underwater!

Fly, the same voice told him. This time he did as he was told and reached for his skysails. They fell open with a snap, and the next thing he knew he was soaring through the water. He laughed, the sound erupting from him in a froth of bubbles. He spun and swirled, twirled and dipped.

In moments he'd made it to shore, and he hauled himself out of the surf. He expected to find the giant wooden piers of the Quay stretching above, the sand dirty at his feet. But instead when he stood he found himself in the middle of a lush garden, surrounded by flowing green leaves and flowers of all colors. Every scent imaginable wafted through the air, and quite a few unimaginable ones, too.

He looked behind him. The Khaznot Bay was gone. But he could still hear the drumbeats of the Rise pounding, and he knew, somehow, that they continued to chase him. He wasn't safe.

Before him stretched a path. He started down it, slowly at first but then gaining speed. He raced through twisted gardens, feeling more and more lost, until he rounded a curve and realized he was no longer alone. He slowed, ducking into the underbrush. A wizard sat on a bench just ahead, her iridescent robes spread around her like ribbons of cloud. It wasn't until we saw her defining feature that he recognized who it must be: Tanea Hollow-Blood. One of the Wizards of Meres.

Ardent had mentioned she had a rather magnificent beard, Fin recalled. He had to agree.

She seemed to be talking to someone. Fin shifted closer, trying to see who. A sharp gust of wind whipped through the garden, bending the saplings almost to the ground. He threw up an arm as leaves pelted him, rain beginning to fall in painful dollops.

"You can't travel back in time!" Tanea shouted, her voice carrying on the wind. "It is possible, yes, but the power it would take to open the way, it's beyond imagining! It's never been done!"

Thunder crashed overhead, a streak of red burning through Fin's closed eyes. His gut clenched, and his heart raced. He knew what red lightning meant. He knew who Tanea was arguing with.

Fin shouted a warning, but it was too late. The Master of the Iron Ship advanced toward Tanea, his white beard whipping in the wind, his eyes cold blue behind his metal mask.

Tanea raised her hands. "Wait, no! Please!"

The Master's cruel iron fingers clutched at her robe. Tanea Hollow-Blood's head twisted to the side. Her eyes caught Fin's just moments before her pupils turned to dull metal. Fin blinked, and all that remained of Tanea Hollow-Blood was an iron statue.

Fin clamped a hand over his mouth, but it was too late. The Master knew he was there. He turned slowly until he was facing Fin and raised a gauntlet-clad fist. Fin fell back, scrambling to put as much distance between them as possible.

His back hit against something solid, and he spun to find a fountain blocking the path. He began to scramble around it when he noticed something odd about the reflection in its water. It wasn't of the garden. There were no trees or bushes, no cloudy sky.

Instead it looked for all the world like a tunnel made of paper.

"Jump," a soft voice told him. It was the same voice that had guided him earlier. But this time it wasn't just in his head. He turned and found a woman standing behind him, directly between him and the advancing Master.

"Hello, Fin," she said.

"Annalessa," he breathed. "Wait, you remember me?"

She smiled and nodded. "Of course I do."

He frowned. "You saved me."

She leaned forward, pressing her cheek against his. "Take care of my wizard for me," she told him.

Then she pushed her fingers against his shoulder, tipping him backward into the fountain. The familiar paper tube surrounded him, carrying him away again into someone else's dream.

CHAPTER 15
Try Wiggling It a Little

Most people didn't understand the Pirate Stream. Not the way Coll did. He may not have had Stream water running through his veins, but he had something close enough etched into the flesh of his body.

He hadn't been born destined for the deep Stream, not even close. He traced his line to princes and kings, to sons of great responsibility meant for even greater destinies.

But all of that was gone now. Some by his choice and some not. Now he worked for Ardent. Or Ardent worked for him. They'd been traveling the Stream together for so long it was sometimes difficult to remember.

Coll only knew one thing: His ship was his home. His crew was his family. And his loyalty to Ardent ran deeper and purer than the headwaters at Meres.

Which was why it made him uneasy to stand and do nothing while the giant void drew ever nearer. He paced across the quarterdeck to the port railing and back, looking once again to the horizon. No more than a thousand yards offshore, the cool blue waters of Oneira ended. They didn't turn gold and spread out into the Pirate Stream. They just ended. The water poured away from them in what had to be the top of an enormous waterfall, thundering into darkness.

The void was already upon them. Coll could feel the pull of its destructive current tugging at the boards of the *Kraken*'s hull.

"Should I weigh anchor?" Remy asked. She twisted a knot of rope nervously in her fingers. It was a habit she'd picked up from him.

He shook his head. "Not yet."

"How much longer?" she pressed.

"Until I give the order."

Her expression turned stormy, and she crossed her arms, leaning back against one of the masts, waiting. Under any other circumstances he might have smiled, keeping it hidden from her, of course.

But these weren't ordinary circumstances. In fact, Coll couldn't really remember what ordinary was anymore.

He sighed. "Fine." He strolled toward the gangplank, Remy close on his heels. "Hey, librarian," he called when he reached the shore. "How long until we get our friends back?"

"His name's Yurl," Remy reminded him.

The librarian stepped toward the towering coral tree with its rows of shells. "So, here's the thing, guys." He tapped the surface of the shell, and it turned translucent. Coll could see Ardent's bony frame and Marrill snuggled in next to him, with some other kid squished down in the corner.

"Oh hey—look!" Remy pointed out. "I found Plus One."

Coll looked closer. All around the three occupants, little paper tubes pushed out from the walls. Brightly colored tendrils spread out from their tips, waving peacefully like a field of feathers.

"Stestor's bones," Coll barked. "What are those things?"

The librarian slapped him on the back. "Those are the Shell Weavers, my good man. Your buddies in there are communing with them. And let me tell you, that's a good thing, because that waterfall out there, it's not looking so hot for the old Shell Shoals of Oneira. Anyway," he continued, "no opening this sucker until all of that is wrapped up. Try as you might, it will not happen." He rapped his knuckles on the surface of the chamber, and it turned opaque again. Coll noticed that where once it had been dull, now the shell was bright as polished ivory.

"How long will that take?" Remy demanded.

Yurl rubbed his oddly smooth chin. "Well, let's see here. I'm not a mathmagician, but I'd say...taking the rate of the imaginfilters...and judging from the shadow creep...squaring the hypotenuse..." He counted quickly on his fingers. "I'd say about slightly longer than any of us has left to live."

Coll kicked at the ground. "What good are you?"

Yurl shrugged. "Who said I was any good?"

Remy glared at Coll. "Okay, there's got to be a way to get Marrill, Ardent, and Plus One out of that shell before the void swallows us. Maybe we can speed up the Shell Weavers...."

"Nope," Yurl said.

"Or slow the void?" Remy offered.

Coll crossed his arms. "If we could do that, we wouldn't be in this predicament in the first place."

Remy threw up her hands. "Well, there has to be something!" Together, they stared at the sealed prison containing their friends.

Coll eyed it carefully, following the lines of the shell into the wall. It struck him that the shell was a single little unit. Its walls curved around, but they weren't joined with the wall of the Library so much as stuck to it. Attached, he thought, like a barnacle to a hull.

And Coll knew from long experience: Barnacles could be scraped loose. Well, most of them at least.

"We're taking the whole thing," he announced. In that same moment, the first wind coming off the great waterfall reached them, tousling Remy's hair. He glanced past her to the void drawing ever closer.

Something in his gut clenched at the thought of her being so close to eternal oblivion. "Remy, you man the *Kraken*. Have Ropebone throw us some lines to help pry the shell free." The tightness in his chest eased when she nodded and sprinted back onto the ship.

"How can I help?" asked a young girl hovering to the side. He glanced around, wondering where she'd come from. Another gust of wind blew across them, reminding Coll they didn't have much time.

"Here," he said, handing her a dagger. He turned and started chipping at the base of the shell. "We have to make a notch for the rope."

"This is really great, you guys," Yurl told them as they set to work. "It's nice seeing you all band together as a team and whatnot. Also, the Shell Weavers are going to really appreciate you saving some of them, you know? I mean, they won't *actually* appreciate it, because they don't really process stuff on that level, but you get what I'm saying."

Coll ignored the librarian as he smashed his dagger down with all his might, creating a notch and then prying at the edges of the shell to loosen them. He tried not to think about the void. About what would happen if they couldn't pull the shell free in time.

Instead he focused on the pull of the water at his feet, calculating the drag it would have on the *Kraken*. He listened to the whip of the wind through the rigging, noting how much thrust it would give them when he dropped the sails.

He took into account all of it—the weight of the cargo, whether the Promenade Deck was present or absent, the tilt of the suns, and the currents in the shoals—to determine just how much time he had before it would be too late to escape.

The answer wasn't good.

"Incoming!" Remy shouted as lines sprang from the *Kraken*. Coll grabbed one, slipping it around the notch he'd cut. A girl grabbed the other, knotting it into place.

"Pull, Ropebone!" Coll shouted.

Over in its mooring, the *Kraken* rocked to one side. The line went tight. The shell wiggled, but didn't budge.

The girl looked at Coll, her eyes pleading. "Can you get the ship any closer?"

If he were the only one at risk, he wouldn't give it a second thought. But he was responsible for the rest of the crew—Remy, the pirats, Ropebone, even the Naysayer. He refused to put them in more danger than they already were.

The reef shuddered underneath them, fissures and cracks running across the shoals. The void had reached the edge of the reef, just beyond where it rose from the water. As Coll watched, an entire shelf of coral broke free and disappeared over the waterfall.

They were out of time. He noticed a girl struggling to help him free the shell, and he balked. "Go!" He shouted to be heard over the sound of destruction. "Get to the ship, where it's safe."

"Are you leaving?" she cried.

He glanced toward the *Kraken* and saw Remy standing on the quarterdeck, her hands gripping the wheel, feet wide and braced as he'd taught her. Her hair whipped around her head, making her scowl of concentration appear even fiercer than usual. She shouted a string of orders, and though he couldn't hear them, he watched as the ship burst to life at her command.

He smiled. She made a fine captain.

And she would be devastated if something happened to Marrill.

He doubled his attack on the shell, chipping hard at the coral around it, not caring when a sharp edge sliced at his knuckles. There was another crack from the reef, and another shudder. Coll felt the land beneath him begin to slide, slipping toward the yawning abyss.

The whole of the Library leaned, the towering coral tree listing away from them. But in the process, it opened up a channel all the way to the *Kraken*. Coll watched in horror as Remy turned the ship, sailing her closer. Straight toward the void.

She was going to get herself killed, and there was nothing he could do.

More and more lines flew from the *Kraken*, anchoring all around the shell that held Ardent and Marrill. It was mostly free, but there was still a bit near the bottom that refused to give.

From out of nowhere, a girl leapt onto the shell. She jumped up and down on it, using her body weight as leverage. A straining groan like the death rattle of a giant filled the air. Behind them, oblivion yawned, sucking in more and more of the coral shoals.

"This is a sad day," Yurl lamented. "All those dreams, all that history, lost. But you know, what do I know? I'm just a simple amalgamation of stray thoughts and ideas assembled into the semblance of a person. Maybe there's a reason dreams get forgotten. And now that you guys have a few Weavers, maybe you can build new shoals one day."

The reef crumbled out from underneath the librarian. The great coral tree shuddered, wobbled, fell. "Oh, here we go, new friends!" Yurl said. "The Library of Dreams is falling. Fallen, fallen, is the Library."

As the great tree toppled beneath them, Coll struck the shell with all his might. The girl jumped and jumped, shouting at the top of her lungs. And just as it seemed the falling reef would pull them away into the void, the shell popped free.

It snapped toward the *Kraken*, landing on her deck with a thud. No longer tethered, the ship shuddered, golden water splashing up over the railings. Remy spun the wheel, hard.

Standing on the last scrap of coral before the waterfall, Coll felt the immense pull of the void. He was close enough now that he could stretch out a hand and brush his fingers against the emptiness.

He had a moment of wondering what that would be like. Being done with his endless stretch of days. Being done with his curse. Being done with his memories.

But then he felt the nudge of a rope against his hand. He grabbed tight. As it began to yank him away, he noticed a girl next to him, about to be sucked into the void. He reached out, snagging her arm, and together they flew toward the *Kraken*.

They landed on the quarterdeck, surrounded by chaos. Pirate Stream water dripped from the railing on the port side, and a gaggle of pirats were using pot lids to protect themselves as they battled a band of fanged cutlery. Nearby, a trio of stools danced in a circle, singing nursery rhymes off key. Square in the middle of them, Marrill's cat hunched, water dripping from his fur as he spoke.

To the man in iron, I leave his wish and the knowledge that the tides of the Stream run patient and true.

Coll glanced at Remy. She stood gripping the wheel, ignoring it all as she steered them away from the void. Her quick thinking and daring had saved their lives. And he had no idea what to say. So he gestured at the Stream-doused cacophony. "This is why we don't leave things lying around on the deck."

She smiled and patted his shoulder. "You're welcome."

CHAPTER 16
A Ribbon and Ink

Tears slipped from Marrill's eyes. Whether they were in joy or sorrow, she didn't know. Maybe they were both. She held her mother's hand on the edge of the cliff they had jumped from years ago, a tropical waterfall pouring into the crystal-blue pool below. Inside it, the Shell Weavers spread their multicolored tendrils, glowing bioluminescent in the dusk.

"See?" her mother said. "Aren't you glad you leapt in feetfirst?"

Marrill nodded. It had been a whirlwind day. It started with jumping off the cliff again, but when she hit the water, they'd been swimming in the Pirate Stream. Only, with her mom there, the waters weren't dangerous.

At first, she'd felt the pulse of anxiety all around her, the nebulous swirl of fear that filled the Shell Weavers, constantly threatening to spill over and turn the dream into a nightmare. But with her mom there, it was okay. They'd swung like Tarzan through the Gibbering Grove, dared each other to climb the heights of Monerva, played doubles on Margaham's Game.

Finally, Marrill was able to share with her mom all the wonders of the Pirate Stream. And with her mom there, everything was safe. Just like in real life, whenever she got scared, her mother was there to walk her through it. Her mom always knew what to do. Even when Marrill knew she didn't, somehow she did.

Slowly, as the day wound on, the anxiety died down. Fear gave way to fun; worry turned to winsome. Now, the whole world hummed with a peaceful contentment.

And yet, there was still a hard core of sorrow. Marrill gripped her mother's fingers tight, trying her best to pretend it wasn't there. She wanted this day to last forever. But she knew it wouldn't. She knew that no matter what she did, it was just a dream. When she woke up, she'd be out on the Pirate Stream, facing the Lost Sun of Dzannin. And her mother would be in a bed in Boston, waiting for doctors in white coats to bring her news.

She looked up into her mom's eyes and sniffed. "I don't want you to go, Mom."

Her mother's fingers ran through her hair. "Oh, honey," she said. "I'm not gone yet. Just enjoy the moment. Even if it is a dream. Because here, dreams really can last forever."

Marrill leaned in, letting her mother's arm drape around her shoulders. She smiled as she watched the walls of ivory and horn stitching themselves into ribbons that wrapped around them both.

A moment later, her eyes popped open. For real this time, not in the dream. Around her, the shell turned brittle, cracked, and crumbled to dust. Before she knew it, she was lying next to Ardent and Fin on the deck of the *Enterprising Kraken*, as if she'd always been there.

"Ohthankgoodness," Remy cried, pulling Marrill and Fin into a hug and squeezing tight. "That one was *way* too close." The babysitter stood. "Full sails," she cried, and the ship burst to life.

As the wind caught them and the *Kraken* gained speed, Marrill looked around. Next to her, the paper that had once made up the tubes of the Shell Weavers lay unspooled on the deck, joined together to make a single long ribbon.

The dream ribbon! she realized. The raw material of the Map to Everywhere. They'd found it!

She glanced around for any sign of the Weavers themselves. There was nothing. The Shell Weavers were gone. But suddenly, she realized she held something in her hand.

It was a white shell. A beautiful, round half-moon like a clam's, with ridges of ivory and troughs of yellow-white horn.

She clutched the shell to her as the others swept her into an embrace. Inside, she could feel the warmth of the Weavers, tucked away and hibernating. Waiting to build a new Library, somewhere far away and safe.

+⊢ ⊦ ⊣+

Later that night, Marrill sat at the table Ardent had pulled out onto the main deck, as he liked to do in fair weather, and held the dream ribbon carefully in her hands. Karny purred happily in her lap. The wizard was pontificating loudly on the origin of the material and the nature of dreams, but she was barely listening. The blank canvas of the ribbon seemed to speak to her of endless possibilities. It seemed to beg to be filled with them.

"...and when you consider that the dreams had not yet been had, well!" Ardent explained to an obviously bored Remy. "I couldn't begin to fathom how one knits with unformed dreams. Ah, the wonders of the Dzane."

"Pretty spiff stuff, that," Fin whispered in Marrill's ear. "Raw dreams and such."

She nodded. "I kind of want to draw on it."

Fin looked one way, then the other. "Thought you might." From a pocket in his coat, he produced a packet of her drawing pencils. "I nicked a set from you." He coughed. "I mean *for* you," he hastened to add. "Figured you'd run out somewhere when you really needed them."

Marrill's eyes brightened as she reached for the pencils. "You're the best," she said, and she meant it. She pulled one free and pressed the graphite down to the blank surface. "What should I sketch?"

He screwed up his features in thought. "How about… me kicking the Lost Sun in the face!" He dropped back into a mean fighter's stance.

Marrill couldn't help but laugh. "How about…a dragon!" she said. Quickly, she sketched out a vicious-looking beast, with a head too big for its body, a mouth full of oversized, dangerous-looking teeth, and a thick tail that wrapped around one of the *Kraken*'s masts.

As she put the finishing touches on the drawing, the image on the page shifted, breathing fire. Tongues of flame lit the night around her, licking toward the table. Marrill yelped, dropping the ribbon and jumping back. Karny bolted from her lap, racing up the nearest mast despite the pirats' protests.

Ardent looked up. "Marrill, what in fourteen suns—"

Before he could finish, a huge scaly foot with enormous claws stomped against the nearby stairs. Marrill's jaw dropped as her sketched dragon lurched down from the forecastle. Its enormous head bobbed from side to side comically, snapping at the air. Its tail lashed in a wide arc, forcing her to drop back.

Marrill glanced down at the dragon she'd just sketched. The image on the ribbon mimicked exactly what was happening in real life!

"By the Dzane, a megacephalic wyrm!" Ardent cried.

"Dragon!" Remy shrieked, darting for the main hatch.

Marrill rolled to one side as another stream of fire burst over her head.

"Never fear!" Ardent announced, standing tall before the furious creature. "This beast will not be the first I have slain. Away with you, lizard!" Bright blue lightning crackled from his fingers, directly at the dragon's overlarge nose.

The blast passed straight through the dragon, shooting out its back and smashing the bulkhead beside Marrill. "Ardent, watch out!" she cried.

The old man stared at the dragon, then at his hands, then back at the dragon. "I say, that's a new one on me," he declared. And then the dragon's maw snapped down on him, swallowing him whole. Marrill's scream joined five others, wailing into the night.

She struggled to her knees. Something about those screams wasn't right. Namely, *Ardent* was still screaming—even though he had been devoured. She looked back to where her friend had been standing... and still was.

"AAAAAAAAaaaaaah... oh. Oh, I see now," Ardent muttered. "Well, that's quite clever, isn't it?"

The dragon growled and snarled. As it turned on the tight deck, its tail passed right through the timbers of the railing.

It wasn't real.

"Fin," Marrill hissed, pointing to the unfurled dream ribbon the creature had come from. "Erase the drawing!" He looked at her like she was crazy. "The dragon is an illusion!" she said, tossing him her pencil.

"Oooooh," he said. Still, he ducked and dodged each time the dragon wheeled on him, before finally grabbing the long parchment and scrubbing it hard with the eraser. The dragon let out a howl into the night, disappearing one swipe at a time.

Marrill heaved a sigh of relief as the beast vanished. That would be the last time *she* drew on dream ribbon, she felt sure.

"Well, that was exciting," Coll deadpanned. He made his way toward the table, Remy following cautiously behind.

Ardent clapped. "Wasn't it? Only the second time I've ever been swallowed whole!" He bit his lip, apparently realizing what he'd just said. "I'd prefer not to discuss the first time, if it's all the same." Everyone quickly agreed that it was.

Marrill walked over to the ribbon, taking it gingerly from Fin. The parchment seemed so innocuous now. And yet, she could still feel the possibility flowing out of it. She had to admit, a part of her still itched to sketch on it.

"Sorry about that," she told everyone.

Ardent shook his head. "Well, I can't say that was obvious. But it would seem that perhaps we should avoid drawing anything on the dream ribbon, at least until we're ready to turn it into our new Map." He took it from her carefully and rolled it up into a furled scroll. "A good thing you weren't using the ink we'll need. I suspect if you had been, your little doodle would have had...more substance."

Remy peered over Coll's shoulder, still looking uncertain. "Which does raise the question of where we're going next? I mean, we're pretty much wandering aimlessly at the moment...."

"Yes, certainly," Ardent said. He held up the Map. The hole in the middle of it was now substantially larger. It had been no bigger than a quarter when they made landfall at the Oneiran Shoals. Now it was the size of a silver dollar, and growing.

"How much of the Stream has been lost?" Marrill whispered. "How much does this hole cover?"

Ardent looked at her sadly. "It may appear small, and in a sense it is, as the Stream is infinite. But this is still a very sizable amount. Many worlds are gone already."

"Now, here is Meres," he continued, trying to get them back on track, "where the Lost Sun intends to inject his power into the headwaters of the Stream." He motioned to a point halfway between the edge of the void and the Neatline, the borders of the Map that kept its endless worlds from spilling right off the edge of the paper. Marrill noted that the hole extended unevenly up in a teardrop shape toward the spot Ardent had pointed to. "The Lost Sun is moving faster than expected. At this rate, he will likely make landfall at Meres in two days. Perhaps sooner."

The thought chilled Marrill to the core. "I guess we'd better get moving, huh?"

Ardent nodded. "Quite. Fortunately, we only need one more thing. Living ink, capable of drawing everything that was or could be."

Marrill sighed. She knew what that meant. She searched the rigging, finally locating her cat awkwardly clawing his way back down the mizzenmast. She hated doing this to him, but there was no choice. They just had to hope that the Dawn Wizard had bequeathed living ink in his will, as well.

"I'll get the cannon," she said.

But Ardent waved his hand, dismissing her. "No need," he said. "We know precisely where to find this ink."

Marrill perked up. "That's great news! Where?"

Rather than answering, Ardent glanced toward Coll.

Coll's hand instinctively touched the coil of rope tattooed on his skin. It snaked down around his forearm now. "Home," the sailor said in a hollow voice.

Marrill traded a confused expression with Fin and Remy. "And that's...a bad thing?" she guessed.

Coll nodded, but didn't elaborate.

As Ardent looked at the sailor, genuine regret flashed in his eyes, but Marrill had no idea why. "It's the only possibility, you know. It's the only place we can find the ink."

"I know," Coll said.

Ardent put his hand on his friend's shoulder. "We have to go, Coll."

Coll nodded again. A strange tension crackled between them. "I said, I know."

"I wouldn't ask it of you..."

"And yet you are."

The wizard considered the captain for a long moment. "Yes, friend, I am." He cleared his throat. "Set a course for the Knot of the Coiled Rope."

Coll straightened his back and tugged his shirt straight. He nodded once and then turned and mounted the steps to the quarterdeck without a word.

Finally, Remy broke the silence. "So. Anyone want to explain why Coll going home is such a *thing*?"

Ardent plucked up the roll of dream ribbon and wound it tightly. He stared at it a moment. His eyes seemed vacant, lost.

"It isn't my story to tell."

CHAPTER 17
The Gloom and the Glow

L ate the next morning, Fin stood on the quarterdeck,
watching uneasily as the Stream drew closer around
them, narrowing from an endless expanse to a river
once more. Scores of sails dotted the horizon. Most were
civilian vessels, ships fleeing the coming of the void. But
some belonged to warships sporting a familiar shape. And
those warships, he realized, were headed straight for the
Kraken.

"It's the Rise!" Fig whispered urgently. "They've found us. There's no way we'll make it past them!"

She was right, Fin knew. Rise warships were racing in from either side to cut them off, while others tacked long courses back and around to circle them. The *Kraken* would soon be pinned, with no retreat and no way forward unless they could break through the rapidly forming blockade.

Fin glanced toward Coll, trying to gauge his expression. The captain scowled fiercely, his mouth set in a firm line, but Fin couldn't tell whether it was the looming Rise that concerned him or the looming destination.

Ardent stood just beside the captain, leaning forward with a hard look in his eye. Only the whipping of his beard and the way his hat danced like a windsock undermined the severity on his face.

"Are you sure you want to do this?" Coll asked.

"As sure as I am that you don't," Ardent replied.

"You know what you're asking of me?"

The wizard nodded. "I do not ask it lightly. Nor do I undervalue your accompaniment. But you must have faith. I didn't let you down the last time we were here, and I don't plan on doing so now, either."

The sailor looked to his other side, where Remy stood chewing her lip. Coll had made clear that if they were going to do this, she had to be next to him the whole time, ready to take the wheel whenever he told her to.

Judging from the number of ships racing toward them,

Fin wasn't sure this was the time for a teaching moment. But it wasn't time for an argument, either. Coll was the captain, and right now he was the only hope they had of outmaneuvering the Rise.

"They're getting too close," Remy gasped. "We can't make it!"

Coll let out a snort. "Calm yourself, ensign." He held out one hand, pointing with his index and pinkie to the nearest ships on either side of them. "Only those two even have a chance of touching us. Now observe."

He tapped the wheel left, and the bow swung right. The war vessel to starboard tacked in to drive the *Kraken* toward its partner. The portside vessel, meanwhile, swung broad, angling to catch them when they inevitably pulled away.

But Coll held course. The starboard ship tacked even more sharply toward them, coming up fast. Fin couldn't help but notice the fortified ram at the prow of the ship. It was just perfect for smashing into an enemy vessel. On the deck, he could see the Rise preparing for battle.

"They're going to ram us!" he cried.

Beside him, Fig fidgeted wildly. "They'll do it, too," she added. "I've seen this before. They don't have mercy. They'll break us to splinters and snatch the orb while we're sinking."

Coll held up a hand. "Calm..."

The Rise ship drew closer, on a dead collision course. Soon, the *Kraken* would be taking on water, enemy boarding hooks would be flying. To the port side, the other Rise vessel had realized what was about to happen and turned back, leaving its ambush position to join the fight. It, too, would be upon them shortly.

Remy gripped Coll's arm as he, in turn, gripped the wheel. "Just like I told you," Fin heard him whisper. "Aaaaaand...now!"

He spun the wheel with all his might. The *Kraken* twisted abruptly, skating so hard it surfed up onto one side, slicing around through the water. The Rise ship sailed straight past them, soldiers on deck running from bow to port to aft as they passed.

"And now!" Coll yelled again. Remy lunged forward, catching the wheel and spinning it with all *her* might in the opposite direction. The *Kraken*, still with full momentum, surfed right up on its other side, slicing neatly around the second vessel.

Marrill clapped as Fin let out a shout of victory. Fig blew out a relieved breath. On the deck, the Naysayer had turned himself so they couldn't see his hands, but Fin could tell he was gesticulating angrily toward the Rise ships.

"And that, folks, is how you captain," Coll said with a smirk. He steered the ship smoothly into the narrowing channel.

Fig looked to Fin, eyes wide with astonishment. "I can't believe we made it!"

He shrugged. "Coll's the best there is."

"But we beat the Rise. For the third time." She stared at

him like his nose had come unglued. "The Rise aren't beatable!" Fin started to point out that she was obviously wrong, but she shut him down with a wave of her hand. "You don't understand. I've seen the Rise take entire worlds. Far-off places, just as *training exercises.* They're ruthless and efficient, and I've never seen them lose a battle before they came up against you guys. Not once. That's what they tell us, anyway, in the pens...." She suddenly trailed off.

Fin arched an eyebrow. "The pens?"

Fig averted her eyes. "Oh, yeah, just...you know, where they keep the Fade children. And the disobedient. And the ones who have to be protected, like you—" She clapped her hand over her mouth.

Fin leaned in toward her. His voice came out a sharp whisper. "What do you mean, *like me?*"

"Nothing," Fig chirped. "Just, like I told you, the Rise and Fade are linked. If a Fade dies, all the weakness returns to her Rise." She shivered. "It's the worst thing anyone can imagine. Dragging down your Rise...the ultimate failure."

Fin sighed. He couldn't figure out what was worse: being no one or being less than that—a living embodiment of failure. "So they keep us in pens?"

Fig shrugged. "Yeah, some of us. Like I said, the young, who have to be trained, and the disobedient, and those with an important Rise, who must be protected. It isn't a nice place, but then...we deserve it for being what we are. Weak."

Fin shook his head, sure he couldn't be hearing her

correctly. "Are you kidding? We don't deserve it. *No one* deserves to be kept in a pen!"

"But—"

"There are no *but*s! They're treating people like cattle. No wonder my mom took me away...."

And just like that, it all clicked. *His mom had taken him away to escape the pens.* To be free. To live his own life. Suddenly, all the hurt he'd felt over the years seemed like a stupid kid's game. His mother had risked everything to free him, so that he wouldn't end up like Fig—believing that he deserved to be treated like a prisoner.

"You know what?" he told her. "You keep saying we're the bad parts. But I've met Vell, and I'm starting to think your definition of 'bad' and mine aren't the same." He pushed his chest out, feeling proud of himself. "So if it's all the same to you, I don't think I belong in a pen. And I don't think you do, either. And based on recent experience, I'd say that if the Rise had never before been beaten, it's because the Rise had never before met the crew of the *Enterprising Kraken*. Marrill, am I right?" He reached over for a high five.

Marrill turned from where she'd been leaning over the gunwales. She lifted her hand, slapping it against his. "Right about what?" Her eyes slid toward Fig and her confused frown deepened.

Rather than explain who Fig was for what felt like the hundredth time that morning, Fin distracted Marrill while

Fig slipped away to the other side of the ship. "Hold on tight—looks like things are about to get rough."

Ahead, the current picked up as the water funneled between banks of jagged rocks so tall their tops were lost to the clouds overhead. The *Kraken* plunged between them, sluicing along the raging river. The towering walls closed tight around them, blocking the sun and casting them into a makeshift twilight, broken only by the glow of the churning water. Fin grabbed for the railing as the sound of whitewater pelted his ears.

At first, he thought they must be approaching a giant waterfall. But then he realized it was more than that. The sound was coming from *beside* them, not just ahead. He peered at the broken stone walls. Through the gaps, he caught flickers of gold.

It was another branch of the Stream, flowing right next to them! "Hey, check it out!" he said. "There's another river!"

"I know," Marrill said. "I see it!"

"Me too," Fig added from across the ship.

Fin spun on one heel. Sure enough, through the jagged rocks on her side, even more glimmers of gold shone through. "Oh, wow," he said. "There's *three* of them."

"Four," the Naysayer said in a sniggering grunt. He stood amidships, one hand pointing at the sky.

Fin looked up. With a start, he realized that they were

in a giant cave. And on its ceiling straight overhead, yet another glowing river flowed.

"Five," said the Naysayer, pointing with another hand, then another. "Six. Sixteen. Sixty-three."

"Whoa," Fin breathed, craning his neck. They were riding on one of what had to be hundreds of identical rivers, all flowing along the arching cave walls with no concern for gravity. They all rushed in the same direction, toward the same unseen point somewhere ahead.

"Have you ever seen anything like it?" Fig asked, rejoining him.

He shook his head. "Never even *heard* of anything like it. I mean, sure, there are places where branches of the Stream meet. Lots of them. But nothing like *this*."

"Come on, Fin!" Marrill called. "Let's find out more!" She took off up the steps to the quarterdeck, where Coll stood, carefully supervising a white-knuckled Remy. Fin and Fig followed, practically tripping over each other as they piled up the stairs.

"You're doing fine," Coll reassured Remy. "Ease up a little. When you're tense, it makes your movements too jerky. Flow with the current when you can, be ready to fight it like mad when you have to."

"So, this is your home?" Fin asked.

Coll raised an eyebrow at him. "One of them got on board," he whispered to Remy. "Must have cut the turn too close. Hand me an ax."

Fin threw up his hands. "Friend! Friend!" Behind him, he could practically *feel* Fig slow-walking back down the stairs.

Coll looked to Marrill, who nodded furiously. "Belay that order," he told Remy. Then the captain shrugged, returning to the earlier conversation. "Sure. Home. Was. Sort of."

"How many rivers *are* there?" Marrill asked.

"Too many to count. All this"—he motioned to the cave walls, the floor, everything—"this is just a small part of it."

"Indeed!" Ardent declared, shuffling forward from the rear of the ship as if he'd been perched there all along, waiting for someone foolish enough to ask a question susceptible to a needlessly long-winded explanation.

"You will recall," the wizard continued, "that the Pirate Stream is not one river, but many, and even the open Stream itself is, in a manner of speaking, just many rivers all flowing on top of and beside one another simultaneously."

"Sure," Fin said. "Let's say we remember that."

Marrill shushed him playfully. "I actually *do* remember it," she giggled.

"FakecoughSUCKUPfakecough," Fin said to her.

Ardent waved his hand a few times and seemed to catch a long handkerchief out of thin air. "Oh dear," he said. "Faking Cough is a terrible disease. Have a pretendssue." Fin reached for it halfheartedly. The fabric evaporated the second he touched it.

"As I was saying," Ardent continued, "on the Stream

proper, all those different rivers may flow by and near and on and through one another, but they flow in different directions. The Knot of the Coiled Rope is the only place where all the rivers of the Stream flow together, all to the same place, all at once."

"So, how come no one knows about it?" Fin asked. "It seems like something like this would get a lot of attention."

"Fin, look," Fig whispered in his ear. She nudged him in Coll's direction. The tangled knot tattoo, the one that traveled across the sailor's body and had once nearly strangled him, peeked out from the sleeve of his left arm. And his right one. And from his collar.

It was growing!

Ardent must have noticed as well. His eyes flitted over it, studying Coll cautiously as he kept talking. "Not just anyone can come here, of course. It's a secret, known only to the greatest sailors on the Stream. It takes a very special person, like our friend Coll here, to navigate the passage."

"But," Marrill piped in, "we've just been sailing straight down a river this whole time."

Coll shook his head, taking the wheel from Remy. "It only seems straight because I know what I'm doing. I assure you, things would look very different if I didn't. There are hidden eddies and whirlpools everywhere. Any captain who couldn't handle them would find himself sucked down one and spit out somewhere random on the other side...if he was lucky."

"Difficult to find, nearly impossible to reach, and almost

entirely unknown," Fin mused. "Hey, Naysayer—I think we might have found your new home."

"No," Coll and Ardent said at the same time.

"This is not a place where one stays," Ardent said. His expression grew oddly glum as he turned to the sailor.

The look Coll gave him was anything but friendly. "Not if you can help it," the captain added. Fin could hear fear, real fear, wavering in his voice. It was an emotion Coll showed rarely. If ever.

The captain tightened his hands around the wheel. "If the Stream weren't ending, Ardent..."

"I know," the wizard said. "I know."

The tunnel twisted, carrying them faster, farther. The rush of whitewater turned into the roar of a giant waterfall, bigger than Fin could imagine, coming up fast. He squinted, trying to make out their destination, but in the gloom and the glow, everything muddled together. Wherever they were headed, they were headed on faith alone. Fin hoped that was enough.

Remy stomped her heel fiercely on the deck. "No."

"Pardon?" Ardent said, cocking an ear.

The teenager wheeled on the old man. "I said no." She turned to Coll. "And that goes double for you, mister. You two are being weird and scary and secretive, and I am *not* having it. Spit it out: What's going on? Where are we going? What's going to happen when we get there?"

Ardent started to reply, but Coll held up a hand. "That's

fair. It's not like we can turn back now. The truth of the matter is, there will be a price for our trip here. Just like there was the first time I made it"—he took a deep breath—"four hundred and seventy-three years ago."

"What?!?" Remy croaked.

Fin looked at Marrill; he could see her eyes, white and wide in the shadow. He was sure his own looked the same way.

There were ways to extend life, without doubt, and many creatures on the Stream who naturally lived beyond that of mortal men. Ardent, for example, was at least two hundred, and probably a lot older. And Coll had always seemed wise beyond his years.

Even so, the sailor didn't look a day over sixteen, much less pushing five hundred.

"Right," Coll said. "I was expecting that reaction." The waterfall sound came louder than ever, forcing him to yell to be heard. "But to your second question, where we're going is *there*."

He pointed, just as the *Kraken* rounded a bend. Ahead of them, the rocks ended. Indeed, the whole giant cave ended, opening into a great chamber with no ceiling or sky Fin could make out, and no floor or walls, either.

On all sides, rivers of glowing water thundered inward. Hundreds of them flowed from the tunnel they'd been traveling through, and their tunnel was just one of thousands twining in from every possible direction, each pouring its own rivers into the vast emptiness ahead.

Where the tunnels ended, the rivers burst into empty air. Some cascaded down in mighty cataracts; others sprayed upward, casting rainbows like spiderwebs through the air. Still other rivers twisted and corkscrewed around one another, tangling and twining impossibly.

And at the center of it all, a great cathedral hung in the air, like a spider in the rainbow webs. It was strung like a pearl on a line of pure magic, buoyed by streams passing below, wrapped on all sides by rivers that flowed around and across and through it. And it was there, at the cathedral, that Coll was pointing.

"Whoa," Fig gasped. Fin nodded in agreement, his mouth gaping.

"The Knot of the Coiled Rope," Coll said. "That's our destination." His next words were so quiet, they were nearly lost in the rush of water. "Now what's going to happen when we get there? I have no idea."

CHAPTER 18
The Knot of the Coiled Rope

A s the *Kraken* sailed along twisting, looping rivers of magic, Marrill stared at the foreboding edifice before them. Up close, what had looked like a solid building showed itself to be a maze of interconnected structures.

They were all built in the same style: long, rounded curves and arches, carved in a coiling motif, twined around the flowing rivers of magic as if grasping onto the Stream itself.

Like a knot, Marrill realized with wonder. The entire thing was built in the shape of a massive, intricate knot tangled around the myriad branches of the Stream.

She squinted, but couldn't tell what exactly it was made of; it was smooth like marble, yet soft and rubbery as well. In the glow of the Stream water, every surface of the place glistened.

"This is the home of the Sheshefesh," Coll told them in hushed tones. "The creature to whom all great navigators owe their loyalty—and their fear. Now prepare for landfall."

Marrill quickly scanned the main deck, making sure Fin wasn't forgotten and Karnelius was secured (in the arms of the Naysayer, where he practically lived these days). Satisfied, she turned back, only to find Remy standing dead in front of the wheel, facing Coll.

"We're not preparing for *anything*," the babysitter said, "until you tell us exactly what your deal is."

Coll leaned to one side to peer around her. The babysitter leaned to block him. He leaned back the other way. She matched him once more. He looked to Ardent for help, but the wizard said nothing.

Seizing the moment, Marrill jumped forward. "Yeah! No one goes anywhere until you fess up"—her eyes narrowed—"*old man*."

Coll smacked his lips. "You really want to know?"

They nodded as one.

"Fine," he said. Taking his hands off the wheel for the

briefest of moments, he pulled up one sleeve. The inky ropes of his tattoo now writhed across his skin, as if he had been etched with live eels. "This thing," he said, "is the gift of the Sheshefesh. The greatest sailors, the ones who can make it to the Knot of the Coiled Rope all on their own—the Sheshefesh rewards them with it. Through it, they can always feel where the currents are turning, and always find their way back to the Knot. But it's a curse, too."

Chills stole across Marrill's flesh. "Curse doesn't sound good."

Coll looked terribly unimpressed. "Yes, by definition a curse is *never* good. The price you pay for the gift of the Sheshefesh is never being able to settle. Stay in any port for more than a day or two, and the mark gets restless. That's what happened when the ropes of the tattoo started strangling me in Monerva—we were stuck there, and the mark was trying to drive me on. If we hadn't left when we did, it might well have killed me."

Marrill gasped. Remy hung her head. Fin looked away, while the new deckhand fidgeted uncomfortably. "So you just have to keep going and going?" Marrill asked. "Forever?"

Coll shrugged. "More or less."

"Because you're immortal," Remy offered uneasily, as if hoping he might contradict her.

Coll shrugged again. "More or less." He looked down at himself. "Good thing I was so young and handsome when I first made it here. Could be stuck in an old man's body."

Marrill crossed her arms. Something about this didn't add up. "If you came here before to get this gift, how come you're so afraid of being back now?"

Coll looked toward the glistening building, with its walls shaped like the coils of a giant serpent, squeezing the very heart of the Stream. "Every sailor who comes here eventually returns. And when they do, the Sheshefesh's mark binds them here...for good."

"What?" Remy snapped.

Coll took a deep breath. "The second time you come to the Knot of the Coiled Rope, you never leave."

"*Almost* never," Ardent broke in, finally speaking up. "Some have come here twice *and* come out again." Coll gave him a long, withering look. "They have!" the wizard exclaimed. "At least one has. And I'm confident it will happen again!"

"But..." Marrill asked. "Why? Why does the Sheshefesh want to keep all those sailors?"

Ardent cleared his throat. "The Sheshefesh is a creature of old magic. It works by rules that do not apply to the more...*finite* among us." He looked at her with dead severity. "To call, to guide, to entangle. Those are the rules that define the beast. It cannot do anything else, or else it would not be what it is."

Marrill and Remy burst with questions, but Coll held up one hand sharply. "I *said* prepare for landfall." His tone was so harsh that no one dared to contradict him.

As the *Kraken* sailed close, the building ahead shifted. Marrill watched with wide eyes as one of the massive coils untwined from the Stream and swung toward them, bearing a stone wharf atop it. Ropebone Man quickly fastened several lines to its pylons, pulling them in close. The pirats scurried down from the yardarms to secure the lines even further, keeping the *Kraken* steady in the fast-moving current still flowing around them.

"When we're inside," Coll said as they disembarked, "don't touch anything." He looked at Marrill with real severity. "I mean *anything*, got it?"

"Don't touch anything. Got it." She glanced toward Fin, making sure he'd heard the warning. But he seemed to be arguing with a new deckhand. Marrill was about to call for him when Coll grasped her elbow, helping her down from the gangplank. The ground she landed on was oddly spongy, and she pushed against it, testing how bouncy it was.

Coll's grip tightened, holding her still. "Or talk to anyone," he added.

When he was certain she understood, he turned to assist Remy. "All the sailors the Sheshefesh has collected are still here," he continued. "And they *will* talk to you. Ignore them. No matter what they say. Just remember, you can't help them."

"Don't talk to anyone. Got it," Marrill repeated, loud enough to make sure Fin heard as he bounded down the gangplank after them. She scarcely noticed the girl who followed him.

"When we reach the Sheshefesh, do not address it directly," Coll finished. "It will speak to me, because I'm a navigator, and to Ardent, because even *it* respects wizards. If it speaks to anyone else, that's trouble."

Ardent nodded gravely. He stood up straight, lengthening his spine. His robe was newly washed and pressed, his cap clean and neat. Marrill had never seen him dress for an audience before.

Her insides squirmed. She wondered what exactly they were getting into.

Without a sound, the great coil they stood on lifted upward, carrying them to the main building. Marrill marveled at the architecture. Every swooping spiral seemed deliberate, every curved line designed with the utmost care and attention. Across every surface, images of mermaids and dragons and sailing ships were etched in dark ink, as if the building itself were tattooed.

And throughout it all, omnipresent, was the curling, knotting motif of ropes.

"As far as anyone knows, the Sheshefesh has existed since the time of the Dzane," Ardent explained as the platform came to rest before a great wall made of coiled bulges that looked like pythons stacked on top of one another. A branch of the Stream swooped in above them, and the top of the wall was built to loop up and around it, allowing it to flow into the building. "Legend has it that from the beginning it made its home here, trawling its fingers in every current of the Stream."

Marrill noticed Coll rubbing at the edges of his tattoo— it had grown so large now that lengths of inky rope spread not only along his hands and arms, but even reached up around his neck.

Suddenly she wasn't so sure this was such a good idea. But then she swallowed, remembering the hole gnawing its way across the Face of the Map to Everywhere. The fate of the Stream depended on them finding the ink and getting to Meres before the Lost Sun.

The wall ahead shifted, bulges unknitting and pulling away from one another, opening up into a long, long gallery. As far as she could see, there were no doors, no windows— only the Stream-branch, flowing straight down the center of the ceiling, lighting the path in muted gold.

Before they went any farther a girl who'd been standing next to Fin stepped in front of Coll and held up a hand, stopping them. "Are you sure there's not another way to get this ink?"

Coll's eyes swayed like the sea as he glanced toward Ardent and then back at the girl. He plunged past her, saying nothing.

Marrill heaved a deep breath and followed. Her steps faltered, however, when she was met with the din of voices. All around, sailors were strung up against the walls, bound tight by ropy tendrils. They shouted to one another ceaselessly.

At first Marrill thought they were wailing in agony, and she shuddered with pity and a burst of cold fear. But then she listened closer to the words that twined like tentacles through the air all around them.

*Twice the whale done rise, and twice I slipped
right past 'er...*

*Then the mate says, the mate says, 'Then
who's got the jib!' GET IT?*

*A storm the likes of which we never seen, and
the manatee, oh, the fangs on the manatee...*

*Now the Stagorn sirens, they sing a little
higher on the ol' octave...*

Marrill shook her head. "They're telling stories."

Coll looked back at her. "Of course they are. Don't listen—ninety percent of it is complete swoggle."

"But..." Marrill said. "But they're laughing."

"Guess some of it's really *good* swoggle," Fin volunteered.

Coll cupped his hand over his mouth. "A lot of them are just being polite," he whispered.

A cacophony of stories wheeled around them as the crew of the *Kraken* marched down the hallway. The whole place smelled of brine and sea breeze. Dangling seaweed clung to the lines that held the sailors tight, and water puddled on the floor.

The coiled rope theme was everywhere—in the loops around the jawing sailors, inscribed on every surface in knotted designs suspiciously similar to the living tattoo that now threatened to cover Coll completely. Even the walls and the floor bulged like gigantic ropes laid next to one another.

"'Ey!" one of the bound men called to them. "Ahoy, sailors! Come abaft, an' have a seat. Join us and tell us some new tales, 'ey?"

Coll's arm shot out before Marrill moved. "Don't. Don't talk, don't engage. Remember, there's nothing you can do to help them." He held her gaze for a long moment as the stories rattled around them.

Marrill nodded intently. But when she finally looked away, she realized that Fin, without anyone paying attention to stop him, had wandered over to one side. An old sailor was talking to him, spinning him stories. With each word, Fin leaned in a little farther. He didn't seem to notice that all around, the knot-drawings on the wall were *moving*, slithering closer inch by inch.

Alarm rushed through Marrill. "Fin!" she shouted. "Watch out!"

Fin's head snapped back. Behind him, just beneath the still-talking sailor, a knot-drawing uncoiled swiftly. A thin spine appeared on its end as it popped out of the wall and reared to strike.

"Unfortunate flaccidity!" Ardent called, dropping his hand through the air. The spine drooped, slapping Fin across the back of the neck like an undercooked noodle.

"Shanks!" he shouted, darting away. "What was that?"

Ardent *humph*ed. "You're lucky Marrill called my attention to you, young man," he said. "A moment later, and you would have been...infected."

"Infected?" Marrill gasped. She looked from side to side. The inky drawings were shifting all around, gathering in the shadows beneath the sailors, scooting stealthily across the colonnades that made up the walls.

Coll nodded gravely as Fin rejoined the group. "Aye. We're at the heart of the disease. One strike, and you're infected for good."

Remy put her hands on her hips. "I thought you got that thing willingly. I thought you came here for the 'gift.'" She made dramatically overemphasized air quotes with her fingers.

"I did, yes," Coll said. "But I was *already* infected, by then. You don't need a tattoo for it to get in you. The disease, it starts in the stories—and the stories are how the Sheshefesh makes itself known in the world."

Marrill's eyes grew wide. If she hadn't seen the things she'd seen, she would have thought he was speaking figuratively. That there was no way a story could literally infect you. But on the Pirate Stream, well...she'd once tossed a grape into the Stream and it transformed into confusion. It had taken them forever to figure that one out.

The sailors all around strained against their bindings. "There's a reason mothers keep their children away from the docks," growled one.

"The sailors' stories," another wailed, "they get into your head." The chorus of voices rose together.

The promise of adventure.
  The life of exploration.
    The lure of the Stream and the sea.

"They pull you in," one said, "and then it's in yer blood. Ye've no choice but to sail, and sail ye must."

The promise of adventure.
  The life of exploration.
    The lure of the Stream and the sea.

"And the more you sail," said another, "the better you get, the more stories you hear, and you're deeper lost yet."

The promise of adventure.
  The life of exploration.
    The lure of the Stream and the sea.

"Until one day, you hear the tallest tale," one said.
"Or ye meet a man with a strange tattoo!" yelled another.
"Or you find a story etched on driftwood!" a third added.

Coll leaned in, cutting them short. "The tallest tale of them all...a secret known only to the greatest captains who ever sailed a ship."

"The Sheshefesh," Marrill breathed.

"The Sheshefesh!" the sailors all cried.

"Just so," Coll said. "And so...you come."

The raucous atmosphere grew strangely somber for a moment. A low groan whispered throughout the chamber. Marrill could have sworn she felt the floor shift, ever so slightly, beneath her feet.

"We should hurry," Coll said. "The Sheshefesh is waiting."

CHAPTER 19
The Shell Altar

Fin rubbed at the welt where the limp tattoo-spine had slapped across his shoulders. He couldn't help staring at the undulating lines of ropy ink stretching up the back of Coll's neck and down to his palms. If it weren't for Marrill and Ardent, he'd be carrying one of those now. He'd be cursed to never have a home, never settle.

Not that it would be much of an adjustment. Though not having a home had to be better than living in a pen, he reminded himself. He shook his head, pushing away the thought.

"You okay?" Marrill asked, stepping over to inspect the welt. Fig peered out from behind her shoulder carefully, her eyes echoing the concern.

He nodded to them both. "No trub," he said. Then he frowned, glancing between Coll's tattoo and the coiled drawings shifting menacingly along the walls, their thin spines poised to pounce. "Think that's the ink we're looking for?"

Ardent shrugged. "Of a kind. They're drawn from it, certainly. But we need to find a source that's a bit less... malignant." He reached the end of the hallway and paused in front of a massive circular door. "Ah, here we are."

As the wizard stepped forward, the door didn't open so much as uncurl. Inside, a huge round chamber waited. Here, the ropy architecture took the form of thick columns, side by side against one another, rising into the distance. Rivers of Stream water threaded in and out through nearly invisible gaps, like golden rings on fat fingers, hundreds of them, as far up as Fin could see.

The room itself, though, was empty. No sailors, no Sheshefesh, nothing. Only a strange curved altar, no higher than Fin's waist, waiting silently in the middle of it all. Its surface was smooth, its top curved nearly to a point, like a hawk's beak. The edges looked sharp as an oyster shell.

"We're here," Coll said somberly. He stepped forward and bowed down before the altar, respectfully. "Hail, great Sheshefesh. Hail to the Knot that ties together the thousand paths."

As soon as the words left his mouth, the altar split down the center and yawned open. A great voice boomed through the chamber.

"None who come here leave forever. And yet, you return to me so soon. Have you sailed your fill for a second lifetime?"

The altar closed with a snap around the final word. Fin wondered how small the Sheshefesh must be to fit inside it without them seeing even a hint of its body. But at the same time, its voice made the very air around them tremble. It didn't make sense.

Fig clearly had the same thought. "Down below," she breathed, just barely audible. "There's another chamber. Got to be."

Coll rose and took a deep breath before addressing the Sheshefesh. "Not even close," he told the creature. "I didn't come because I want to stay."

"And yet, here you are. With the cursed wizard who tried to take from me and leave nothing behind. Wizard, wizard, why do you trouble me so? Did I not lend you my finest captain?"

Coll glanced at Ardent. The old man reached out and gripped the younger—well, seemingly younger—man's arm, a gesture of support and friendship. "You did. The finest and best captain the Stream has ever known, without doubt."

"Speak, then. I listen."

Ardent clasped his hands behind his back. "Your fingers trail in every current; you are no doubt aware the Stream faces grave danger."

"Many currents have drained dry," the Sheshefesh answered. **"Many threads have been severed."** The altar in the center of the room closed and then opened again.

Fin caught Fig's eye. She nodded. They were definitely having the same thought: There *had* to be another room below this one. A hidden chamber, with only one way in: by crawling through the sharp-edged, snapping shell of the altar. If there was something here worth protecting—say, a supply of magic ink, fit to fix the Map to Everywhere—that would be the place to keep it.

Fin licked his lips. He could feel a heist coming on.

"Is that why you've come to me, sailor?" the Sheshefesh continued. **"Do you seek sanctuary? Safe harbor, against the blowing storm?"**

Coll ground his teeth. "We're here to seek your help. That and nothing more."

The walls around them shifted slightly. **"You've already received my blessing. What more can I offer? What aid can I give that your wizard cannot?"**

Ardent cleared his throat and stepped forward. "We come in search of something you have."

The very floor seemed to ripple beneath their feet. A

deep bass hum filled the chamber as though the building itself responded to the Sheshefesh's mood.

"So you've returned at last for the Compass Rose," the voice boomed.

Fin arched an eyebrow. Rose? That didn't make any sense. They'd last seen Rose in the grips of the Master of the Iron Ship, back at Margaham's Game. What would she now be doing here?

Ardent, too, popped up one long, owl-haired eyebrow. "The Compass Rose?"

The floor rumbled once again. Fin was beginning to think it was the sound of the Sheshefesh's laughter. If the horrible sound could be considered laughter. It was more like an evil cackle.

"Yes, wizard. Years ago you came to me for a captain to help you find it, and yet I held the Compass Rose all along."

Ardent stumbled back a step. "Rose was here when I came before? How?"

"Entrusted to me here, where all paths come together, by the Dawn Wizard, last of the Dzane. For even he was subject to the rules of this place. None leave—"

"But leave something precious entangled," Ardent finished. He dropped his chin to his chest and exhaled, slowly. "Except for me."

"Except for you!" The Sheshefesh sounded almost

giddy. **"Oh, the arrogance! Did you truly think you could break the rules that bind this place? Did you think they applied to all but you alone? No. You simply did not realize what you left entangled—your hope of finding the very thing you were seeking."**

Fin gave Marrill a questioning look, but she was already tugging on Ardent's sleeve, face scrunched in confusion. "What's he talking about?" she whispered.

Ardent sighed. "Long before I lost Annalessa, I came here on a quest for the Map," he explained. "Of course, I never found it then. And apparently one of the pieces was right under my nose." He closed his eyes. "Oh, how did I miss that?"

Marrill gripped the old man's hand in a show of comfort. But Fin wasn't sure why it should matter that Ardent failed to get Rose so many years ago. After all, eventually he'd gotten ahold of all the pieces of the Map.

Fig tapped him on the shoulder, motioning with her head. With everyone distracted, it was the perfect moment to make their move.

As the shell snapped open, the chamber filling with the Sheshefesh's gloating, Fin began to creep toward the altar while Fig circled it from the other side.

"You failed in your quest then," the Sheshefesh continued. **"And another came and took the Compass Rose from me. A wizard who understood**

the rules of this place. She took my Compass Rose, but left a piece of herself in return."

Fin's footsteps faltered. *She?*

Ardent's entire demeanor suddenly changed. He was sharper edged, his body tense as though ready for a fight. "Annalessa?" he asked evenly.

The chamber trembled with the low roll of the Sheshefesh's laugh.

"I warn you, creature, do not toy with me," Ardent said, his voice as cold and hard as metal. "Recall what happened at my last visit."

Fin swallowed, trying to focus on the task before him. Maybe Annalessa had been here. Maybe she'd been the one to take the Compass Rose. It was ancient history as far as he was concerned. While Ardent was jousting with the Sheshefesh, the void was out there, eating worlds. Growing.

He kept his eyes on the spongy floor, watching his step as he tiptoed closer to the altar. Across from him, Fig mirrored the movements.

"What is it you would have me recall, wizard? How you seared your way into my chamber? How you burned my flesh until I agreed to release one sailor? A sailor who had already sailed his days and was by all rights bound to me for eternity?"

At the edge of Fin's awareness, he heard Remy gasp. He dared a glance back, in time to see her spinning on Coll. The captain's dark eyes were downcast, looking almost beaten.

"You were already here!" Remy accused. "You had already become one of them!"

"Who speaks?" the Sheshefesh boomed. The floor trembled with the power of it. Fin, one leg outstretched in a footpad's step, was thrown off balance. He fell, but caught himself in the way all Quay kids knew, using the momentum to roll behind the altar. Landing on his back, the tip of his head just rested against the hard, shell-like surface of the altar.

For the first time, his bare hands touched the floor. It felt strange—tough and rubbery, cool but trembling. He glanced back to see if Marrill had noticed what he was up to yet. Thankfully she was completely focused on the brewing argument.

"Remy, shh!" Coll hissed. But his eyes were squeezed shut. Even from behind the altar, Fin thought he saw tears forming in the corners of them. "Yes, for over a century I was here," the sailor gasped. "At first, it feels good to settle. But then you remember the sea, the Stream. You feel the wanderlust. But you can't leave. You're stuck here forever. The stories... the stories are all you have."

"And if I give you what you ask, wizard, for the second time?" the Sheshefesh spoke. **"What will I keep in return? None leave but leave something precious. That is my rule, and it cannot be broken. What will you leave entangled in the Knot of the Coiled Rope?"**

"You say I left my hope of finding what I was seeking

when I came here before, and yet eventually I found the Compass Rose and assembled the Map. So you see, I left nothing behind then, and I'll leave nothing now," Ardent growled. "Annalessa left *you* something, and I would have it!"

The altar heaved open once more. A great, bitter wind blew out over Fin. It smelled of waterlogged ropes and pungent, acidic funk, and something very, *very* fishy.

"You have asked me for the wrong object in the past," the Sheshefesh boomed. **"Is it your intent to make the same mistake again, wizard?"**

"I did not come to bargain, but to demand!" Ardent stomped a foot against the ground with a force that caused the floor to tremble. A low howl of pain rumbled through the chamber. "You will give me all that I ask! What did Annalessa leave?"

"Ardent, this isn't what we're here for!" Marrill begged. "The ink—"

"Who speaks?" the Sheshefesh demanded again. **"Who dares address me without right or power?"**

"I have power enough for all!" Ardent bellowed. "You know well the power of a wizard in this of all places!" He threw up his arms. The hairs on Fin's head threatened to stand and run down his back. Overhead, the rivers ran more turbulently; the sound of splashing echoed from all around. The air was heavy with magic.

Things were escalating, fast. There wasn't much time to

grab the ink and get out. Across the altar, Fig waved him on. She, at least, was focused on the real job: thieving.

"Great Sheshefesh," Coll cried reverently, "the fate of the Stream is at stake and what Ardent means is—"

"Silence, sailor!"

Fin seized the moment, popping his head over the altar just as it opened. No fish, no creature waited inside, no treasure room, no ink. Below him, a sticky, fleshy tunnel yawned. Oyster-shell hooks lined mucous-covered muscle, undulating downward as far as he could see.

It was one giant creature, he realized. It was *all* one giant creature.

He was looking down the throat of the Sheshefesh.

A second later, Fig shoved him, pushing him aside just as the oyster shells snapped shut, nearly taking his head off. "Watch out," she hissed.

"Another speaks again!" the Sheshefesh thundered.

Fin could feel it trembling with rage. Out of the corner of his eye, Marrill desperately waved for him to return to the group.

But Fin was focused on one thing: the blackness of the mucous he'd seen dripping down the creature's throat. It was the exact same color as Coll's tattoo and the drawings slithering across the rest of the walls of this place. It was just as alive, but without form.

It was ink.

"Not only do you threaten me, but you pollute my chamber with the unworthy!"

Fin dug into his thief's bag, fingers closing around an empty jar he kept for just such an occasion. Quickly unscrewing the lid, he waited for the next outburst.

"Cease your blustering, squid!" Ardent snarled. "Give me what she left, or I will pull the power of the Stream down on you!"

Fig counted on her fingers. One...two...

"Fool Wizard! I will send you to your—gak!"

Fin dove between the two shells as the great beak opened. In a single swooping motion, he scraped the jar along the creature's throat, filling it with ink.

"Akh...yuhk...hrr..."

All around, the great columns of the walls swayed and untangled. The coils of the door slipped apart, the gallery beyond dissolving into a chaos of tentacles as the creature unwound itself.

Fin jumped to his feet. "I've got it!" he shouted, holding the jar of ink into the air.

"Dooooooooooooooooooooom!" the Sheshefesh finished.

CHAPTER 20
Song of the Sheshefesh

Marrill struggled to stay on her feet as the whole world unraveled. What had once seemed to be columns, as thick as sequoia tree trunks, now lashed and slashed all around them. Through the gaps between the great tentacles, ribbons of golden water twisted and twined in every direction.

The entire structure, she suddenly realized, was one giant creature! There was no land, no sky. Only air, raw magic, and the enormous bulk of the Sheshefesh.

"What did you do?" Coll shrieked as Fin raced toward them. In his hand, Fin clutched a vial of something dark and thick.

"We've got the ink!" he cried, holding it up triumphantly. "Let's get out of here!"

"Thief!" the Sheshefesh bellowed.

It whipped a tentacle toward them. Marrill ducked. Fin yelped, and she looked up to see him gliding through the air on his skysails. A second later, a girl she hadn't even noticed crashed into her out of nowhere.

"Hey," the girl said.

"Hi?" Marrill said reflexively.

She didn't have time to ask questions. The floor itself bowed beneath them.

Suddenly they were sliding then they

were

falling.

Marrill screamed, her voice joining a chorus of the others.

The air rushed from her lungs as she slapped against the rubbery skin of another thick tentacle. She struggled to her hands and knees as she felt herself lifting again. She looked up.

Beside her, Coll and Remy and the new girl wrestled to their feet. Alongside them, Fin glided frantically on his sky-sails, twining through the mass of moving flesh and deadly water.

The tips of smaller tentacles whipped by them,

merely the size of telephone poles and covered in dancing tattoos.

Sailors waved past, tethered to the tips,

hooting and hollering

on what must have been the most terrifying carnival ride imaginable.

"Oh, you're going to get it now," one said as he whizzed by.

"Look who woke the Sheshefesh!" shouted another.

"Hope you like being smashed!" cried a third.

Ahead, what had been the ground turned into a wall, then literally turned, revealing a bulbous body the size of a stadium. An eye as big as a swimming pool focused its gaze on them.

"**I am as old as the Stream,**" the great beast boomed, "**born in the early rush of its waters. I am the lord of sailors, the master of the flow. Behold my form and tremble!**"

Marrill forced herself onto her heels, looking down to be sure she didn't slip. On the pallid flesh beneath her fingers, a braided pattern coiled like a band of muscle.

She jerked her hand away, falling backward. A long spine stabbed the empty air where she'd just been. "Tattoos!"

"Don't let them touch you!" Coll cried. They scrabbled backward, Marrill crab-walking as the living patterns closed in. Hanging over them like a movie screen, the great eye of the Sheshefesh watched.

"**None leave but leave something precious entangled. Who will leave their freedom? Who will wear the ink of my mark in exchange for the ink you have taken?**"

Panic spread fire through Marrill's chest. No matter which way she looked, a new pattern was moving in. The nearest one coiled, ready to strike. Marrill braced herself.

Just then, an invisible force rushed by her face. A swath of ink vanished in front of her, as though it had been swiped by an eraser from a whiteboard.

"A tattoo is a big decision, young lady," Ardent said from above her. "And that design is one I suspect you would very quickly regret."

The wizard balanced on a Frisbee-thin disk made of pure energy. A long arm made of water reached out from one of the infinite branches of the Stream, holding the disk gingerly in place. Even for Ardent, it was downright amazing.

The Sheshefesh's eye turned to the wizard. The colossal body curled and shifted. Tentacles slashed toward Ardent. Marrill gasped.

But the water-arm just tossed him, sending disk and wizard sailing. Ardent laughed as another arm shot out from another glowing river, snagging him smoothly out of the air. This arm tossed him to another, and then to yet another, and another. Energy shot from his fingertips as he twirled. The air smelled oddly like fried calamari.

"If this is the best you can muster," Ardent yelled, "I was too generous in my last visit! Now give me what Annalessa left behind!"

"You take and take and take," the Sheshefesh boomed, **"and still offer me nothing?"**

The tentacle they were standing on swung into motion. As Marrill battled for balance, the inky tattoo Ardent had severed knit itself back together. There was no way they could stay here. "We have to go!"

"Go where?" Remy yelled.

"We have to get to the *Kraken*!" Coll said. Inky veins

bulged across his forehead. Ropes curled over each of his ears. "Even if Ardent burns this thing into submission, the Sheshefesh will never let you two leave unmarked. And it can definitely hold him off long enough to get that done."

Marrill peered down into the tangled tentacle abyss, searching not just for the *Kraken*, but for Fin. She didn't find either. A chill passed over her. She could only hope he was okay.

The Sheshefesh was in full motion now. Its great body curled through the mass of coiled streams, chasing Ardent as the watery arms tossed him from one to the next. The whole world was a tangle of flying tendrils and twining rivers. It was hard to even know where *up* was.

"There!" cried a girl beside her, pointing. Far below, the *Kraken* skidded along like a water skier, tethered to the Sheshefesh's trailing tentacle. Marrill searched for a way down to it, one eye on the deadly designs re-forming all around her.

From below, another big tentacle swept up toward them—or maybe they were sweeping toward it. Whatever was happening, the tattoos on it were spread out, far easier to avoid than the ones surrounding them.

"We have to jump!" she told Remy. Before the older girl could react, Marrill grabbed her hand and the arm of the unfamiliar girl next to her and cannonballed over. *It's not the craziest thing I've done recently*, she reminded herself midair.

They landed with a huff on the lower tentacle, Coll a

moment later beside them. His face was grim, his teeth gritted. The ink of his tattoo waved all across his skin, rippling his very flesh as it moved.

Above and around and beside them, Ardent and the Sheshefesh were locked in vicious battle. The massive creature struck at the wizard with ropes and tendrils; Ardent burned them back with fire and lightning. It was all Marrill could do to hold on and avoid the swirling tattoos. With Ardent occupied, there was nothing to keep the living ink at bay.

"Jump again!" Coll commanded. "Here!"

They leapt to another passing tentacle, then another, running from the oncoming tattoos, dodging the deadly Stream water twining through the air around them. Sailors sang as they whipped by, still tethered to the tentacles that held them.

Wouldn't you like to sail with us forever?
Join the chorus, tell the tales of the sea!
Wouldn't you like to taste the salt wind forever?
You'll say you're free, but you'll never be free!

Marrill rolled out of the way as they passed mere feet beneath a spiraling loop of raw magic. Their tentacle swooped, turning as it went, forcing them to run in place. They leapt and rolled, struggling through the maze of tendrils and water. Around them, the bound mariners continued their song.

Wouldn't you like to sail with us forever?

"What did she leave?" Ardent yelled, his voice a high counterpoint to the sailors' refrain.

Join the chorus, tell the tales of the sea!

"Tell me!"

Wouldn't you like to taste the salt wind forever?

"Tell me or I will burn you down to stumps!"

You'll say you're free, but you'll never be free!

Marrill threw up her hands as they rose once again, away from the ship. Every time they jumped to a lower tentacle, it lifted them higher. "We can't get down there," she realized. "We have to get the *Kraken* up here!"

It was Remy who nodded. "That would do it! She's fast enough to keep up with the Sheshefesh, for sure!"

Coll grinned wide, the first smile Marrill had seen from him since they'd set sail for the Knot of the Coiled Rope. "That's good," he said. "You know your ship like you know yourself. You'll be a great captain before you know it."

Marrill rolled her eyes. "Someone has to actually *get* to the ship," she reminded them.

Just then, she saw Fin swooping past them. She let out a sigh of relief to know he was safe. His skysails cut through the air as he banked toward the ship, landing on the deck a moment later with a stutter. His eyes swept the tangle of tentacles, and when he found Marrill he held up the jar of ink so she could see that he still had his prize.

"Fin's already on the ship, and he's got the ink," she announced excitedly. "He can help..." She trailed off. She could just make out Fin racing frantically around the deck, struggling to free the mooring lines. The *Kraken* wouldn't respond to him. Of course it wouldn't, she realized; like everyone else, the ship itself didn't remember him.

"Never mind," she finished. "One of us has to get the ship!"

A girl, maybe one of the sailors, piped up beside her. "What about the Naysayer?"

Marrill, Coll, and Remy looked at one another for a long moment.

"One of *us* has to get the ship," Remy repeated. They all nodded in agreement.

Coll stood tall. The inky cords of his tattoo threatened to burst along his arms. "Well, she's my ship," he said. "Leave getting her to me."

And then he jumped.

Marrill couldn't believe what she saw next. As the battle between wizard and sea monster raged all around, as sailors sang their chorus and living designs inched toward them, Coll fell, reaching out his arms, and screamed in pain.

Wouldn't you like to sail with us forever?

Ropes uncoiled from Coll's skin, snaking out to anchor on nearby tentacles. One yanked him one way, the other another. He swung between them, pivoted, and pulled with all his might, wrenching one rope loose from its anchor, then the other.

Join the chorus, tell the tales of the sea!

They immediately shot for other swaying tentacles, clearly seeking to pull him in tight to the Sheshefesh's embrace. But even as they did, he fell farther, swung, arrested his fall, controlled it. It was great and it was terrible; he was like a superhero and a captive prisoner, all at the same time.

Wouldn't you like to taste the salt wind forever?

At last, with a final shout, Coll dropped to the deck of the *Kraken*. Instantly, the ship's sails jumped to life.

Marrill was so focused on watching his descent that she didn't even notice the tattoo coiling beside her. Not until a spine stabbed straight out. Time slowed, crawling toward a stop. In a heartbeat, she would be stuck at age twelve forever, doomed to one day spend eternity as the Sheshefesh's living, breathing wall decoration.

She felt Remy grabbing her from behind, tossing her off the tentacle. Marrill landed on another with a thump that forced the air from her lungs. A second later, her babysitter dropped next to her, letting out a sharp cry as she hit the ground.

Marrill caught the older girl's eye. "Too close," she whispered. Remy nodded solemnly. "Thanks," Marrill whispered again.

"I'm northern Arizona's best babysitter," Remy replied. "You think I'm going to let one of *my* kids spend all eternity stuck to a giant squid?"

"You dare taunt me?!?!?" Ardent shouted from somewhere above. Marrill looked up to see him spinning through the air, waves of bright lightning darting from his fingertips. Just out of his reach, a tendril no thicker than an arm waved a scrap of paper.

"This is what you're looking for, wizard," the creature chided. **"The words of a love lost, and they can be yours. Just follow my rules. Leave something behind. Tell me who will bear my mark, and this letter will be yours."**

"Ardent, come on!" Marrill yelled. Her legs ached. Her

ribs and back were sore from close calls and rough landings. It wouldn't matter if she ever made it to the deck of the *Enterprising Kraken* if Ardent refused to join them. They couldn't very well leave *him* behind.

Ardent lifted his arms wide. Arcs of lightning leapt from his body, searing against the flesh of the sea creature. The Sheshefesh roared and squirmed, writhing as Ardent pelted it with the full force of his rage. Marrill cringed; she couldn't bear to see any creature in pain, not even a stubborn, greedy, angry one.

But just then, as the *Kraken* dodged through the tangle of tentacles beneath them, she saw it. The tentacle bearing Annalessa's letter swooped between her and the deck of the ship still several stories below.

Marrill didn't stop to think or second-guess or even plan. She simply jumped.

"Marrill, no!" Remy cried behind her.

She barely had time to realize her stomach was twisting. Barely had room to register the barbs of coiled ink lashing out as she tumbled past. Her whole being focused on the slip of paper, the whipping tentacle that held it.

Wind stung her eyes, bringing fresh tears that made everything blurry. Her fingers brushed against the letter and she grabbed it, hoping against hope it wouldn't tear as she crushed the paper in her fist.

Something snagged around her ankle, whipping her out

of the way. "Nooo!" she shrieked, sure a tentacle had her. But then, before she knew it, she found herself on the pitching deck of the *Kraken*, a length of familiar rope unwinding from her leg. Remy landed next to her, a young girl clinging to her back. Fin raced over to help untangle them.

"Thanks, Ropebone," Marrill panted. She opened her hand and glanced down. The letter hadn't ripped! She thrust it in the air. "Ardent! I've got it!"

The Sheshefesh roared with fury. Its vile breath washed over her.

"Thieves, thieves, and thieves again! You will never escape!"

Coll let out a growl and cupped his hands around his mouth. "Ardent, come! *Now!*"

A second later, Ardent's disk spun to the deck. The wizard stepped off it, and the disk twirled, shrank, and became a single golden coin that he tucked into his robe. Blue lightning and green fire continued to crackle over his knuckles, and his face was still folded with fury.

"Full sails," Coll cried at the top of his lungs. The knotted tattoo practically consumed him now, crossing his cheekbones, tangling down over his jaw and chin.

The *Kraken* gained speed, looping-the-loop down a Stream branch, in and out through the maze of tentacles. The Sheshefesh watched them. Its great eye was bloodshot, its surface scratched, tentacles drooping. It lashed out once, twice, but halfheartedly.

The monster had been beaten.

The sailors' song faded as the great monster retreated back through the heart of the stream-tangle. The Knot of the Coiled Rope fell into the distance.

Ardent let out a deep sigh. He plucked the letter from Marrill's fingers without a word and stared at it a moment before slipping it up his sleeve. "Well, then," he said. "That was an adventure. And nothing left behind after all." He brushed at his robes, tugged at his beard. "I suppose we now have everything we need. It's time to put an end to the Lost Sun."

The crew just stared at their wizard. Marrill wanted to say something to him, anything. About the Sheshefesh. About Annalessa. About how he had acted, how it had scared her. But she wasn't sure what.

"Coll," the wizard announced. "Set course for Meres."

Coll looked down from the quarterdeck for a long moment. The inky ropes still swirled furiously across his skin. "I . . ." he started.

And then he flew backward, over the railing and out of sight.

Remy screamed. A young deckhand threw herself against the bulkhead as though she could still catch him. Marrill raced to the side of the *Kraken*, just in time to see a tentacle withdrawing, dragging Coll deep into the darkness below. The laughing voice of the Sheshefesh boomed up from the abyss.

"None leave but leave something precious entangled!"

Marrill's mouth hung open. She looked to Fin, then Remy, then Ardent. All three wore the same expression she did.

Coll was gone.

You'll say you're free, but you'll never be free!

CHAPTER 21
What Was Left Entangled

F in stared at the spot where Coll had been standing only moments before. He was stunned. Numb. Speechless.

Remy, on the other hand, was not.

"What just happened?" she demanded. When Ardent didn't immediately answer, she stomped her foot and shouted, her voice even more panicked than before. "*Where did Coll just go?*"

Ardent shook his head. "It would appear the Sheshefesh reclaimed him."

Remy blinked at him. "I'm turning this ship around." Fin could tell it was as much a statement to herself as to the rest of them. "We have to go back." She spun on her heel, headed for the quarterdeck.

"We can't go back," Ardent said softly.

Remy froze. "What?"

"Yeah, what?" Fin echoed. He couldn't believe what he was hearing. Coll was part of the *crew*. They didn't leave crew behind. They didn't even leave the Naysayer behind, and he was a useless, greedy curmudgeon who spent all his time stealing food and insulting everyone. This was *Coll*. This was their captain. How could Ardent even think about not going back for him?

"We can't," Ardent repeated. "I understand now. We can never face the Sheshefesh and win. Not really."

Remy didn't give anyone a chance to jump in. "Are you kidding? You were beating the ink out of that thing. It gave up. Go *take* him back."

Ardent sighed and shook his head sadly. "I fooled myself into believing those rules did not apply to me. That I alone could take from the creature without being caught in its tangles. I was wrong."

Deep wrinkles hung from the corners of the old man's eyes. He looked old and sad and tired. "The creature let me take Coll long ago because it knew I would have to return, or else give up the chance of ever finding the Map to Everywhere. One way or another, I left feeling victorious, when in truth my greatest ambition stayed behind, entangled with the Sheshefesh.

"Now," he continued, "it has taken Coll in exchange for the ink and Annalessa's letter. If we return for him, it will extract something even more valuable. And if we return for that, it will take something more. And in the meantime, the Stream is dying."

From within his robes, he produced the Map to Everywhere. The tear-shaped hole in its center was as big around as Fin's wrist. Even as they watched, more worlds vanished into it.

Ardent pointed to the very tip, the sharp point the tear hung from as though ready to fall. Just above it, marked with the sketch of a fountain, lay Meres.

"He's nearly there," Marrill said, her voice hushed. Ardent nodded. Fin felt acid churning in his stomach. They didn't have much time left.

As one, they looked to Remy. Her lip curled, showing the end of one canine tooth. "We need Coll. He sails the ship, remember?"

Ardent gave her an encouraging smile. "I have faith in you. You seem a capable captain."

Remy's eyes narrowed into slits. "I'm an *awesome* captain, actually." She turned away. "But I'm not the *best*. Coll is. And only the best captain is going to be able to get us out of this mess."

Fin's heart broke as he saw the wrinkles around Ardent's eyes fold in sympathy. The old wizard's voice was gentle as he approached her and said, "Coll was my friend as well. I shall feel his absence more than you know."

Remy's bottom lip trembled. She rubbed at her side, as though gripping at the pain Fin knew she must be feeling inside. "Then why did you make him go to that awful place? We could have found a way to do it without him. We—*you*—could have kept him safe. He only went because you asked."

Fin could hear the frustration and pain in her voice. He felt it himself.

Ardent let out a weary sigh and reached out to reassure her. "Because he is a great and loyal companion and friend."

Remy thought about this for a moment, then said, "Well that makes you a pretty terrible friend for asking," she bit out. "And maybe if you hadn't been so obsessed with getting that letter..." she sputtered, too angry to even finish the statement.

She shrugged away from Ardent's touch and stormed across the deck, headed for the ship's wheel. Fin scrambled to get out of her way.

Marrill's head dropped to one side in concern. Fin was glad she was there; he had no idea what to say in this type of situation. Marrill always knew what to do. She stepped forward, to follow. "Remy..."

The older girl whirled around, one finger held up sharply.

"No," she snapped. Marrill stumbled backward, clearly stunned by the force of the command. Fin gulped. He'd never seen Remy this mad. And he had seen her *pretty* mad before.

Remy's eyes jumped between each of them; they even locked on Fig. Apparently this level of wrath made *everyone* noticeable. Not even Ardent had the nerve to challenge her.

"The Lost Sun is approaching Meres from the south," she said at last. "We'll come in from the north. That'll give us time to reach the Font without worrying about him smashing up the *Kraken*."

She turned and bounded up the stairs two at a time. Her expression was stony when she wrapped her hands around the wheel. "Full sails," she called.

Nothing happened. Without Coll there to give permission, the ship wouldn't listen to her. "Full sails!" she repeated, louder.

"Ropebone," Ardent said weakly. "Pirates...you have a new captain. Abide by her." The ship surged to life, pirates scampering across yards and the Ropebone Man hauling lines.

Just then, the Naysayer burst from the main hatch. "Hey, barnacle brains, know what might be nice when your ship has a deck that up and wanders to different locations? A *sign*. Spent the last day and a half negotiatin' my freedom from a crew of jam-worshippin'..." He paused. They all stared at him. He looked up at Remy. "Wait, the cheerleader's captain now?"

Ardent sighed and headed for his cabin. Remy, for her part, glared at the lumpy creature. "Call me a cheerleader again and I'll toss you in the brig."

The Naysayer picked at his teeth with the claw tip of a prollycrab. "Eh," he said, shrugging all four of his shoulders as he ambled off. "Unless it's fulla brutal savages with an unhealthy respect for preserves, I been worse places."

Remy said nothing. Merely gripped the wheel tighter and scowled at the horizon.

"Someone should talk to her," Fig said, nodding to Remy.

Marrill looked at Fin. "You're right," she said, as if the words had come from him and not the Fade girl. "But I already tried. Your turn. *I'm* going to talk to Ardent."

"But—" Before he could finish the protest, Marrill nudged him toward the quarterdeck and spun, knocking on the door to Ardent's cabin. A sharp voice called for her to enter, and she slipped inside, leaving Fin and Fig standing in the middle of the deck, staring at each other.

"Well, it can't be *me*," Fig said. "She won't remember *me*."

"She doesn't remember me, either," Fin said. "To her I'm just another kid she has to keep up with. Marrill, plus one."

Fig crossed her arms. "That sounds like being remembered to me."

Fin sighed. She was right. Besides, every time Remy called him Plus One, it sent a little thrill down his spine. He nodded grudgingly to Fig, took a deep breath, and headed up the stairs to the quarterdeck.

At the ship's wheel, Remy stared straight ahead, looking angry. But he could see her eyes were glassy with unshed tears. Fin had no idea what to say. So he went with the first thing that came to mind.

"So...do you know where you're going?"

The moment she heard him, she squared her shoulders and raised her chin. Her answer was quick and curt. "Yes."

Fin waited. She said nothing more.

He cleared his throat. "*How* do you know where you're going?"

Remy didn't even look at him. "If you don't mind, I'd rather be alone."

It wasn't the first time Fin had been brushed off in his life. Or the second. Or the thousandth, for that matter. He nodded. "Right. Okay. I'll just be over there." He gestured vaguely as he sauntered down the steps to the main deck.

"Well," he told Fig, "I tried..."

She counted on her fingers. "Three...two...and now she's forgotten she ever talked to you. Time to try again!"

Fin sighed again and walked across the deck to the stairs on the other side. Having someone who *really* understood what it was like to be him was starting to get old.

"So, I hear you've just been promoted to captain," he said, strolling toward her. "Pretty impressive, *especially* at your age!"

Remy cut her eyes toward him. "Some people are older than they look," she said. She let out a long sigh. "If you don't mind—"

He held up his hands. "Oh, sure, want to be alone, no problem. I'll just be over…" He let the statement trail off as he climbed back down the stairs.

"Three…two…" Fig counted.

"Right, right," Fin grumbled. A few beats later and he was back on the quarterdeck.

"So…" he mustered. "Whaddya get when you cross a skink-riding plantimal with the Khesteresh Empire?"

Remy looked at him, eyebrow raised.

"Genocide."

She ran a hand down her face. "If you don't mind…"

She didn't have to finish. He was already down the stairs.

Fig held up her hand. "Give her a few extra seconds," she said. "That one's going to be hard to forget."

As they waited, she leaned back against the base of the stairs. "Remy's right, though," she mused. "We needed Coll if we're going to escape the Rise. They know the Lost Sun's on his way to Meres and that we'll head there eventually to try to stop him. They'll come for us there, I'm sure of it."

"I don't think that's why she's upset," Fin told her.

"I know," Fig said. "And it was stupid of Ardent to make Coll go back there, knowing we could lose him."

Fin held out his hands. "Hold up a tick," he said. "Ardent didn't *make* Coll go. He *asked* him to, sure, but Coll could have said no. It was as much his decision as Ardent's."

"What?" Fig laughed. "It was not! Why would anyone do that voluntarily?"

"I would," Fin said reflexively. "I mean, if Marrill asked me to do something like that to save her mom, I would say yes, too. But it would be my choice, not hers."

Fig looked at him funny. "You'd risk yourself like that just to help her save her mother, who you haven't even met?"

"Of course," Fin said. The question didn't even make sense to him. "She's my friend. I'd do anything for her."

"Without a Rise, or anyone, ordering you to?"

Now *that* question didn't make sense. "No one *orders* me to do anything," he told her. "The crew of the *Kraken*, they're my family. I'd do anything for them because I *love* them, not because I have to." He paused. "Same as my mom did for me."

The Fade girl shook her head, a small smile on her face.

"What?" Fin asked.

"Nothing," she said. "Just...that's not something you hear among the Rise and the Fade, that's all." She glanced away.

Fin waited a beat, then said, "I saw you reach for Coll. When the Sheshefesh took him. You tried to save him."

She lifted a shoulder, but didn't say anything.

Fin pressed the point. "If you'd actually succeeded in grabbing him, you could have been dragged back along with him. Trapped in the Knot with all the other sailors for eternity."

She still didn't respond or meet his eyes.

"And back in Oneira, when Remy described how close

the void got while Coll tried to pry our shell free from the shoals, I could tell from the story there was something missing: you. *You* were there helping him. *You* risked being swallowed by the void to save us."

He stepped toward her. "No one ordered you to take those risks, Fig." He dropped a hand on her shoulder and squeezed. "In fact, it's exactly the kind of thing someone who's truly part of the crew would do."

Fig fidgeted, clearly uncomfortable with the attention. But the truth was clear: she *wanted* to be a member of the crew. She actually cared about them, whether she even knew it herself. Why else would she have risked herself for them on multiple occasions?

Fig shifted again and cleared her throat. "Countdown's done. Time to give Remy another go."

"Right," he said. His thoughts were still on their conversation, though, as he climbed the stairs. He paused at the top and turned back, slipping his hand into his thief's bag to grab something important. "Hey, Fig—"

She looked up at him.

"Catch!" He flung the object toward her and she raised her hands reflexively. Her silver bracelet glinted in the glowing light of the Pirate Stream as she plucked it from the air. Fig's eyes shone as she slid it onto her wrist.

She opened her mouth, then closed it, swallowing several times before saying softly, "Thanks."

He smiled and nodded, before continuing to the

quarterdeck. His mind still swirled with thoughts of Fig, the crew of the *Kraken*, the Rise and the Fade, Coll, Ardent, his mother. He didn't know what to say to Remy. He just wanted to be there for her. He just wanted her to feel better.

Without saying anything, Fin leaned against the railing and stared up at the sky. The Stream was still a braided knot before them, but they'd left the cave of the Sheshefesh. It was dark out, and Fin's star—the one his mother had pointed out to him long ago—shone near the horizon. He smiled at it.

She was still out there, he knew. The woman who had saved him from the pens where poor Fig had grown up. The woman who'd risked everything so that he might have a chance. Just like Coll had done for all of them.

A sharp ache pinged his chest. He glanced over at Remy. Even with her back rigid and eyes straight ahead, her misery was obvious.

"I'm going to miss Coll," he said. It was the truth. Coll was a good captain. Even if he never remembered Fin, he also never hesitated to stand by the side of his friends.

Remy's chin wobbled. "Me too."

He hesitated. "Do you want to talk about it?"

"Not really."

Fin stood by for moment, thinking about what he'd want if he were in her shoes. "Do you mind if I stay out here a bit longer? I promise not to bother you."

She glanced at him. "Actually, Plus One…" Fin pushed

himself off the railing, ready to head back down the stairs. But the ghost of a smile played around her lips. "I'd like that," she said. "I'd actually like that a lot."

Fin smiled back. "Spiff," he declared. "I'll just be here. You know, if you need me."

Remy nodded. When she returned her focus to navigating the intricately braided threads of the Stream in front of them, her shoulders seemed a bit more relaxed.

Fin resumed his position against the railing, knowing that he'd likely already been forgotten but still not wanting to leave. So it was a surprise when a few minutes later he heard a soft "Thank you" from Remy.

CHAPTER 22
Ripples on the Ocean

A rdent?" Marrill asked, pushing her way into the darkened cabin. The wizard stood, hands clasped behind his back, staring out the far window. Through it, the *Kraken*'s wake glittered like golden fire, casting sparks into the night.

"When I first went to the Sheshefesh," Ardent said without turning, "I believed the Bintheyr Map to Everywhere would lead me to the secrets of the Dzane."

Marrill had to laugh grimly. "Well, it did."

"That it did," he agreed. "Though the Lost Sun of Dzannin was not quite what I had in mind. This was before Serth drank Stream water, before the Meressian Prophecy; I had scarcely even heard of the Lost Sun back then. No, what I wanted more than anything in life was to achieve the power of the Dzane. The Map was my utmost ambition. Knowing now that the Compass Rose was with the Sheshefesh...The creature fooled me good."

Marrill let the door shut behind her, slipping closer to the wizard's desk in the center of the room. It was strewn with junk, as usual. One corner, however, was clear, save for a thick scroll, partially unraveled. "So, that's what I don't get," she said. "You said the Sheshefesh took something precious from you because it had the Compass Rose. But then it gave the Compass Rose to Annalessa, and you ended up getting it after all."

Ardent turned to her. One hand hung limp at his side, the crumpled letter dangling from it as if stuck to his fingers, ready to fall at any moment. "Indeed," he said, "it found something even more valuable to me to take instead."

He took a deep breath. "In my quest for the Map, I would spend weeks researching before I went anywhere, making sure my leads were real, that I knew what I was looking for, that I would recognize any clues that I might stumble upon. When Annalessa went missing, I forgot all of that. I hunted wildly, heading anywhere I thought might even be possible, as fast as I could travel, for years, to no avail."

He waved to the scroll on the corner of his desk. Marrill

approached it cautiously. Scrawled down the length of it was a list of what looked to be locations: the Boastful Coast, Kittargh & Yaracdala, Scarbride Furrow, Strange the Grange. Most had been scratched through, but not all. Three in particular glowed a soft yellow at the bottom of the list, as though inked in candlelight. These three, she recognized.

Monerva
Margaham's Game
The Knot of the Coiled Rope

With a flick of Ardent's fingers, the scroll began to unravel. It reached the edge of the desk and fell to the floor, unrolling across the length of the cabin. Marrill sucked in a breath—there must have been thousands of locations scratched out. "You went to all of those?"

Ardent sounded tired when he answered. "Many of them twice."

Marrill recognized the expression on his face. It was the same one her father always tried to hide from her—the one he wore late at night, when his thoughts were consumed by her mother's health. It was fear and worry and deep, aching sorrow. Ardent and her dad had that in common, she realized. Both were unable to shape the fate of the person they loved.

"What was in the letter?" Marrill asked.

Ardent sighed and shrugged, his fingers twitching as he

held it toward her. "You were the one to retrieve it for me. You have a right to know its contents."

Marrill swallowed back her surprise and scurried across the cabin to retrieve it before he could change his mind.

Dear Old Fool, it read.

> *When we met in Monerva, I knew I could not stop Serth and his Prophecy of destruction. My future was your past—how could I change it? I could only track him, learn from him, and hope that an answer would reveal itself. What I didn't understand was that my steps led in a circle, and even as I hunted, I was hunted in turn. I am pursued now by the walking shadow of the man I once knew, a grim reflection of the person I once held as dear as myself. He already knows where the path leads us; there is no escaping it. But even he doesn't know what we will find there.*

> *Still, I found what I needed. I cannot stop the Prophecy, I know, but I believe I __can__ influence the manner in which it comes to pass. And that may be just the chance the Stream needs to survive the coming of the Lost Sun.*

> *To do what must be done, I needed the Compass Rose. And to get it, I had to leave something precious behind. The Sheshefesh had but one demand: that I promise, bound by the magic of the Knot of the Coiled Rope, that I would not see or speak to you again until my task was completed. The Sheshefesh assures me that you will return*

someday and retrieve this letter. Indeed, he insisted that I write it. Part of his price on both of us, it seems, is for you to know exactly the terms of our bargain.

How I wish you had come with me, back when I visited you in your tower. Now, there are no more chances. I must do this alone.

The lodestone, the Compass Rose you tried to find so long ago, weighs heavy in my hand. It guides me to the Font of Meres, where wizards and magic mingle. What will happen there, I do not know. Perhaps one day, I will send you a letter telling you the job is done, the Sheshefesh's curse is lifted, and we can see each other again. Perhaps not.

One way or the other, trust in me, and believe this: You __will__ see me again someday, though time and tide render us both unrecognizable.

Until then, I remain, for always,

Yours,

Anna L

"That's why I could never find her. Annalessa made a deal with the Sheshefesh so that she might never *be* found." Ardent pulled off his hat and ran his fingers over his forehead, as though trying to ease tension. Without his cap his soft white hair fluffed around his head like a cloud, making him look even more absurd than usual.

Marrill frowned. The way *she* interpreted the letter, Ardent had it all wrong. She thought back to her first visit to the Stream, the very first time Ardent had told her about his quest to find Annalessa. A quest that started when she *sent him a letter.*

"Um, Ardent? This is great news!" she cried.

"How do you figure?" the wizard asked, arching a white eyebrow.

"The letter," she said, vibrating with excitement. "The one Annalessa sent you that started your search for her. If she sent that letter *after* writing this one, that means her promise to the Sheshefesh is already over!"

Ardent's brow furrowed. "Well, certainly it would, Marrill, but we have no way of knowing the order in which these things happened. And besides, she didn't actually send me a letter. She sent me…" He trailed off. His eyes suddenly opened wide. "The Compass Rose," he breathed.

Now it was Marrill's turn to be confused. "Huh?"

Ardent's eyes, however, flashed with understanding. "I never told you that bit. She sent me the Compass Rose itself. I opened her letter, and off it flew. You see, Annalessa never approved of my quest for the Map. She worried that my obsession with finding it would destroy me; indeed it was she who once persuaded me to give up on it. For her to send me the Compass Rose, a piece of the Map, well…"

He kicked on the hem of his robe and began pacing. "She never would have tempted me to resume my quest for the Map unless things were dire. Unless there were truly no other options. I knew right then that I had been a fool. That

I had turned my back on the person I cared about most. That if she was lost for good, it would be my fault. I swore I would not let that happen."

Marrill grinned, glad to see him more animated again. "So if she sent you the Compass Rose, that *definitely* had to happen after she wrote this letter." She crossed her arms. "You know, I think the Sheshefesh was just toying with you. Annalessa seems convinced you'll see her again—maybe she's waiting for you in Meres. And if she is, and the Sheshefesh is just a big blustering jerk...then after that, maybe we can go get Coll back after all!"

Color infused Ardent's cheeks. "You have a point, Miss Aesterwest. You have many good points." He leaned over the desk to tousle her hair fondly. They both laughed. It felt good—after seeing Ardent act so cruelly and so callously with the Sheshefesh—to hear him be himself again.

The old man smiled a grandfatherly smile and turned back to the window. "Well," he said, "the night grows late. Tonight, let us sleep soundly, dreaming of fond reunions and glorious victories. For tomorrow, we make landfall at Meres."

⇥ ✝ ⇤

The next day did not dawn so much as leak into the world.

Marrill had seen some pretty incredible places on the Pirate Stream. She'd imagined that the Isle of Meres, where wizards conferred, must be the most magical of all. Beyond magical. *Super* magical.

But when she emerged onto the deck the next morning, there was none of that. Rocks jutted up from the wave-tossed Stream, some of them bigger even than the *Kraken*. They formed a maze so dense that it seemed impossible to sail through. Not that anyone would want to. Because from what glimpses she could catch, nothing but a squat scrap of land awaited, covered in dead trees. They looked lost and dull beneath the sorrow-colored sky.

Marrill climbed to the quarterdeck where Remy leaned against a post, one finger on the wheel to keep them steady. "Are you sure you know where you're going?" Marrill asked.

Remy let out a huge yawn, blinked her bloodshot eyes. "Of course I know. This is the current for Meres." She nodded her chin toward the rocks around her, rubbing absently at her side. "Which should make that the Isle of Meres."

Marrill scrunched up her face. She couldn't hide her disappointment. "But…it's so empty…and ugly."

Remy shrugged. "I guess they can't all be the land of unicorns and rainbows."

"Nah, went to that one for my third anniversary," the Naysayer grunted from a nearby table. "Overrated."

Marrill gave him a sidelong glance. "Third anniversary of what?"

"Third anniversary of mind your own business, that's what," the monster snapped. "Oh, wait, you minding your own business hasn't happened yet. I'll make a note to celebrate if it does, though."

"Are we celebrating something?" Ardent asked in mid-yawn as he stepped from his cabin.

The Naysayer pushed from the table and slumped toward the hatch. "Not unless you call doing something stupid to get us all killed a celebration. 'Cause if you do, then every day's a party with you thumbheads." He reached the stairs just as Fin appeared at the top.

"Morning," Fin chirped.

The Naysayer gave him a withering look. "Congratulations, ya mastered the time of day. Learn to count your fingers, and you'll officially be not as dumb as you look." He stuck a thick hand out at Fin's face. "Classic Naysayer," the beast snarled before lumbering belowdecks.

Fin shook his head sadly as he scooched next to Marrill. "Good to know the Naysayer's still here. I keep taking down that sign he posted on the Promenade Deck, but he just won't wander onto it anymore." He swiped a cheese rind off a nearby table and gnawed on it thoughtfully. "Speaking of signs, any sign of the Rise and Fade?"

Marrill shook her head. "Horizon's clear. Looks like smooth sailing."

He nodded. "Good. Fig says they'll be here, though. She's sure of it."

Marrill gave him a long look. *Fig?* Did Fin have another friend she didn't know about? She'd felt like he'd been a little preoccupied lately. Most of the trip actually. As if half the time, he wasn't even talking to her.

Something familiar nagged at the back of Marrill's mind, like she already knew the answer to this problem. She just couldn't focus on it....

"So this is Meres," Fin interrupted, scattering the thought away. "Not much to look at, is it?"

Ardent shot them a mischievous smile. "Not yet, perhaps. But Meres doesn't reveal its secrets to just anyone. Observe." He kicked aside the hem of his robe and strode toward the nearest railing, took a deep snort, and hocked a loogie straight into the Pirate Stream.

"Ew," Marrill said. "Why did we have to observe that?"

As she said it, though, ripples spread from where his spit hit the water, and it was like a bloom of color sweeping the Stream. Everything that had been sepia before shifted, the hues growing more and more vibrant. The rocky shoals seemed to separate, clearing a path for the *Kraken* to sail. Beyond them, the island stretched out into an impressive coastline. The leafless trees twisted and grew, branches tangling into one another.

Marrill blinked. It was like a veil had been lifted from her eyes. What had been barren and brown before was now strikingly lush. "Whoa," she whispered.

"It takes the waters of a wizard to unlock the waters of Meres," Ardent said, straightening. "The others always preferred the dramatics of blood, but I was never partial to needles or knives."

"Best loogie *ever*," Fin declared.

Ardent bent down between them. "You should have seen what happened when I peed in it," he whispered.

"Oh, gross. I heard that," Remy moaned.

Ardent cleared his throat and swept out an arm. "Mmm-hmm, yes. What I meant to say was, welcome to Meres! The birthplace of the Pirate Stream! Now that the path is clear, take us into shore please, Madam Captain."

"Way ahead of you, old man," Remy murmured. Sure enough, she'd already guided the *Kraken* into the main channel. In moments, they were weaving their way through newly formed gaps in the great rocks, hemmed in on either side by the massive boulders.

With only the island ahead of them, Marrill realized that this would be an awfully easy place to get trapped. She looked aft, just in time to see the warships slipping out from behind the largest of the rocks.

"THE RISE!" a girl shouted from the main deck, giving voice to Marrill's fears.

Remy stayed the course, white knuckled. "We're in trouble, folks," she said. "Nowhere to turn, nowhere to run. Either we head to the island and risk getting pinned, or we're gonna have to try to reverse this thing past them."

"Keep going," Ardent commanded. "The Lost Sun is nearly at Meres. We must reach the Font before he does... even if we lose the *Kraken* in the process."

"Lose the *Kraken*?" Marrill whispered. It would be like losing Coll all over again. She swallowed, trying to force the thought from her mind. If she dwelled on everything they might lose in all of this, it would paralyze her with fear.

"Quickly," Ardent continued, "gather everything we need to make landfall. This will be a race, it seems."

"Dream ribbon, check," Marrill said, snatching it up from where she'd been inspecting it by her sketchpads. She shoved it into a bag she used to carry her drawing supplies. "Fin, you got the ink?"

"Check," Fin nodded, passing her the jar. She added it to the bag.

Ardent nodded at him. "Thank you, unfamiliar young man." The wizard patted at the sleeve of his robe. "And I have the Map and the wish orb." He leaned closer, adding, "Wouldn't do to leave it here for the Rise to use while we're facing the Lost Sun. One apocalypse at a time, I say."

He started toward the railing, but a girl stepped in his path. "This is a race you can't win," she warned him, grabbing his arm.

Marrill jumped back. For a moment, she thought they'd already been boarded. But Fin put his hand on her shoulder, then on the girl's. The name *Fig* sounded in Marrill's head. It sounded...familiar.

"It's okay," Fin said. "She's one of the good ones. And she's right."

"Now see here," Ardent blustered.

Fin pointed off the stern. "The Rise are fast behind.... They'll catch up long before you reach the Font."

They were all silent for a moment, distracted as they watched the Rise ships move into the channel behind them. They'd be on them in less than ten minutes. That wasn't much of a head start.

Then Marrill realized what Fin just said. "What do you mean, 'before *you* reach the Font'?"

Fin gave her an odd smile. "You go ahead with Ardent. I'll stay here and buy you time."

"That's crazy," she pointed out, crossing her arms. "They're an unbeatable army. How in the world do you think you can stop them?"

Fin rocked back on his heels, his usual cocky grin splitting his face. "Don't worry about me. I have a cunning plan."

Marrill rolled her eyes. "Fin, this is serious. It's just that... it feels weird to split up. We've always faced the end of the Pirate Stream together." She took a deep breath. "And besides... this whole journey was supposed to be about helping you find your mom. I just feel... I feel like I completely lost sight of that and abandoned you. Just like in Monerva."

The next thing she knew, Marrill found herself swept up in an enormous hug. "Marrill," Fin said, "you're the best friend I have in the whole Stream. You don't have to be helping me every second for me to know that you want to."

"Land ho!" Remy shouted. The *Kraken* ground to a halt, her squid-shaped anchor dropping with a loud grind of its chain.

Fin pulled back, his hands gripping Marrill's shoulders. His expression grew serious—or as serious as it ever did.

"The Rise may be an unbeatable army, but that doesn't mean they don't have a weakness. Everyone has a weakness, and I intend to use theirs against them. Besides, they'll never hurt me. Vell needs me."

Marrill lunged forward and grabbed Fin in another hug. "Be careful anyway."

Despite the looming danger, Fin smiled and waggled his eyebrows at her. "*Pffft*, my job is the easy one. Now you and Ardent go save the world."

"I'm staying, too," Remy declared. Marrill gave her a stunned look. But the older girl was dead serious. "This ship has already lost one captain," she said. "I'm not leaving her. Besides, you'll be with Ardent. I may be northern Arizona's best babysitter, but I'm still no match for a wizard." Remy nodded at her. "You've got this, Marrill."

Taking a deep breath, Marrill joined Ardent at the stern. "I guess it's just you and me again," the wizard said. He held out a crooked elbow. "Shall we?"

Marrill looked back as Ropebone swung them across to solid ground. The shore was narrow, not much more than a strip of rugged rock edged by the maw of the dark woods. Fin waved from the bow as they headed into the forest.

Up ahead, shadows loomed; it was impossible to know what awaited them.

But whatever it was, the *Enterprising Kraken* had their back.

CHAPTER 23
The Rise Before the Fall

Fin held his chin high and chest out until he was sure Marrill and Ardent had disappeared into the forbidding forest. Then his head dropped, and his shoulders sagged. Overhead, a wheeling seagull gave a mocking cry, and the salt-and-seaweed air felt acrid in his lungs.

"Well," he said, "I don't actually have any ideas. So if anyone else has thoughts, I'm open-minded."

Fig paced up and down the deck beside him. "There's

nothing we can do," she muttered. "The Rise can't be beaten. They can't be stopped."

"Okay," Fin said, clapping his hands together. "That's not really helpful, so does anyone have any thoughts that *aren't* of the we're-all-going-to-die variety?"

Behind them, the warships crashed through the surf, racing between the rocks far faster than any sane captain would dare. Because sane captains feared for their lives, Fin realized. The Rise had no such fear. They would be on them in moments.

"I should have stayed in Arizona," Remy muttered to herself. "Oh, wait, I never chose to *leave* Arizona."

Fin gulped. "All right, grab whatever you've got on hand," he said. "All we need to do is slow them down for a while. So we'll fight them until they take us, then I'll pretend to lead them to the wish orb in Ardent's cabin." He chuckled to himself, already thinking about Vell covered in screaming gel. "Any questions?"

The first boarding hooks whistled through the air, digging into the wood of the main deck. Fin took a deep breath, loosing his climbing daggers. Beside him, Fig continued pacing nervously. On the quarterdeck, Remy swiped the cutlass Coll kept by the ship's wheel, holding it away from her body as though she was scared of it.

Another boarding line struck the *Kraken* and another. The Rise soldiers crouched at their railing, preparing to jump between ships.

"Okay," Fin said. "This is it. Time to buckle some swash!"

The first of the Rise landed on the quarterdeck. Remy lifted her cutlass and charged, only to be tripped by a Fade who jumped out of nowhere. She careened into the side of Ardent's cabin, where more of the Rise and Fade appeared, securing her.

Additional soldiers reached the main deck, advancing on Fin. He dodged the first, rolled around the second. A third blindsided him, grabbing for him. Fin parried the man's hand away with his dagger and bounded off the railing, spinning as he hit the middle of the deck.

More Rise had made the ship, though, starting to fill it. They had Remy, and Fig seemed to have put up no fight at all. Even the pirates had their arms in the air, toothpick-swords dropped in surrender.

The crew of the *Kraken* hadn't lasted long. It was now up to Fin to draw out the battle.

"Hello, Brother Fade," his own voice said behind him.

Fin whirled, lashing out with his dagger instinctively, fully expecting a parry, preparing to redirect the rebound energy into a dodge. But Vell just stood there, taking the blow straight across the chest.

Cloth gave way like paper. The blade made a sweeping sound as it passed across Vell's bare flesh. Fin gasped. He heard Remy gasp, too.

But there was no blood. Vell didn't wince. Fin stared up at him in shock, raising his dagger again halfheartedly.

His twin didn't even blink. In one swift motion, Vell batted the dagger to one side, grabbed Fin's wrist, and twisted it until he dropped the blade. He then brought up his elbow to smack Fin straight in the face.

Fin stumbled back, pain shooting through his head, dropping him to his knees. His Rise watched him impassively. "We don't cut," Vell said, cracking his knuckles. "We don't burn. We don't bleed. We are the Rise. Do you see now we cannot be beaten?"

Another voice broke across the ship. "Stop toying with him, Vell." The Rise ranks separated.

The Crest herself had come to the *Kraken*.

She snapped her fingers, and Vell obediently stepped back, just beside her. "You know what we are here for," she said. "The wish orb." Her eyes flitted up and down Fin as he crouched on the deck, one hand nursing the rapidly forming bruise on his cheekbone. "And to secure you, of course. It's a miracle you haven't died out here without our guidance. The way you act so...rashly. Do you have any idea how painful it would be for Vell if you became a part of him again? All your fears and doubts and insecurities pouring into him, making him mortal?"

Tears welled up in Fin's eyes. He couldn't honestly say where they came from: the pain from Vell's blow, or the sting of the Crest's words. He looked at the two of them—they didn't seem real, standing here before him. Himself and his mother, together once again...and yet, they didn't care for *him* at all.

It was so difficult for him to understand. He thought of all the love and loyalty he felt for the crew of the *Kraken*, for his adopted family, the Parsnickles, back in the Khaznot Quay, even for the Naysayer: people who didn't remember him, yet who he loved nonetheless. Vell was his Rise— they'd been the same person once. His mother was the same way with the Crest. That had to make them some form of kin. That had to *mean* something.

He didn't fight the tears. They'll help the con, he told himself. The battle was lost. Time for stage two of the plan.

"Fine," he said. "You want the wish orb; you can have it. We won't fight you anymore."

"Fin, no!" Remy called. Her tone was so fake that it made Fin cringe. On top of it, when he looked at her, she gave him a big, dramatic wink. An actress, she was not.

He took a deep breath, hoping that Remy hadn't blown the ruse. Slowly, he raised one shaking finger, pointing to Ardent's cabin. "It's in there. On the far side of the wizard's desk. There's a chest. The wish is inside. Just... take the whole thing, and I'll come with you."

The Crest didn't seem to even register his words. Instead, she looked past him, to Fig. The Rise had pushed the Fade girl forward so that she stood just behind Fin. Her arms were crossed, one hand tucked inside her vest. Her head was bowed, and her eyes met neither the Crest's nor Fin's.

"Did you retrieve it?" the Crest asked.

Slowly, Fig nodded.

Fin's heart beat faster. Confusion and fear bubbled up inside him. What was Fig doing? Did she have some other plan he hadn't known about? Why wouldn't she have told him?

All his questions were put to rest when Fig pulled free her hand. Clutched in it, glowing brightly with the concentrated magic of the Pirate Stream, was the wish orb.

"Oh no," Fin groaned. He slapped a palm against his forehead. He had a faint memory of Fig grabbing Ardent's arm, trying to stop him before he and Marrill disembarked. She must have nicked it then, and no one even noticed.

Fig was a better thief than he'd given her credit for. Not for picking the wizard's pocket—that was easy enough. But for making him believe she cared about them.

For stealing his trust.

Fig's hands were shaking. "I'm sorry, Fin," she stammered. "I didn't have a choice. Vell ordered me to, back at Margaham's Game, he ordered me to secure the orb before the next time we met...."

Despair and betrayal flooded Fin's heart like a ship's hold taking on water. "And you did it. You chose them over us. Over me."

The Crest stepped forward. "Come now," she said. "The Fade are not real. They have no choices. A good Fade must do as the Rise command. And now, I command you to give me the orb."

Fig hesitated, eyes locked on the softly glowing wish in her hands. Fin could see she was struggling. He seized the moment and stepped toward her. The Rise were rows of statues, standing rigid on the decks of the *Kraken*. The Fade peered through them, nondescript faces filling out the ranks.

"No," he pronounced. The sun fell hot on his cheeks. The salt air that had so recently burned acrid in his mouth now fueled a fire in his lungs. "No, you can't have it."

The Crest's eyes fell on him. Fin wasn't used to people seeing him so directly, to being scrutinized, examined. His every instinct told him to run, to hide, to slip away and be forgotten. But he couldn't. Not now. And more than that, he didn't want to.

His eyes locked on the Crest's. Fin forced himself to meet the iron in her gaze with all the power of his will. And when he did, he saw a flicker of something he hadn't expected.

Uncertainty.

Suddenly, everything he knew about the Rise, or thought he knew, came into question. He had an advantage now. And he had to press it. "You say the Rise are unbeatable," he spat. "And yeah, maybe you can't be cut or hurt or whatever. But the way I see it, you *have* been beaten. Over and over again."

"Still your tongue," the Crest said. But she didn't make a move.

Fin felt the edge of a smile dancing across his lips. "Fact is," he continued, "seems like we've beaten you every single time you've shown up."

"Yeah!" Remy shouted from the quarterdeck. "Like how Coll slipped past your little blockade on the way to see the Sheshefesh!"

"And at the game..." Fig mumbled.

Fin's smile turned into a full-blown grin. "And when we outran your warship back at the Soporific Straits." He crossed his arms. "Seems like the unbeatable army is pretty *beatable* to me."

For the first time, a squirm seemed to pass through the statue-still ranks of the Rise. Out of the corner of his eye, Fin could even see Vell looking uncomfortable. It was true. And they all knew it.

"You don't understand what you're saying," the Crest barked. "Now stop standing between me and my wish!"

She started toward him, reaching a hand to his shoulder. Fin slapped it away with a sharp rebuke. "Don't touch me." He felt her fingers catch against the zipper of his skysailing jacket. She drew back with a hiss that sounded almost like pain.

The Crest's gaze dropped to her hand. There, blooming on the tip of her finger, was a bright red drop of blood.

"You're bleeding," Fin whispered.

She nodded slowly. Her eyes met Fin's once more. This time, a wash of emotion filled them: fear, regret, resignation.

Across the deck of the *Kraken*, a murmur of disbelief passed through the ranks of the Rise and the Fade. Even Vell, who up until now seemed incapable of showing emotion, was stunned. "This can't be," he protested. "Rise don't bleed. Not unless..."

Understanding hit Fin far harder than the force of Vell's elbow had. The Rise were invulnerable because their weakness had been removed from them and turned into the Fade. And so long as their Fade still lived, they remained immortal.

So long as their Fade still lived.

"No," he gasped.

The Crest nodded. It wasn't arrogance in her eyes. Not hardness. Just sorrow. "So you've found out my secret."

Fin couldn't believe what he was seeing, what he was hearing. The leader of the invincible army could be hurt, just like him. She felt fear, just like him. She could fail, just like him.

The Crest of the Rise was mortal. Which could only mean one thing. Her Fade... Fin's *real* mother...

"My mom is dead," Fin breathed.

CHAPTER 24
As in the Beginning...

Marrill stared at the tiny path ahead of them leading into the depths of the forest. It was like a nightmare of every fairy tale she'd ever read put together; every scary one, anyway. She half expected hungry wolves or cackling witches to leap from the shadows.

But then, this was the Pirate Stream—wolves and witches were way too tame for whatever terrors lurked here.

Ardent stood at the edge of the tangled trees, hands on his hips as he surveyed their surroundings. "Only three rules you need to remember," he said. He ticked each off on his fingers in turn. "First, stay on the path. Second, don't get lost. And third…" He paused, brow furrowed. "I could have sworn there was a third. And come to think of it, maybe staying on the path and not getting lost are the same one…." He shrugged. "Well, just don't die, I guess. Anyway, on we go."

With that, he straightened his cap and started down the dark path.

This was the point where Marrill would normally look to Fin for a wry joke to make her feel better. But Fin wasn't here—he was back at the *Kraken* holding off the Rise and the Fade.

Marrill sucked in a deep breath. If he could face down an unbeatable army, with no hopes of success, she could take a walk in some scary-looking woods.

"No problem," she whispered to herself. Then she plunged into the forest.

The temperature plummeted almost instantly. The very air felt weird: thicker in some spots, thinner in others. Every atom in her body vibrated at an odd pitch as she struggled to keep up with Ardent's confident stride. At times, she felt like different parts of her were moving at different speeds.

On either side, the forest closed tightly around them. Branches leaned toward her with a creaking hiss, as though Marrill had some sort of magnetic pull. Out of the corner of her eye she thought she saw lights. But when she tried looking at them, they disappeared, blinking out of existence like fireflies.

Then there were the noises. She swore she could hear whispers, giggling even, layered with the calls of strange creatures and the slippery shifting of parting leaves. Underlying it all was a hum that changed pitch whenever she turned her head.

Disconcerting shadows danced at the edge of her vision. "Am I the only one seeing phantoms?" she asked.

Ahead, Ardent slapped his hand against his forehead. "Right, of course! How silly of me. *That's* the third rule." He spun back to her. "What you are seeing are not phantoms. They're echoes. I'd avoid them if I were you."

He turned and continued down the path. Marrill scrambled after him. "What do you mean by echoes? Echoes of what?"

"Oh, all sorts of things! Old magic, usually. Remember that a pirate stream is a river that flows away from another river. So if you think of the Pirate Stream as a branch out of the River of Creation, then Meres is an island in the juncture of that branch. Some would even say it *is* the branch."

He turned to face her. "That's what makes this place so magical! It's the only world that touches both the River of Creation *and* the Pirate Stream at once. All the waters of the Stream flow through and out from here."

A chill stole up Marrill's back, like a cold finger tracing the ridge of her spine. And then she realized that there *was* a cold finger tracing the ridge of her spine. With a squeal she jumped to the middle of the path, spinning to see what had been touching her.

Nothing greeted her but the darkness of the forest. She was pretty sure she heard a tinkling of laughter hidden in the rustling of leaves. "That's it," she said, pressing a hand to her screaming heart. "I'm officially declaring this place worse than nightmares."

"This?" Ardent waved a hand. "This is the safe path. All this is nothing but a ripple on the ocean that is Meres."

Marrill swallowed. "It gets worse?"

Ardent threw his head back and laughed. "Oh my, yes. Much worse." He started back down the path. Marrill was pretty sure she heard him chuckle to himself, "Much, much, much worse."

From that point on, Marrill stuck close behind the wizard. Ardent droned on about various esoteric points, and though she wasn't completely listening to him, she was grateful that his voice drowned out the strange noises of the forest. Eventually, though, a rushing sound began filling the air, making Ardent harder to hear. It started out low and soft, but the farther they moved along the path, the more insistent it became. Soon, it grew to a thunderous, almost physical presence.

Up ahead, the bitter blackness of the forest gave way to light and air. As Marrill cleared the edge of the trees, her stomach dropped to her toes. She gasped, clutching the wizard's robe to keep her balance.

"The Font of Meres." Ardent's voice was reverent, his eyes shining as he took it in.

They stood at the precipice of a circular chasm so massive that the other side was almost lost to distance. It was completely ringed by the dark forest, the impenetrable mass of trees stretching right up to its edge. In the center, as though the chasm were a great moat around it, a spire stretched up to the sky.

Halfway up the spire's height, golden water gushed from great maw-like arches on each side, the raw magic cascading into the depthless chasm. Clouds of shimmering mist wafted from the depths, exploding into colors, as if sunset itself had evaporated and hung in the air.

This was the source of the roaring hum; it was the sound of thundering water. This, Marrill realized, was the source of all magic. The spring from which the Pirate Stream flowed.

At the tip of the spire perched a building, looking as though it hadn't been built so much as carved from the stone itself. Ardent gazed at it a moment before flipping the tip of his cap over his shoulder. "Now then, all we have to do is get to the Font itself, repair the Map, and re-cage the Lost Sun of Dzannin before it destroys all of creation."

"So, you know," Marrill muttered, "the usual."

"Exactly," Ardent said, apparently missing the sarcasm. "Now, to the Font!" Before she could stop him, the wizard stepped off the edge of the cliff and dropped out of sight.

"Ardent!" Marrill squeaked, lunging forward. She fell to her knees, scooting as close to the edge as she dared. A pair of blue eyes greeted her, scarcely a foot below her own. They crinkled with a smile.

"Oh, you should see your face," Ardent chuckled. "That never gets old; it truly doesn't. Anyway, come on, follow me. Mind your step now, it can get a bit tricky in the middle." And with that, he strode out over the open chasm toward the spire.

Marrill realized suddenly that the glittering mist had congealed itself into an iridescent line just below the edge of the cliff—a shimmering rainbow bridging one side of the chasm to the other. It looked a bit slicker than she would have liked. Taking a deep breath, she slid a leg over the side, positioned herself as best she could, and dropped down onto the bridge made of sparkling dew.

The wind off the water buffeted them as they made their way closer to the spire, coating her skin with its glowing mist. It tingled and tickled at the same time, turning into little bubbles and occasionally causing a random hair to crawl down her arm. But thankfully it wasn't enough to work any *real* magic.

Eventually the bridge morphed into stairs, and so she climbed. Ardent was so far ahead of her that he was nothing more than a purple smudge in the distance. Her legs burned, and her breath came in strained pants by the time she caught up to him.

"Couldn't the wizards have built something more convenient?" she gasped.

Ardent shook his head. "One cannot approach the Font of Meres but through difficulty. If we tried, we would find it had simply moved farther away."

"Wizard logic makes no sense," she mumbled to herself.

He continued upward, hands cavorting through the air like birds as he lapsed back into his favorite activity: long-winded explanations of obscure magical concepts. "Indeed," he declared, "some have speculated that space and time on the Pirate Stream are related to each other solely through the amount of effort expended to travel between them. That's part of what makes the Master of the Iron Ship so fascinating!"

"The Master of the Iron Ship?" Marrill asked, her eyes on the sides of the barely visible staircase. With each step she struggled between hurrying to keep up and going slowly to keep from tumbling into oblivion. "Do you think we'll see him here?"

Ardent paused, looking back over his shoulder at her. "My dear Marrill, I would almost be stunned if we didn't. Recall that the Wiverwane showed me the Master meeting the Dawn Wizard, though the two should never have existed at the same time. *And* Tanea Hollow-Blood's reported last words show he was interrogating her about means of time traversal. To do that would require more power than I have ever even heard of. Perhaps as much as only the Lost Sun itself could provide…but how that would work…"

He stroked his beard thoughtfully. "At any rate, the Master has gone to an unbelievable amount of effort to bring the Lost Sun into being. Whatever his reasoning, I cannot imagine he will absent himself from this confrontation."

"Great." Marrill shuddered at the thought. She was tense enough as it was; the last thing she needed was to add the Master to the equation.

At long last, they reached the base of the building. Marrill collapsed against the stone wall. If it took effort to reach the Font of Meres, she'd definitely earned her way in.

Ardent, on the other hand, barely appeared winded. He placed a hand on her shoulder, and she felt warmth flow through her. "Ready?" he asked.

She nodded as he kicked aside the hem of his robe and stepped into a narrow sliver of an entranceway, so thin he had to turn sideways to squeeze through. Marrill started to push her way after him, but as she did, she caught sight of the far side of the chasm. What she saw made her throat close and her gut clench.

On the other side of the island from the *Kraken*, out beyond the edge of the forest, the arc of the sky ended. *Everything* ended. The glowing waters of the Pirate Stream poured into the darkness in perverse mockery of the waterfalls flowing out from the Font all around her.

The void of nothingness. The wake of the Lost Sun,

eating its way toward them like a black hole, consuming everything it touched. A figure in silver strode purposefully ahead of it, walking along the surface of the Stream as though it were a flat highway. From his footprints, the trail of emptiness spread.

The Lost Sun of Dzannin was nearly upon them.

CHAPTER 25
Life's Blood, Spilt

"My mom is dead."

Fin choked on his own words. Around him the Rise and Fade muttered to one another. Vell paced, fingers pressed to his forehead, grappling with the revelation.

The Crest ignored all of them, never taking her eyes from Fin. "Yes," she said, curling her finger into her fist. Her blood stained the lines on her palm in ruddy crimson.

Fin let out a strangled cry. All this time he'd been

searching for his mother...all the nights he'd looked up at the star she'd pointed out to him, dreaming that one day he'd see her again, that she would hug him again. Every hope of having a home, a family. And she was dead.

She'd *been* dead.

All of his dreams were lies.

"How long?" His voice was a sob, a cough, and a whisper, all jumbled up together.

Vell stormed forward, knocking Fin to the side. "Yes, *Mother*," he said with a sneer. "How long? How long have you been hiding your weakness? How long has this *atrocity* been allowed to stand?"

She cut a cold gaze at Vell, reminding Fin that every bit of cruelty she'd showed had been genuine. "That is none of your concern," she hissed. Whatever weakness or vulnerability she may have had, she was still the Crest. Still the woman who had sent Fig to steal from them, still the one who was intent on releasing the Salt Sand King. She was still ruthless.

"So long you won't even admit it then?" Vell snarled. "Why allow that weakness to reside in you? Why not cut it free again?"

But Fin didn't care about that. He was focused on something much, much more important. "When did my mother die?"

The Crest stepped back, surveying both of them at once. Her back was still straight. Her gaze was still harsh. But the edges of her eyes twisted down, carrying in them real emotion. Her posture, too, seemed more open—not welcoming, perhaps, but not guarded, either. She was an odd mix of cruel and compassionate, harsh and yielding, weak and strong.

She was a *person*, Fin realized. Not an emotionless Rise, not a shrinking, indeterminate Fade. Just a person.

The Crest let out a sigh. Not one of impatience, but one of exhaustion. As though she'd been carrying the weight of her weakness for too long. She looked to Fin. "Your mother isn't truly dead," she explained. "She's a part of who I am, who I've become."

Her expression had softened slightly, and he searched for anything familiar—for that part of her who'd held him in her arms as they sailed into the Khaznot Quay.

"Wait...so you...*are* my mom?" Fin asked, voice breaking.

The Crest nodded. "In a way. Her individuality, her personality, her thoughts—those are gone, now and forever. But her memories, I have those. They come with the essence of who she was. And that's still here, in me. After getting it back, I couldn't just let it be cut out again."

She reached out and took his hand, crouching so that they were face-to-face. "I know it's hard to see. I know I can seem...I can *be* cruel. But believe me, I *would* have protected you."

Fin pulled back. He was pretty sure what had happened

up until now wasn't protecting anyone. "By throwing me in a pen? By enslaving people like me and telling us we're nobody?" He looked back to Fig. Her face was a mask of fear, sorrow, and confusion. Her hands clutched the glowing wish orb tight to her chest. "By stealing the wish orb and unleashing the Salt Sand King?"

The Crest grabbed his arm and pulled him back to her. "Yes!" she said. "When the Salt Sand King comes, everything will change for the Rise and the Fade. We have a real chance to undo the way we've lived for millennia! But somebody has to be there to explain it to our King. Someone with the station of the Rise, but not their heartlessness."

Fin snorted. "So you expect me to believe that even though you want to free the Salt Sand King and help him conquer all of the Pirate Stream, you *also* want to help me and the Fade." He shook his head in disbelief. "Next thing you'll say you're proud of me and Vell equally."

"I am," the Crest said. For the first time, possibly ever, a real smile stole across her face. "People are complicated, Fin."

"People are 'complicated' because people are *weak*," Vell broke in. He sneered at Fin. "She's been *your* mother," he said with an impatient wave of his hand, "for far too long."

He pushed Fin aside so he could confront the Crest directly. "I understand this happens. The Fade are weak and stupid. They do foolish things, they die, they have to be removed. What I don't understand is why you allowed that weakness to live in you."

"Humanity isn't weakness," the Crest began.

But Vell cut her off with a sharp shout. "This is why we lost the game! This is why they escaped our blockade, why they got away from us in the first place!" He gained speed as he talked, body coiling like a cat. "This explains why we've yet to take the orb. Why we've yet to free our King and conquer the Stream." He leveled his eyes on the Crest. "Because you're weak."

The Crest ignored him, turning back to Fin. Behind her, Vell's expression shifted as something seemed to suddenly occur to him. "Because you're *weak*," he repeated in a whisper.

Fin realized too late what Vell's statement meant. Already Vell had stepped forward. Already he'd slid his knife free of its scabbard.

And before Fin could move. Before he could even utter a warning, Vell thrust the blade into the Crest's back.

Her eyes went wide. A hiss of shocked pain slipped through her lips. A moment later, blood bloomed across her chest in a violent gash of scarlet.

"No!" Fin screamed.

He lunged for his mother, catching her in his arms before she could fall. Slowly, carefully, he lowered her to the deck.

It was all too much, all too fast. He'd just found her again. Even though he wasn't sure who it was he'd found. "Why did you—why did she take me?" His voice quavered as tears spilled down his cheeks. "Why did you *both* leave me?"

"Because love isn't a weakness." She gripped his arm. Her breathing came short and fast, her eyes black with pain. "Remember our star, Fin." Her words became labored. She pressed trembling fingers against his cheek. "I never forgot."

There was so much Fin wanted to tell her. So many things stored up in his heart from all the years apart. But the words wouldn't come.

And then she was gone.

Fin's heart shattered into so many pieces that he wasn't sure he'd ever be able to find them all again. Uneasiness rippled through the ranks of the Rise and the Fade, but Fin ignored it. Closing his eyes, he let his forehead drop, pressing it against hers.

The Crest. His mom. He didn't care which she was, because she'd never forgotten him. All these years she'd still looked up into the sky at night, searching for the star that reminded her of Fin.

Vell let out a cry of victory. With a whirl and a flourish, he turned to the ranks of his soldiers. "As the new Crest of the Rise, it falls to me to secure the orb," he announced. "I shall be the one to call forth our King. I shall be the one to unite us to his will!"

He then glared down at Fin menacingly. "Move aside, Brother Fade. You're in the way of my destiny."

Fin took a deep, shuddering breath. He'd been demolished, beaten. Resisting at this point seemed hopeless. And yet, as he cradled the body of his mother, he knew he couldn't give up. Someone had to stand between the Rise and the wish orb. Someone had to stop the coming of the Salt Sand King. And he knew now that he could be the one to do it.

He'd been loved. He'd been remembered. He was worth something. *And tonight,* he thought as he struggled to his feet, *tonight when the sky slides into darkness, my star will still be there.*

If the Lost Sun didn't pull the sky down first.

CHAPTER 26
Making Things Whole

Inside the spire, the whispers from the forest were back, louder and stronger than ever before. Waves of uneasiness washed over Marrill. She took an involuntary step back and was startled to brush up against something semisolid, like a wall of thick, frozen air.

She spun. Shadows marched toward her, filtering past as if she didn't even exist. They were somehow solid and insubstantial, dark and light at the same time. And yet she could *feel* them. The hair on the back of her neck stood on end.

Her skin felt heavier, burdened with the weight of them, as they passed through her on their way to the intricately carved doorway ahead.

Marrill let out a squeak of alarm and pushed closer to Ardent, grateful at least for the reassurance of his presence.

"Do not fear them," he murmured as he watched the shadows pass. "The echoes are but memories, anchored to this place by its magic and the power of the events that happened here. They may disturb you, but they cannot harm you."

One of the shadows paused at the doorway, turning slightly toward Ardent and Marrill. Almost as if it could sense their presence.

Ardent smiled softly at it.

Marrill gasped as the echo's features wavered into detail. The similarity was terrifying and uncanny. The echo man's shoulders were broader, his back straighter. His expression was more severe, his eyes piercing, his chin sharp without the softening lines of a wispy beard.

But the way he carried himself. The way he turned and kicked aside his robes as he entered the chamber. It was the same familiar gesture Marrill had seen over and over on the deck of the *Kraken*, on the Wall of Monerva, even just now, here, at the entrance to this very tower.

The echo was Ardent. Younger Ardent, but Ardent nonetheless.

"The memories become more distinct when someone

who lived them is near," Ardent told her. "I fear we will see echoes of the day the Prophecy was born, imprinted on this place by a magic so strong it left a mark on time and space."

Another familiar figure swept in behind the Ardent echo. "Oh, Annalessa," the real Ardent murmured. She, too, was younger, her elegant features almost haughty, rather than the generous woman Marrill knew. She hesitated at the entrance to the chamber, waiting.

Marrill's insides squeezed tight when she saw who the echoes were waiting for.

The figure bringing up the rear of the procession was tall and narrow. Even as an echo, she could make out the familiar pattern of stars scattered across his robes. Though Marrill knew instantly that this echo was a younger Serth, it was difficult to reconcile his appearance with the mad prophet—and now mad vessel of the Lost Sun—she knew. His features were relaxed, even happy. His skin was smooth and unlined, completely free of the black grooves carved by centuries of tears.

He was so young. So strong and determined. "He looks...normal," Marrill murmured. *If wizards can be considered normal*, she mentally added.

Seeing him that way made her mind jump to the figure that was even at this moment walking toward them. The Lost Sun of Dzannin, wearing Serth's body, on his way to pour all of his destructive power into the source of the Pirate Stream.

Ardent's eyes had fluttered shut, his chin dropped to his chest as his friends from so long ago swept forward into the chamber together. Marrill grabbed his arm as he slumped against the wall and let out a long, trembling breath.

"Come on," she said. "We've got to repair the Map before the Lost Sun gets here."

The wizard nodded. "Yes, of course. Of course, you're right. I...hadn't expected that to be quite so difficult. And it will get worse." He pushed himself to his feet, waving his hands as Marrill tried to comfort him. "I'm fine, I'm fine. Don't worry, I'll manage."

Marrill nodded and nudged the carved door open. But as soon as she saw the inside of the chamber, her steps ground to a halt. She stared in wonder, overwhelmed by the pure grandeur that surrounded her. Stone walls rose dozens of stories into the air before curving toward a domed ceiling made of multicolored glass.

What really caught her attention, however, was the Font dominating the center of the room. It was made of the same stone as the walls and floor, as though the room itself had been carved around it. A raised dais surrounded it, making access to the wide bowl easier.

There was no question this was the Font of Meres. The light emanating from the bowl bathed the room in a magical glow.

Ardent paused beside her. "The headwaters of the Pirate Stream," he murmured reverently. "Forthorn Forlorn crafted the fountainhead as you see it today, but the wellspring, it has always been here."

His words were nearly lost in the cacophony of noise emanating from the echoes that filled the chamber. The crowd was so thick Marrill couldn't move without touching them. Their cold darkness slithered across her skin, tugging against her. The murmuring echoes overlapped, making the empty room sound busier than Grand Central Station at rush hour.

"I thought there were only eight Wizards of Meres." Marrill had to raise her voice to be heard.

"There were," Ardent told her. "Most of these echoes were here already." She stared at him, blinking. "Meres is a place of great power," he explained. "What you see are shadows of the Dzane. This was their seat of power, where the waters of the Pirate Stream are their purest and most concentrated."

He spread his hands wide. "This is where they bound the Lost Sun before. And where we shall bind it again! Indeed, if we're lucky, we might even see the shadows of that first battle while we're here."

"Lucky?" Marrill asked, incredulous.

Ardent *harrumph*ed. "Yes, right. Not the time, is it?" He kicked at his robes and started toward the dais. "Let's get started, then."

Marrill cringed as they plunged into the maze of echoes. In the midst of it, she could see that the shadows were flickering, changing. Different scenes played out and stopped, a thousand roles re-created by shadow actors, all overlapping on each other like a three-dimensional montage.

As Ardent passed, some of them resolved, gaining features and growing vivid. Triggered, she supposed, by his memories. She recognized Margaham, though she'd only seen him in iron, chanting and weaving strange rituals. As he moved his hands, the specter of Forthorn Forlorn brought forth a stone bowl that merged perfectly with the top of the Font. She was witnessing the original placement, she realized. The securing of the fountainhead that now stood before her.

Her eyes were drawn to the echo of young Serth approaching the Font. The shadow Annalessa carried forward a stone cup, and Serth took it, then plunged it into the Font before him.

Now she knew exactly what she was watching. She'd heard the story so many times. "This is the beginning of the Prophecy, isn't it?"

Ardent's gaze drifted to the dais. "It is," he said solemnly. "If we'd only known," he added in almost a whisper.

"See how the waters do not harm me," the Serth echo declared. He lifted the cup, holding it aloft. Water dripped over the rim, splashing his fingers but causing no damage.

He lowered the cup to his lips. There was a moment of hesitation, when Marrill thought she might have seen the slight curl of a smile. Then he tossed it back and drank deeply from the Pirate Stream.

This was the point when everything changed, Marrill knew. Serth would fall and spout the words that would become the Meressian Prophecy. From this moment the events that led to now unfolded.

As if in emphasis, a great crash like thunder echoed through the room. Outside the south-facing windows, the sky had grown black. There was a rush of wind, but no sign of rain. No dark clouds filled the sky. Just darkness, pure and endless.

The void approached.

"Ardent," Marrill warned, making sure he knew how little time they had left.

Shadow Serth writhed on the ground, the stone chalice dropping from his fingers, spilling Pirate Stream water across his robes.

"I see it," Ardent said. From a hidden pocket he produced the Map to Everywhere. The hole in its middle looked like someone had punched clean through it. The teardrop pinnacle just touched the outline of Meres. The Lost Sun had made landfall.

"Quickly, now," Ardent said, mounting the stairs to the top of the dais. "The ribbon and ink. We've little time."

Marrill was already ahead of him. She pulled out the bag with the ingredients in it and rummaged through as fast as she could. As before, when her hand closed around the dream ribbon, it sent her imagination immediately into overdrive. Her fingers itched to find a pencil and begin sketching, her mind's eye already conjuring up all the fantastical images she could bring to life.

She forced the compulsion down, racing the ribbon and ink up to Ardent. But as she climbed the stairs, a face appeared, scaly and red, with teeth that scintillated in the darkness. It roared, and flames washed over her.

Marrill screamed, but she didn't feel the burn. The flame billowed back toward the far end of the chamber. "What was *that*?"

Ardent strode over and snatched the ribbon and ink from her hands. "It appears we will see the Dzane's battle against the Lost Sun after all." He started back toward the Font. "I didn't expect it to be in quite that much living color. But then, I suppose someone who remembers those events *has* come to Meres." He glanced toward the window and the blackness beyond.

Marrill swallowed. All around, strange beings she'd never imagined resolved themselves out of echoes, writhing in furious conflict. Their efforts flew toward a shadow just at the edge of the room, a shadow darker than all the rest.

The shadow of the Lost Sun. While outside the real Lost Sun drew dangerously closer, his memories were already bringing the echoes of the Dzane in the chamber to startling life.

Carefully, Ardent set the remains of the Map on the lip of the Font beside the other objects. He stared at them, brow furrowed in concentration.

"So…you know what you're doing, right?" Marrill asked.

He shot her an impatient glance. "Of course. I am the great wizard Ardent. And today, I am the most powerful wizard alive on the Pirate Stream. If anyone can command the magic of the Dzane…I can. I *will*. Now stand aside, and make sure I'm undisturbed."

He unspooled a section of dream ribbon and slid it under the Map so that it filled the hole created by the void. Then he uncorked the jar of squid ink and hesitated, glancing between the two. With a shrug he tilted the jar, letting a sludge of ink spill onto the middle of the ribbon. It fell with a splat and slowly seeped into the delicate material.

Marrill waited, breath held, watching. Fingers of ink spread, crawling across the ribbon in a blotchy pattern that reminded Marrill of a Rorschach test. But that was it.

Nothing more happened. The ink didn't morph into islands or continents. No worlds appeared. No islets or hamlets.

"Hmmm." Ardent frowned and poked at the ribbon, pushing it until a corner drooped down into the Font far enough to touch Stream water. The ribbon disintegrated like cotton candy in a glass of water.

Nearby, the echo of Serth continued to babble prophecy as the echo of young Ardent furiously scribbled down everything he said. All across the chamber, in an even earlier timeline, the echoes of the Dzane waged war against the oncoming shadow of the Lost Sun.

"I can't concentrate," Ardent said flatly. "This place, there's too much distraction. I need some quiet."

Marrill took a deep breath, searching the room for some way to help. Next to her, the echo of a catlike face she recognized as the Dawn Wizard swirled his hands together, drawing water from the Font to create an entire world in miniature. He hurled it toward the shadow at the door, who caught it effortlessly, then disintegrated the world into oblivion.

How was she supposed to stop the howl of wind being sucked into the Lost Sun's oblivion? How was she supposed to quiet the babble of the Meressian Prophecy, or still the warring Dzane? It was impossible!

Ardent's lips clenched in annoyance as he lined up another section of ribbon and called forth another dollop of ink.

Suddenly, Marrill had an idea. "Ardent, can I borrow a scrap of ribbon and some ink?"

The wizard gave her a withering look. "Marrill, now is not the time for doodling...."

"Trust me," she begged. "This will help."

Ardent sighed and tore the long roll of paper in half. From the air, he conjured a small bowl and filled it with ink.

Marrill reached for them but hesitated. "Any chance you happen to have a brush on you?"

Ardent's patience was clearly running thin, but he snapped his fingers and a trio of brushes appeared. She grabbed one with a "thanks," and dipped it in the ink.

Working quickly, she sketched an outline of Ardent and the Font, with a glass wall surrounding them. She paused, then added sketches of musical notes, bouncing off the wall.

A second later, the drawing jumped from the paper into life. Marrill caught her breath as the walls walked themselves around Ardent. The wizard stopped, looking at her through the inky outline of the newly drawn chamber. His mouth opened, but no sound came out.

Marrill laughed. It worked! She'd drawn a soundproof chamber, and it had come to life!

Ardent smiled hugely, gave her a thumbs-up, and bent back to his work.

Marrill let out a sigh of relief. Now she just had to sit back and enjoy the show while the wizard saved the world. It felt nice to have the pressure off. Beside her, a shape-shifting Dzane changed from a living rock into a tiger made of ice, throwing frost at the echo of the Lost Sun.

But as she watched, the Lost Sun's shadow seemed to split apart. As its dark hands raised to deflect the blast, another set of arms slid into place behind them. These arms, though, were not hollow or faded. They were solid, filled with color. Silver sleeves draped down around the wrists.

The faceless vision flickered. Beneath it, a porcelain visage emerged from the formless depths. The shadow wasn't becoming clearer, she realized. Something was moving through it.

"*I have arrived,*" a voice that wasn't Serth's pronounced, stepping through the echo of the Lost Sun.

CHAPTER 27
What Is Real and What Is Not

Fin pulled himself to his feet. His limbs felt like they'd been cast in lead. The deck of the *Enterprising Kraken* may as well have been a yawning abyss, its gravity pulling him down to the body of his mother. Lost to him now, forever.

Vell—his Rise, the boy whose existence defined him— had just murdered their mother. And now he would free the Salt Sand King, unleash the Iron Tide, and send the whole Stream to its doom. As if the Lost Sun of Dzannin wasn't enough for the job.

If he ever needed proof that the Rise were ruthless and unfeeling, this was it. They may look the same and have come from the same whole, but he and Vell were nothing alike.

"Sister Fade," Vell said, his voice cold and emotionless, "bring me the wish orb."

Fig hesitated, looking between the two identical boys. Uncertainty played across her features.

"Don't, Fig," Fin said calmly. "He doesn't control you."

Vell rolled his eyes. "Sister Fade, that was an *order*."

Fig's hands trembled around the shimmering wish. "I can't resist him," she said. "He's *Rise*. We have to obey their orders."

Fin's entire body vibrated with fury, but he bit back the scream of rage clawing at his throat. "You don't have to do *anything*, Fig," he growled. "You're a *person*. You make your own choices."

She shook her head. "No, Fin," she whispered. "We're not. Neither of us is. From the moment we come into existence, we're nothing more than the cast-off remains of someone else's weaknesses. We're not *real*."

"Fin," Vell snorted. "*Fig*. You've even given each other names. How absurd." He shook his head and looked at Fin. "She's right, Brother Fade. You are everything weak, to my strength." His eyes fell back to Fig. "The orb, Sister Fade. *Now*."

"Kick him in the face, Plus One!" Remy yelled from the

quarterdeck. "Show him who's weak—*mrphh!*" A tall Rise clapped his hand over the teenager's mouth, silencing her.

But it was too late. Remy's words were enough. Suddenly, everything clicked in Fin's mind. He finally understood exactly what Vell's weakness was. What all of the Rise's weakness really was. Now, he just had to show them.

And he was going to enjoy every moment of it.

Placing his body between Vell and Fig, he looked to his Rise, a huge smirk squirming its way across his face. "Go ahead and take the orb," Fin said evenly. "All you have to do is kill me."

Vell sneered, stepping backward.

"What's the matter?" Fin laughed. "I'm just a Fade. I'm nothing but weak weakness that's weak. You're super strong. Just stab that dagger straight through me, like you did our mother."

Vell's nostrils flared. His hands dropped to the dagger at his side. But he didn't draw it. He couldn't. And now they both knew it.

"Come on!" Fin chided. "I mean, of course, you *would* end up like our mother. With me inside you. With all my doubts and fears and insecurities, clawing at your mind. Able to bleed, able to suffer, able to die." He shrugged. "But it's no big deal. I do it every day." He waved a hand across the deck. "All the Fade do!"

A murmuring rippled through the ranks of the Fade. The Rise soldiers all looked to their sides, nerves playing across their faces. Everyone, Rise and Fade, seemed to be having the same revelation all at once.

Fin pressed his advantage, talking as much to Fig and the Fade as to Vell. "Or is it..." he said, drawing out the argument like the show that it was. This was how he lived in the Khaznot Quay. Playing out the game. Running the con to its perfect effect. Only this was no con. This was definitely, indisputably, the truth. "All this time you've convinced the Fade they aren't real. That *we* aren't real. When all along, it's the Fade who hold the power."

Vell nearly trembled with rage. "You hold nothing because you *are* nothing," he spat.

Fin shook his head, refusing to believe that any longer. "Nothing but the key to your mortality."

"And what value do you have beyond that?" Vell barked. "What value do you have on your own, without me? Who are you, *Brother Fade*, other than a phantom haunting the shadows of *my* glory?"

There was a beat of silence. A cold smile of victory split Vell's face.

Maybe he was right. Now that Fin had the answers to all the questions he'd spent his life asking, it changed nothing. He was still Fin. He was still forgettable.

He forced the feeling down. Because the truth was, there was nothing wrong with him. Being forgettable was part of who he was. It had its drawbacks, sure, but it had its advantages as well. If he hadn't been forgettable, he'd never have met Marrill. He'd never have recovered the Map. He'd never have beaten back Serth on the deck of the *Black Dragon*, or stopped the Iron Tide in Monerva, or locked away the Salt Sand King, the very burning fire that his cruel Rise wanted more than anything to free.

And that was what it all came down to. Vell wanted Fin to believe he was worthless, with no will of his own. And yet, *Fin* chose his own path, while *Vell* existed to serve the king he'd never met.

Vell wanted Fin to believe he was nothing because if he did, then Vell had all the power. But that trick only worked if Fin believed him.

And he didn't.

"Who am I?" Fin drew himself tall, lifting his chin. "I am Fin U. Lanu. The son of the Crest of the Rise. I'm the Ghost of Gutterleak Way. I am the Master Thief of the Khaznot Quay and a crew member on the *Enterprising Kraken*. I'm Marrill Aesterwest's friend, Fig's comrade, and Remy's Plus One. *I'm* the one who stole ink from the great Sheshefesh, and *I'm* the one who kept your king locked away in his prison."

He stepped forward, reveling in Vell's shocked expression. "I may be Fade to your Rise, but that also makes you Rise to my Fade. Bow before me, or cut me down and *become* me."

Vell's eyes clouded with rage. "Rise," he pronounced, "please restrain my Fade."

All around them, harsh faces stepped forward, headed for Fin. "Blisterwinds," Fin muttered. Well, at least he'd tried.

"NO!"

Fin, Vell, and the Rise all paused as one. Fin turned to see Fig with her legs splayed, the wish orb clutched in a death grip in her hand. Her expression was strained, her teeth gritted.

"No?" Vell said.

"No?" Fin echoed.

"No," she pronounced. She waved her hand through the air in a circling motion. "Brothers and Sisters Fade," she called. "Protect our Brother Fin."

For a moment, nothing happened. Then, slowly, the Fade moved forward. They shoved their way out from the ranks of the Rise as the soldiers stood stunned. One by one, they created a ring around Fin.

Fin tried not to show his surprise as warmth spread through his chest. It had worked. The Fade understood now. Fig understood now. She was on his side after all.

She was his friend.

He had to bite his cheek to keep from grinning.

Vell sputtered, but Fig held up a hand, cutting him off. She stepped forward, next to Fin. "Any Rise makes a move, they have to cut us all down. And then feel what it's like to be *weak*. Each Fade who falls, a Rise becomes mortal. Every blow you strike, you strike yourselves."

Fin smirked at Vell. "Seems the Fade know when to *rise* to the occasion." Vell groaned. Fin shrugged. "Guess a sense of humor is a weakness."

Fig jabbed him sharply in the ribs. "That actually wasn't very funny," she said. She shoved the wish orb into his hands. "Seriously, though," she whispered, "you better take this and go. The Rise have never met a problem they couldn't stab. Eventually they're going to turn on us out of habit."

"What about you?" he asked. He touched her hand, genuinely concerned.

"Don't worry about me, *blood*," she said, adopting his word. "I'll be fine."

He nodded. A pat on the arm didn't seem to be enough to show his gratitude, so he gave her a quick peck on the cheek. "Thanks, friend."

She rolled her eyes and gagged. "Oh, come *on*, gross!" But she squeezed his arm, and he could see by the shine of tears in her eyes just how much she meant it when she said, "Stay safe, Fin."

"No trub!" He laughed. Then he raced between the lines of the Fade, past the stumbling Rise, toward the front of the ship.

Just as he climbed onto the forecastle, the Naysayer burst out of the main hatch. A tricorn hat perched on his head, a cutlass waving in each hand. "*En garde*, scum munchers!" he shouted.

Fin looked back at him quizzically.

The Naysayer snorted, surveying the deck. "Am I late again? I'm late again." He tossed down his swords and pointed around with all four arms. "I hate each and every one of you. *Equally*," he grunted. Then he turned and stormed back down belowdecks.

"Classic Naysayer," Fin said. He grabbed a rope and swung to shore. He glanced back once, watching the soldiers on the bow slowly backing down from the nondescript forms of their own weakness. Then he turned and headed into the forest, leaving the Rise and Fade far behind.

CHAPTER 28
Things Get a Bit Sketchy

As Marrill watched, echoes evaporated before the Lost Sun. The chamber filled with his searing light. The shadows of the Dzane poured their power out against him, but the memories couldn't touch the very real form now entering the room. The Lost Sun of Dzannin strode forward into the heart of Meres, his footsteps keeping pace with his own echo, cloaking him in a shimmering veil of light and darkness.

The voice of a Dzane sounded, like daybreak and

thunder, speaking from the depths of history. "Prepare yourselves. The Star of Destruction is upon us!"

"How fitting you are here to greet me." The Lost Sun spoke through the wizard Serth's lips, but he wasn't talking to Marrill, or even Ardent. His words were directed at the echoes of the Dzane, the memories of his last battle.

As he moved through the crowded chamber, every shadow his robes touched flickered and dulled out of existence. As if his very presence overwrote the remnants of whatever magic had kept the memories bound here.

Marrill swallowed, her breathing tight in her chest as the Lost Sun's eyes swept the room. *"The Font of Meres,"* he said as his cold gaze fell on the dais. *"At the point of my first defeat, I will have my final victory."*

Behind her, the echo of Serth as a young man babbled out the lines of the Meressian Prophecy. "...And as in the beginning, so it will end..."

"Ardent!" Marrill cried. "What do we do?"

But the wizard was oddly quiet. She looked back to see him pouring ink onto the Map, which he'd rolled into a tube and wrapped in dream ribbon. Little squiggles of ink burst forth, as if someone had scribbled on the air, then flickered and died.

Ardent shook his head, tossed the used ribbon aside, and pulled out a fresh length. His eyes were completely focused on the task at hand. His lips moved, but no sound came out.

He can't hear anything, Marrill realized. Her brilliant plan had backfired horribly. And worse, Ardent didn't seem to be making any headway on repairing the Map.

She turned back to the Lost Sun. From where she stood, Marrill felt the energy pouring from him. Fissures cracked the floor at his feet, reaching back to become yawning crevices that spread up the far wall. Inside them, the void grew. She had no doubt that with a simple touch, the Lost Sun could destroy anything he wanted to. *Including* Ardent. Including *her*.

She had to buy Ardent more time. And she could think of only one way to do it.

Trying hard to still her shaking hands, Marrill pulled over the half roll of dream ribbon Ardent had given her. She perched herself on the edge of the dais, balancing the ink beside her, forcing herself to be calm and focus. Carefully, she dipped her brush into the ink.

Around her, the echoes of the Dzane fought so furiously she could almost feel the power of their attacks across the millennia. The Lost Sun swatted away the blasts, moving in time with his own shadow as if the battle were happening even now.

"Hold him," croaked the thin voice of the Dawn Wizard. "The Map is nearly complete!"

Marrill closed her eyes, took a deep breath, and began to draw. With each stroke of the brush, ink splashed across the ribbon, unspooling into images as though pulled from her mind. First she drew the harsh outline of a cage. Then she began to fill it in, taking care to make the bars extra thick and strong.

At the edge of her vision, the cage burst to life, even as a Dzane in the shape of a clockwork griffin pounced at the Lost Sun. The shadow-Sun reeled backward before the assault, separating himself from his contemporary counterpart, who jarred to a halt before her. The drawn cage continued to form around him, as though some magical hand had sculpted the ink into three dimensions and made it real.

It was mesmerizing, watching each sweep of ink materialize in front of her. But Marrill didn't have time to stare. Scribbling quickly, she added more bars, weaving them tighter and tighter together until the Lost Sun was completely contained inside an inky prison. Outside the cage, the shadow of him struggled with Dzane, wrapped in a serpent made of ice and flame.

Inside the cage, the present-day Lost Sun swept an arm at the bars as though they were nothing. He was met with a resounding clang as his body struck metal. He staggered back. At the same time, the shadow Lost Sun staggered, the coils of the serpent squeezing him, the griffin clawing at his arms and legs.

Marrill smiled. He hadn't been expecting *that*! Triumph surged in her chest.

But it was short-lived. The Lost Sun gripped two of the bars. With a flick of his wrists, they bent and snapped apart.

The ribbon in Marrill's lap tore clean through, just as the Lost Sun shredded the cage she'd drawn.

At the same time, the shadow-Sun freed one arm and waved it. The clockwork griffin blew away like sand on a beach. With his other hand, he grabbed the serpent by the throat, squeezing until it dissolved into smoke.

"Before me, all was chaos," past and present announced in unison. *"I gave shape and definition to the primal maelstrom."*

"Keep going!" the Dawn Wizard cried. "Stop him from pouring his essence into the wellspring until the Map is finished!"

Marrill knew that the Dawn Wizard was just a memory, calling out to the other memories around him. But it felt as though he were talking to her, urging her to keep drawing until Ardent could complete his task.

She unspooled another length of ribbon and bent over the fresh page. This time she sketched a wall, stacking the bricks one atop the other. "It doesn't have to be pretty," she told herself. "It just has to be strong."

Marrill drew sketch after sketch, just as Dzane after Dzane threw their power at the Lost Sun. But as fast as she drew, he ripped her sketches to pieces. Walls, cages, fences, ramparts, barricades—anything she could think of—he shredded them all. In echo and in substance, the Star of Destruction tore through his opposition, slowed but unstopped.

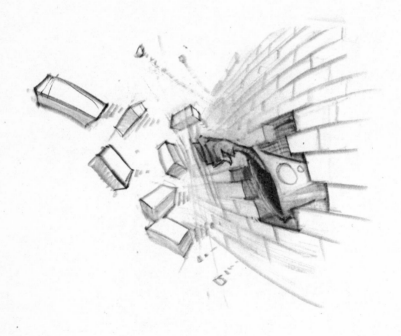

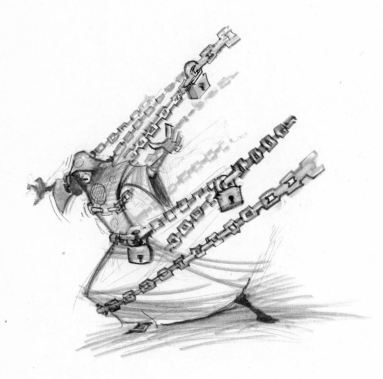

"Almost there!" the Dawn Wizard called at last.

"*I alone am order,*" the Lost Suns intoned in unison. "*I alone am finality. And when my essence pours into the wellspring of magic, I shall bring that finality to all of the River of Creation.*" The shadow of the Lost Sun's past held his hand high, dark-light gathering on his fingertips.

Marrill looked back, hoping. In the echo, the Dawn Wizard raced to where the Font now stood, waving the Map like a cape before him. "Come, then, bright star," he cried, unfurling the Map as the shadow-Sun's light poured forth toward him. "Shine yourself into *this*!"

But here and now, there was no such victory. Instead, Ardent still stooped over the Font, stained scraps of dream ribbon littering the dais at his feet without any sign of progress.

Marrill tried not to give in to the panic eating away at her. The fate of the Stream lay heavy on her shoulders. They needed more time.

Ignoring the cramping in her hand, Marrill grabbed at the dream ribbon, slashing her brush across it with a fury born from desperation. This time, she drew a series of metal chains crisscrossing the chamber, bound together with massive locks. Then she drew more chains on top of the locks, and even more locks on *those* chains, then drew thorns on the locks on the chains on the locks on the chains.

All around, the Dzane chanted in unison as the Map

swallowed the shadow-Sun's light. In real life, the silver-clad figure of Serth fell back a step, encircled in chains as his own past defeat played out before him.

Marrill's heart pounded, sketching the final details of her masterpiece into place. But no sooner had she put the finishing touches on the last lock than the whole drawing began to tear, ripping to pieces just like all the others.

The echo of the Dawn Wizard snapped shut his Map. The shadow figure of the Lost Sun faded. Before her, the present-day Lost Sun stepped through the wisp of his own echo, shredded chains falling at his feet.

"*This is where past and present come apart,*" he pronounced.

Marrill gulped. She reached for another length of ribbon. But the roll beside her was gone—she'd used every last scrap.

She scrambled toward Ardent, slamming her fist against the soundproof wall she herself had drawn into existence. "I need more ribbon!" she cried, keeping one eye on the Lost Sun.

But Ardent wasn't even moving. His arms hung at his sides. His head nodded sadly. Slowly, he lifted his eyes until they met hers. His lips moved, but no words came out.

"What are you saying?" Marrill mouthed.

The Lost Sun opened his arms wide. "*No more barriers.*"

And just like that, the inky walls surrounding the Font

shattered like glass. The soundproof drawing tore to pieces. Marrill stumbled backward. Before her, Ardent stood alone over the tattered remains of the dream ribbon. The last of the Sheshefesh ink leaked out of its jar. The Map to Everywhere floated gently to the ground, the hole in it grown even larger.

Ardent let out a shuddering sigh. "I failed," he breathed.

CHAPTER 29
...So It Will End.

F in burst from the forest, its whispers still clinging to his brain like cobwebs. Across from him, far past the great spire, the other side of the chasm had rent open, the very ground yielding to the void that grew like a slow rip in the fabric of reality. Above the hum and roar of the waterfalls, lightning crashed and thunder boomed from the windows of the building perched at the tip of the spire.

A battle was raging.

Fin's heart squeezed. The Lost Sun was up there with

Marrill and Ardent—they needed his help, fast. Not that he knew *how* to help, but he had to try.

There was no sign of a bridge, and no time to try to find one. Acting before he had the chance to talk himself out of it, Fin leapt off the cliff edge, yanking the strings in his jacket sleeves to fan out his skysails. He plummeted into the mist roiling up from the depths. Magic danced across his skin, sometimes literally. The corners of his eyes felt like they wanted to trade places and the inside of his nose *smelled*. The air tasted like cardamom and longing.

Just as the magic reached dangerous levels, the force of the rising mist caught him, buoying him upward. Fin let out a shout of joy as he rode the updraft around the spire. But any sense of relief was short-lived.

The higher he climbed, the more he realized just how close they were to utter destruction. A wedge of nothingness widened from the point of the Lost Sun's path outward into the distance, as though the world was a cake and someone had taken out a massive slice.

Fin wheeled toward the highest windows of the towering building, snagging the sill of one with his fingertips. For a moment, he clung to the side of the spire, a thundering torrent of Stream water far beneath him, and beneath that, the seemingly endless drop of the chasm. He took a deep breath, steeling his resolve, then hauled himself up into the room.

He thought he'd been prepared for anything. But there

was no way he could have anticipated the chaos that greeted him inside the great chamber. Before him, a sea of shadows seemed to be playing out a thousand different scenes from a thousand different times, all at once. Some of them were full and dark, like the ones he'd seen from the path in the forest, but others were half faded, as if bleached by the light of the Lost Sun. Still others spoke to partners who were no longer there at all.

Cautiously, Fin dropped from the window onto the stone floor by the base of a raised dais. At his feet, the shadow of a young man who looked suspiciously like Ardent crouched by a weeping younger Serth, jotting furiously as the Oracle spouted Prophecy. An equally young Annalessa hovered over them, trying to comfort the madman and shoo away Ardent all at once. A shredded pile of drawings lay nearby, edges already beginning to curl. Beyond that, in the center of the dais, a font bubbled Stream water, surrounded by ink-stained scraps of dream ribbon.

That's where Marrill stood—beside the Font, her face white with terror. Next to Ardent, his chin sagging, looking broken. And past them, tall and sinister as he mounted the stairs, came Serth.

Not Serth, Fin reminded himself. *The Lost Sun of Dzannin.*

"What did I miss?" Fin murmured.

"Fin!" Marrill cried. They rushed toward each other, and

she leapt at him to wrap him in a huge hug. "We're in trouble," she explained under her breath.

"Looks that way," Fin said, gesturing to the shadows filling the chamber.

Marrill waved a hand. "Those are just echoes—old memories magicked into place." He started to ask her to explain but she cut him off. "The plan didn't work. Ardent couldn't fix the Map."

Fin scarcely believed what he was hearing. If Ardent had failed, then their last chance at stopping the end of Stream... was gone. It didn't seem possible. It couldn't be. Could it?

Marrill's eyes met his, and his gut clenched as he recognized the defeat twisting her features. "What do we do?" she breathed.

Fin turned to Ardent. There had to be a backup plan. A secret solution to their problem that would come through at the last minute and save the Stream. But the wizard merely shook his head.

"I don't know," the old man murmured.

A hole opened up inside Fin, and his knees buckled. It wasn't just Ardent who'd failed. It was all of them. After everything they'd done—after all the fighting and struggling, after finding his mother only to lose her again—they'd accomplished nothing. The Stream would still be destroyed.

Fin watched, heart pounding, as the Lost Sun climbed the last of the steps to the dais.

"**Do not feel shame,**" the Star of Destruction told them. His arms spread wide, as though they offered a welcoming embrace instead of a quick death. "**You fought hard and well. But your task was never achievable. From the first time I shone my cleansing light into the raw madness of creation, this day was inevitable. For everything, and everyone, there must be an ending.**"

To Fin's surprise, Marrill jumped forward, hands clenched in fists. "No," she shouted. "You're wrong! The Pirate Stream *doesn't* have to end. It doesn't have to be this way!"

The Lost Sun's head tilted to one side, his eyes focusing on her. Even from where they stood, Fin could see the dark star's power pulsing under his skin, seeping through tiny, almost invisible cracks. As though it was too much energy for a human vessel to contain.

"**It does have to be this way,**" the Lost Sun told Marrill. "**The chaos of the Stream yearns for my light to give it shape, to define it with certainty. I am drawn to its purest waters, the last concentrated vestige of raw, unchained possibility. They call to me to leave this vessel, to shine my light into them, and through them touch—and end—all possibilities at once. There is no way around it. It is destiny. It is certain.**"

"Enough!" Ardent shouted. His expression had grown darker, hard and harsh like a weathered rock face. The temperature in the room dropped, sending chill bumps racing down Fin's arms. Energy sparked along Ardent's knuckles. "The Pirate Stream is not yours to destroy," he growled. "And if you want to try, you'll have to go through me to do it."

The Lost Sun did not look at him or speak. He merely swatted a hand through the air, a gesture as gentle as a cat pawing at a loose piece of paper.

The impact, though, was enormous. Ardent was lifted from his feet and thrown across the room, smashing against the far wall so hard that it sent cracks screaming up the thick stone. He dropped limply to the ground, rolling over with a groan.

"Ardent!" Marrill's screech seemed to come from far away. Fin stood paralyzed, struggling to absorb what was happening as she raced to their fallen mentor.

"That should have destroyed him," the Lost Sun mused. *"Your friend truly is powerful. Perhaps he would have made a better vessel than this one...."* His cold eyes looked down at Serth's porcelain hands. *"No matter, I leave this body soon enough."*

Fin scarcely heard him. Everything about the moment felt hollow and wrong. In his mind the same vision repeated over and over again: The moment blood had blossomed on the Crest's fingers. The way she'd clutched at Fin as she'd fallen. The sound of her voice—so familiar and foreign at the same time.

The heaviness of her body in his arms when she'd died.

Down in some small, wounded place, part of him wondered if the Lost Sun was right. An end to everything meant an end to pain, too. It meant an end to all the anguish and all the suffering that people felt every single day. It meant that no one would see their mother die, that no Fade would be kept in a pen or told they were nothing.

The Lost Sun swept across the dais, pausing as the birth of the Prophecy replayed itself before him. Black tears poured from Serth's eyes as he recounted the images implanted in his mind. The echo of Annalessa struggled against his frozen robes, trying to comfort him.

"The Lost Sun of Dzannin is found again...." Serth muttered, clutching at Annalessa.

"The Dzane believed they could contain certainty in a prison of endless possibility," the Lost Sun said, his voice coming through Serth's lips. **"But in endless possibility, there must, too, be the possibility of an end."**

"Help me with him," Annalessa begged a young Ardent.

"I'm writing as fast as I can," the echo of Ardent snapped.

"What he's saying doesn't matter! He needs our help," she insisted.

The shadow of young Ardent didn't even bother looking over at her. "What he's saying is *all* that matters."

"And as in the beginning…"

The Lost Sun reached out Serth's hand to his former self. With hardly a touch, the echo vanished from existence.

"So it will end," the Lost Sun finished, moving at last to stand before the Font of Meres. The glow of the Stream's purest water lit his face, causing the black grooves etched along his skin to stand out in stark relief. His empty eyes grew wide and eager. His hand raised, held out toward the Font.

Fin forced down the pain, the despair. He looked back to Marrill, cradling Ardent gently. If the Lost Sun destroyed everything, she would never be hurt again.

But then, she would never smile again, either. An end to pain also meant an end to happiness. A world without fear was a world without laughter. A world without tears was a world without friends.

Fin shook his head, breaking the paralysis that had gripped him. He had to do something. He had to stop the Lost Sun. But how? There wasn't any more time!

Serth's raised hand began to crack and glow, the power of the Lost Sun gathering. The room hummed with energy. Light coalesced around his fingertips, preparing to pour forth. *"They call to me even now,"* the Lost Sun intoned. *"The pure waters of the Stream,*

their chaos begs for order—*I am drawn to them!*

Suddenly, that phrase triggered something in the back of Fin's mind. *Pure waters.* The Lost Sun said it over and over; that's why it had gotten stuck in Fin's head. *The pure waters of the Pirate Stream. They call to me...I am drawn to them.* But that wasn't the only time he'd heard that phrase recently.

Fin's eyes widened, remembering the lines of the Dawn Wizard's will, recited via Karnelius:

> **To the King of Salt and Sand, I leave a wish ungranted, an ambition unfulfilled, an army leaderless...**

"...and an orb of gold," Fin finished, "its waters as pure and true as the headwaters of the Stream itself!" He patted through his jacket frantically, finally pulling free the wish.

The Lost Sun's hand glowed like white-hot metal, blasting away the shadows of Meres with its bright light. The power seemed to drain from Serth's body, focusing into his palm.

Outside, the wind howled, the void growing feverishly as the Lost Sun approached the moment of his triumph. The end was here.

It was now or never.

Jumping to his feet, Fin thrust the orb into the air above

his head. His heart pounded furiously. He had no idea if what he was about to do was incredibly brilliant or incredibly stupid.

If it was the latter, at least he wouldn't be around long enough to regret it.

"Hey, Sunshine," he called. "Catch!"

And then, with all of his might, he hurled the wish orb straight at the Lost Sun's porcelain face.

The power barely contained in Serth's body surged, flowing forth toward the Font of Meres. But the last bit of Serth's humanity reacted out of reflex. Before it could strike him, the Lost Sun snatched the hurtling orb out of the air with his raised hand.

The Lost Sun shook and trembled. The blinding light rushed forward and faded, pulled in by the purified waters of the wish orb. The essence of the Lost Sun drained from Serth's body, but never reached the Font of Meres. The wish orb captured it first, sucking it in greedily.

Serth's body convulsed as the power bled from it. The silver faded from the wizard's black robes. The stony face softened to pale flesh as the Star of Destruction left it.

"This prison...will not hold me...." The Lost Sun's voice was a thin rasp, draining away along with his power. *"It cannot contain me...."*

Serth's body dropped to its knees. The wish burned bright in his hand, thrust into the air as though it were the orb that held up the man.

"*The end...can only be...delayed,*" the Lost Sun gasped. "*Soon J...will...be...free....*"

The last light drained from his lips, his eyes. Then the body that had once held the Lost Sun of Dzannin, the Star of Destruction, the Dzane's most powerful creation, collapsed flat onto its face.

CHAPTER 30
The Compass, Rose

Marrill stared at the crumpled body. "Did you just…" She tried to untangle her thoughts. "Did that just…"

She let the unconscious Ardent down gently and pushed to her feet. Together, she and Fin approached the Font and the lifeless body beside it. Outside, the wail of the void died. The cracks in the walls stopped growing. The deep *nothingness* within them dissipated, turning into just empty air.

Marrill shook her head. "Did we just save the Pirate Stream?"

Fin shrugged. "Yes?"

A tide of giggles erupted from Marrill's mouth. It felt amazing to laugh after everything they'd just been through. "We won!" she said, letting the excitement and relief overcome her. "We saved the Stream!"

They grabbed each other by the arms, bouncing up and down with glee.

"Again," Fin pointed out.

Marrill let out a high laugh. *"Again,"* she said. But a moment later, her jubilance dimmed, remembering Ardent. The wizard may have been shockingly tough for his frail frame, but the Lost Sun had hit him pretty hard. "We better get Ardent out of here and back to the *Kraken*."

"Uh," Fin said. He pointed. Ardent was no longer collapsed in a heap. He'd risen to his feet and moved to the center of the chamber, where he stood wordless, staring at the entrance to the Great Hall.

As one, they rushed to him. "Ardent?" Marrill asked. "Ardent, are you okay?" She leaned forward, trying to catch his eyes. "You might have a concussion," she tried to tell him.

"No," the old man said. "No, Marrill, I'm fine."

She sighed in relief. "Well, in that case, you *totally* missed it! It was end-of-the-world time, and the Lost Sun was all WAHMP-wahmpwahmp-WAHMP." She held out her hand, mimicking the sound of the Lost Sun gathering its energy to pour into the Font. "And then Fin was all like, 'Hey, catch!' and then..."

But Ardent didn't seem to be paying attention. He didn't even glance her way. Instead, his eyes remained locked on the entrance. "Annalessa," he breathed.

Marrill spun. At the far end of the room, a new figure swept into the chamber. Annalessa looked exactly as Marrill remembered her from Monerva: long black hair, elegant gown, gentle but prominent cheekbones.

Marrill's heart jumped with joy. They'd found her! "Annalessa!"

But Annalessa didn't seem to hear. Indeed, she looked hurried, harried even, as though she were in a great rush. She moved quickly across the room, as if she didn't see them there watching her.

And that's when Marrill realized. "She's an echo," she said aloud.

All the other echoes had vanished, burned away by the light of the Lost Sun. But Annalessa's was here, as clear and vivid as though she were in the room in real life.

"Someone must be here who remembers this," Marrill said aloud, thinking back to what Ardent had told her when they'd first arrived. "Which means maybe Annalessa *is* here in real life?"

Ardent nodded curtly, but his eyes never left Annalessa's

image, which mounted the dais and moved to position herself behind the Font of Meres.

"I know you're here," Annalessa whispered. Her eyes swept the chamber. Her chin lifted. "Nothing will sway me from this course."

Marrill's breath caught. She sounded so severe. But there was no one else in the room. Who could Annalessa have been talking to?

Beside her, Ardent shifted, moving to stand at the base of the dais. He positioned himself directly before Annalessa's echo, as if she were talking to him, as if she might see him. The pain written on his face brought tears to Marrill's eyes.

Perhaps, she thought, this *was* a message to Ardent. Perhaps Annalessa had known that one day he would be here, listening, watching what she was about to do. Perhaps this was her way of bringing them together in the same time and place, to speak to him directly even though she couldn't be here in the flesh.

"Marrill," Fin hissed. He gestured toward the entrance.

The figure waiting there blew away Marrill's theory in the space of a heartbeat. He was tall, expressionless, wreathed head to toe in cold metal. From one of his hands, an empty cage dangled.

The Master of the Iron Ship.

Panic spiked through Marrill's system. She tripped backward, scrambling to put distance between herself and the terrible figure. Fin shot out an arm, steadying her. "It's not real," he murmured. "Just another echo."

Marrill gulped, nodding. She could see that now: the way the light wavered around the Master, the distance of time making his body vaguely insubstantial. She was thankful Ardent had been wrong about him showing up for their final confrontation with the Lost Sun. But what was his echo doing here with Annalessa?

"We were wrong," Annalessa said to the Master. Her voice came hollow, distorted and distant. "We should have tried harder to stop Serth back then. Say what you will, but the truth is, we didn't try at all. The Wizards of Meres wanted the power of the Dzane. The power of creation. And look what we found instead: destruction. We are as responsible for this as he is, and you know it."

Marrill swallowed. So it was true. Whatever had happened to make him what he was today—time travel, evil pact, or some kind of spell gone awry—the Master of the Iron Ship had once been a Wizard of Meres.

She dug her fingers through her hair, trying to make sense of it. "Everything comes back to the Master," she whispered. "He was there when Serth first opened the Gate aboard the *Black Dragon*. He was the one who drove us into the whirlpool to Monerva."

"He was the one who filled the wish orb at the Syphon," Fin pointed out.

And of course, the Master had set free the Lost Sun at

Margaham's Game. And now here he was yet again—well, not *now*, but in the echo-now—with Annalessa. Marrill shook her head.

Why? What did he *want*?

As she pondered, the Master's echo strode forward to the heart of the chamber.

The echo of Annalessa paused. "You can't stop me," she said. "You *know* you can't." From within her robes, she produced a stone cup. It was a perfect replica, Marrill realized, of the cup Serth drank from long ago.

"I made the original, remember?" Annalessa said with a halfhearted laugh. "You didn't think I could craft another?" She stepped toward the Font, the cup clutched in her fingers.

Ardent, who up to this moment had watched in frozen silence, burst free of his trance. "Oh, Anna, no!" His cry seemed to suck the heat from the chamber; Marrill staggered back, shivering in the cold. The wizard's emotions were out of control; they were bleeding out into the world around him!

It was impossible for Annalessa to have heard him—she was just a remnant from an event that had already taken place. But she raised her head all the same. Tears shimmered in her eyes.

Ardent took a step toward the dais. "Anna, please," he begged.

But Annalessa, locked in another time, could not listen. Instead, she pulled something else from her robe. It was an odd little object, looking to Marrill like a cross between a spoon and a pitcher, rounded and empty like a bowl on one end, thin to a point at the other. As Annalessa held it balanced at the center of her hand, the strange device turned of its own power, swaying back and forth. It pointed to one side, then the next, then back again, finally coming to rest pointed straight at the Font in front of her.

Ardent sucked in a breath. "The lodestone...it's the Compass Rose!"

Marrill didn't understand. *That* wasn't the Compass Rose. The Compass *was* Rose—the scribbled bird.

The echo Annalessa dropped the lodestone straight into the stone cup.

Ardent seemed to understand what was about to happen, though Marrill didn't. "No, Annalessa!" he gasped, leaping onto the dais and rushing forward until his face was inches from hers. "No!"

Pain and panic radiated from him in physical form, spilling forth a torrent of jagged energy that whipped through the chamber. Marrill and Fin had to duck to hide their faces, for fear that it might scorch them.

"Ardent, calm down!" Marrill cried. But if the wizard heard her, he definitely didn't show it. Just as Annalessa showed no sign of hearing *him*.

Annalessa smiled, a tear falling from her eye. "I do this to save us all." She plunged the cup into the Font. Fin and Marrill gasped as her skin touched the naked

Stream water. "See how the waters do not harm me," she intoned.

Marrill knew those words. They were the same ones Serth had uttered, just before he drank from that very cup. The uneasy feeling in the pit of her stomach morphed into fear.

Annalessa took a deep breath. "My love for you, Ardent, is as wide and deep and wild as the Stream." She lifted the cup to her mouth and drank.

"Anna!" Ardent reached for her. But his fingers found only echoes and shadow.

Marrill pressed her face against Fin's shoulder. She couldn't stand to see whatever nightmare the Stream had inflicted on their friend. But at the same time, she kept one eye uncovered—she didn't dare to truly look away, either.

Annalessa's image flickered, dimming to almost nothing. Then it surged back to life, so vibrant she could have been in the room for real. Her eyes went wide. "I can't—" She dropped the cup and staggered back, falling to her knees. "What have I—"

Ardent ran to her, his hands passing uselessly through the image as she doubled over. The echo of Annalessa shook her head violently. Her long black hair whipped the air, twisting around her. The strands of it seemed to thicken, lengthen.

"Ardent!" she cried. It came out strangled, almost a screech.

The echo faded—or had Annalessa herself faded? The very color drained away from her, leaving nothing but

lines, like a drawing brought to life. Then even those lines twisted. Her body seemed to snap into scribbles. The scribbles reordered themselves, turning into wings. The wings stretched wide, flapping furiously.

A moment later, a familiar bird burst into flight, wheeled once around the chamber, and came to perch on the lip of the Font.

It was Rose.

Or rather, it was the echo of Rose.

Marrill gaped, not quite sure she could trust her eyes. "I…she…" She shook her head. "Annalessa…became Rose?"

Beside her, Fin seemed equally stunned. "So when Rose guided us to the pieces of the Map back when we first met… that was Annalessa?"

Marrill frowned, struggling to come to terms with what had happened. "She was the one who first brought me to the Stream…and brought us together way back in the Khaznot Quay." Her mind raced. Annalessa had been with them from the very beginning. Fused, somehow, into the Map to Everywhere.

"Ardent?" she asked, hoping he would help her understand. But Ardent didn't even look at her. His eyes were focused on the bird. His lips curled in a sneer. "Ardent!" she tried again.

Without even glancing her way, the wizard squeezed his fingers into a fist. The words she'd been about to speak lodged in her throat until she choked on them. For a moment she struggled to breathe, her eyes watering with panic.

Fin raced to her side. "Ardent, what's wrong with you? Let her go!" Ardent snapped his fingers, and Fin's voice cut out, too. For a beat there was just the sound of them choking, the tightness of Marrill's chest growing painful. Then the wizard's fingers loosened, and with a cough, her airway cleared. She fell to her knees, gasping.

She tried to tell Fin she was okay, but she was too terrified to speak. Too terrified to invite the wizard's wrath once more.

When she glanced toward Ardent, a sense of betrayal cut through her, so sharp it was almost physical. *Ardent the Cold*, she thought. So this was what that meant. This was what he'd been like, back before Annalessa vanished. Back when he was a Wizard of Meres, Serth's right hand, helping— arranging even—for the ceremony that would lead to the Meressian Prophecy. All the rumors of him being selfish and single-minded flooded her mind. She hadn't wanted to believe any of it, but it was true nonetheless.

A sickening realization dawned on her: Denial doesn't change reality. Just because she wanted something to be true didn't make it so. Marrill had to face the truth: No matter how much she wanted to believe otherwise, Ardent wasn't who she thought he was.

CHAPTER 31
The Man in Iron

Fin crouched by Marrill, his arm around her trembling shoulders. Her eyes brimmed with tears. But Fin was furious. No one treated his best friend that way, even if he was a centuries-old, powerful wizard. He stood, ready to take Ardent on.

But Marrill grabbed his hand, pulling him back down. "No, Fin," she whispered. "He's not himself."

Fin couldn't believe she was making excuses for him after what he'd done. "Marrill, are you kidding? He just—"

"I mean he might kill you," she snapped.

Oblivious to them, Ardent reached trembling fingers toward the echo of Rose, tracing the air around her feathered form. "This is all my fault," he whispered to himself. "I failed her." He dropped his head to his hands. His shoulders shook softly. "Oh, Annalessa, my love. Why do this stupid, stupid thing?"

Rose lifted from the Font and spun twice around the chamber. For the first time since entering, the echo of the Master of the Iron Ship moved. He lunged, reaching for the scribbled bird. She fluttered away, just barely escaping his metal fingers, inky wings beating against the air as she careened out of the chamber.

The echo of the Master turned to watch her go. As ever, if he had emotions, they were buried deep beneath a shell of iron.

Fin understood, then, why he'd been holding the empty cage. He'd come for Rose. To take her like he'd done at Margaham's Game. The difference was that then he'd had perfect timing, as if he knew the exact moment Rose would fly toward the door, whereas this time she'd remained elusive.

Fin shook his head. If the Master had succeeded in capturing Rose back then, when she'd originally transformed, before she'd made it to the crew of the *Kraken*… Fin would never have met Marrill. They would never have assembled the Map or stopped Serth from opening the Gate back on the *Black Dragon*. The very Stream might have ended, with no one there to stop it. He shuddered at the thought.

"He missed her here," Marrill said, her thoughts clearly following the same trail as Fin's. "Did he do everything else—sinking the *Black Dragon*, starting the Wish Machine, freeing the Lost Sun—just for another chance at catching her?"

Fin shook his head. He didn't even know what to think anymore. But one thing was clear: Every step of the way, the Master had been involved. Even the storm surge that had brought Marrill to the Stream in the first place was his doing.

"He was the architect of everything," he concluded. "All of it. All along."

They just didn't know why.

At the edge of the dais, Ardent pulled his head from his hands and pushed himself to his feet. "I should have seen," he whispered. "I should have been able to stop her." He turned to look at them. The man seemed truly, deeply broken.

Behind them, iron clanked. Fin whirled to find the echo of the Master, cage dangling from one hand, standing just where Fin had seen him last. Only something was different now. The cage jangled. Black scribbles flapped and fluttered within it.

"That's not an echo," Marrill breathed.

"It's the real Master!" Fin shouted. He spun toward Ardent. He didn't know if he could forget how callously the wizard had treated them just moments ago. But right now, it looked like that would have to wait. "Okay, Ardent," he said, "time to go!"

But Ardent didn't move. No lightning crackled across his fingertips. He didn't look ready to fight—or even seem to be thinking about it. Instead, he simply stared down at the Master, and the Master, in turn, looked up at him.

"So here we are again," Ardent said at long last. "Back to where we began."

The Master nodded slowly.

Ardent gestured to the cage. "You have her," he said. The iron head nodded once more. "I have to save her," Ardent added.

The Master nodded again.

Fin caught Marrill's eye. The worry on her face made it clear that she wanted to say something, to intervene, but feared what might happen if she tried. Fin didn't blame her; he felt the same way.

"This magic is too powerful," Ardent murmured. "It can't be undone. Annalessa and the Map are fused...but..." Ardent sprang down from the dais, landing like a cat. "She *can* be saved," he muttered. "There's a way. I know it! The Stream touches not just all places but all times...."

He paced back and forth furiously as he talked, forcing Fin and Marrill to move across the chamber just to stay out of his way. "But you know that, don't you?" he said, turning to the Master. "You found a way to travel back to the very dawn of the Stream. How? The sheer power involved..."

The Master moved. Slowly, he held out his hand, turning

it upward. Gripped in his sharp metal talons, pulsing light and dark like the beating of a heart, sat the wish orb.

Fin's stomach twisted. He cursed himself for not grabbing the orb the second the Lost Sun had been sucked inside. The new prison of the Lost Sun, the key to the cage of the Salt Sand King, and the barrier holding back the Iron Tide, all in one. Now the Master alone controlled the fate of the Stream.

Fin slipped his hand into Marrill's, waiting for the Master to wish and release it all. But instead, the cold figure pushed the orb toward Ardent, as if in offering. Inside it, flecks of black marred the golden glow.

The two wizards stood face-to-face, the gleaming sphere between them. Ardent stared straight at the Master, as though seeking out the eyes that peered from within the cruel visor. Blue eyes, just like Ardent's own.

Fin wondered what he saw in them, standing so close. If there was any humanity left. Or if the Master truly was just a dark wraith of the Stream, as Ardent had long ago surmised.

"I know who you are," Ardent said at last. His gaze dropped to consider the wish, his head tilting to watch the black flecks dance and spiral. "It is a weak prison," he mused. "It won't hold the Lost Sun for long. So much power, and yet not enough."

He looked toward Rose in her iron cage. His chin trembled and he sighed, shaking his head. Then, almost cautiously, he took the orb from the Master's grip. The flecks inside it began to swirl, streaking the golden light with trails of darkness. Ardent slowly turned, holding it aloft before him, eyes fixed and staring as the contents of the orb spun faster and faster. The dark streaks grew thicker and grayer, until Fin realized they weren't *darkness* at all.

They were metal.

"I *will* save her," Ardent stated simply. "If I must undo all of the Stream to make it happen."

And before Fin could even shout, the orb in Ardent's hand *melted*. Horror gripped Fin as gold and iron coated the wizard's fingers, flowed down his wrist, raced up his arm.

"Oh no," Marrill breathed. "Ardent, no."

The liquid metal flowed over Ardent, consuming him. Encasing him. Even as it swallowed him, it hardened, turning his fingers into sharp-tipped claws, covering his skin in impenetrable armor. Cold darkness closed over his face, encasing it in a mask of wrought iron.

Fin stumbled backward, tugging Marrill with him. His entire body shook with shock and horror. "It can't be," he whispered, his voice tight.

"Ardent!" Marrill screamed. But even if he could hear her, it didn't matter. The iron enveloped him, leaving no trace of the man they had known. No trace, save for his long white beard and his cold blue eyes.

Ardent was gone. In his place stood a familiar ironclad figure.

Ardent had become the Master of the Iron Ship.

"This can't be real," Fin choked. His mind scrambled to make sense of what had happened. There were two Masters now, identical in every way. The same flowing white beard. The same cold eyes. The same stance. The only difference was the iron cage dangling from the first Master's hand, with Rose still trapped inside it.

Outside, the world itself seemed to let out a howl, a sound at once so shrill and deep that it raked fingers down Fin's spine. The new Master reached out his hands to either side, red lightning bursting from them. The walls of the chamber, already cracked and weakened by the Lost Sun, exploded in every direction.

Marrill screamed and grabbed Fin, dragging him toward the dais. Fin shook his head, clearing the confusion to focus on self-preservation. As the ceiling fractured, raining stone and rubble down around them, they scrambled for the small shelter the Font provided, pushing past Serth's lifeless form to crowd themselves beneath the lip of the bowl.

"What's happening?" Fin cried over the cacophony of destruction.

Marrill's eyes brimmed with tears and terror and disbelief, all meshed into one. "Ardent used the orb," she choked. "He *wished*."

From the Font above, Fin could hear the Stream water churning. Outside, embers and lightning swirled through the air as the chamber collapsed. Walls and ceiling crumbled, until nothing remained but the dais, the Font, and a patch of fractured floor perched at the tip of the spire.

Everything else was gone save for the new Master and the old, standing side by side, surveying the carnage.

Fin's gaze swept across the utter devastation surrounding them. In the chasm below, Stream water twisted and roiled as it spun in a current around the spire. Waves formed, crashing against the cliffs as the current grew fiercer—the whirlpool of Monerva, reborn by the power of the wish.

To the south, the void had left a hole in reality, covered now in a thick fog that seemed to swallow the Stream. To the north, a fire ravaged the forest of Meres. The Rise army streamed through the burnt and broken trunks, racing toward the cliff edge, where a cloud of glowing embers gathered into the outline of a man.

The Salt Sand King had returned to take his place at the head of his unbeatable army.

Fin let out a shudder. But before he could truly even comprehend the depths of the disaster around them, Marrill dug her fingers into his arm, wrenching his focus back to the threat at hand.

The new Master stalked toward them as his twin watched dispassionately. Fin grabbed Marrill tighter, pushing her behind him as the iron figure neared. Wind buffeted across their tiny perch, howling around them. It whipped the new Master's white beard like a windsock as he stepped over Serth's lifeless body and approached the Font.

Marrill scooted backward, pulling Fin with her. But the new Master seemed to care little for either of them. Without even glancing their way, he plunged his hand into the magical waters that were the very source of the Pirate Stream.

There was something vicious about the act; it reminded Fin of Vell plunging the knife into the Crest's back. The horrible brutality and awful finality of the gesture. A hissing sound erupted from the stone bowl as the water in the basin, already churning, frothed and boiled. A dull film tarnished the golden bubbles.

Almost instantaneously, a new sound rose from the chasm below. The roar of the Stream waterfalls changed pitch as though flowing more forcefully. Fin risked a glance over the fractured edge of the chamber floor toward the base of the spire.

His heart froze with dread. Metal marred the once-bright cascades that carried the Font's magical water out to the Stream. The whirlpool below grew streaked with dark slashes of metal.

The Iron Tide was rising.

Rose cawed and beat her wings madly in her cage. Her captor looked at his twin and pointed with his free hand toward the whirlpool. The new Master stepped from the dais without acknowledgment, and made his way toward the edge of the platform.

Fin clutched Marrill, struggling to keep from being swept away as the storm around them gained force. The monster who'd so recently been their friend glanced toward them once more. But if there was anything of Ardent left in him, Fin couldn't see it.

And then, without warning, the new Master stepped over the edge, dropped into the heart of the whirlpool, and vanished.

"Ardent!" Marrill cried, tears streaking down her cheeks.

The remaining Master turned to them, staring, but he made no move. Fin forced himself to meet those blue eyes, knowing now who they belonged to. He wasn't sure how this magic worked, but he knew the two Masters were one and the same. That somehow, the Master who had menaced them had been Ardent all along.

No, Fin mentally corrected himself. There was nothing left of their friend in that creature. Ardent had been right: The Master of the Iron Ship truly *was* nothing more than a dark wraith of the Stream.

"Fin!" Marrill shouted, pointing toward the Font. "We have to get out of here now!"

Sure enough, metal crept across the stone basin, spreading down toward the dais. Apparently the Iron Tide wasn't just pouring from the waterfalls. If he and Marrill hoped to survive, they needed to get out of there before the entire spire was swallowed by it.

As far as Fin could see, there was only one option for escape. He reached for the ties to his skysails. Marrill's eyes widened as she followed his movements. "Oh no," she said. "There's no way you can carry us both across the chasm!"

She probably had a point, but Fin felt like it was best to ignore that. It wasn't like they had a choice. "Give you three seconds to come up with a better plan," he said.

She frowned, looking at the creep of the Iron Tide. "Uh..."

"One..."

Marrill bit her lip, turning to the Master. He tilted his head slightly. Curiously, even.

"Two..." Fin counted. He forced the Master out of his mind and turned to brace himself for the jump.

"Oh, just do it!" Marrill wrapped her arms around his neck as she situated herself on his back.

"You got it," Fin said, taking a deep breath. "Here goes everything!" He ran as fast as he could with Marrill clinging to him, threw his arms wide, and leapt off the edge of the platform, praying they wouldn't drop like a stone or be blasted to bits by the Master.

The massive whirlpool created enough of an updraft that the wind caught them instantly. Marrill let out a whoop of success. Fin allowed himself a moment of euphoria.

But it didn't last. They started to sag almost immediately. Marrill had been right—there was no way they were going to make it. Fin's heart thundered in his chest. Below them, the whirlpool yawned like the maw of a hungry animal.

Then something slammed into them. They spiraled, starting to plummet.

"Fin!" Marrill screeched. Her grip around his shoulders slipped.

Fingers wrapped tightly around Fin's ankle, a hand dragging them down even faster to their doom. Heart in his throat, Fin glanced down as a second hand circled his leg. His blood ran cold.

It was Serth. He was alive. They were definitely, unequivocally doomed.

"*Lift*," Serth's voice rasped.

Suddenly, the wind caught them, pushing them upward. A strong breeze blew from just the right angle to stabilize them and put them back on course. Fin's skysails filled, sending them soaring. He yelped with joy as they soared past the lip of the whirlpool.

In moments, the gust had blown them over the burning forest, past the gathering forces of the Rise, and out to the coastline. Fin was relieved to see the *Kraken* waiting for them, already with anchor weighed and a clear line to the sea. He banked, angling them down toward the ship.

Landing gracefully was impossible, so they tumbled across the deck in a tangle of arms and legs, coming to rest against the steps of the quarterdeck. Remy leaned over the railing, mouth open and gaping.

"Well, this is somewhat unexpected," she said, gaze lingering on Serth. "What—?"

Fin brushed himself off, helping Marrill to her feet. "A lot," he said. He spun toward Serth, ready for the Meressian

Oracle to change from savior to menace. He found the wizard crumpled in a pile, still and lifeless once more. Whatever power he'd used to save them, it seemed to be gone now. For the moment, then, they were safe.

"I repeat," Remy said. "What—?"

Fin met Marrill's eyes. She just shook her head, as if words had failed her. He glanced back toward the shore. Fig stood at the stern, fingers twisted through the rumor vines coiled around the railing, eyes looking lost and beaten. Behind her, smoke curled up into the sky. The sound of the whirlpool growled low in the distance, spinning the Iron Tide out to devour the Stream.

Fin turned back to Remy. He didn't miss the telltale sign of recent tears. Perhaps the babysitter didn't need to know how bad things really were just yet.

He raised his arms in a halfhearted shrug. "Mission accomplished?"

Epilogue

Marrill leaned against the stern railing, looking out at the devastation behind them as the *Kraken* made its way past the rocks of Meres, out toward the open Stream. With a deep sigh, she cradled Karnelius tighter, the feeling of his soft belly fuzz the only thing that gave her any comfort. The rumor vines softly echoed his contented purrs.

On the one hand, at least there was something behind them to see. They'd come to stop the Lost Sun from destroying the Stream, and they'd succeeded. They'd lost nearly everything in the process, however.

Coll was gone, trapped eternally in the tentacles of the Sheshefesh. Annalessa, they now knew, had voluntarily given up her humanity to become one with the Map to Everywhere. Rose, who Annalessa had become, was caged even now in the grasp of the Master of the Iron Ship.

Fin had found his mother, but now she was dead. His people were slaves to their own twins, and the rebellion he'd started had ended as soon as the Salt Sand King returned from his eons-long exile in Monerva.

As for Marrill herself, she'd always assumed the crew of the *Kraken* would be able to find her a way home—after they figured out a way to cure her mother, of course. Without a wizard or a navigator, she now had no hope of finding either. And of course, they had no power to stop the Iron Tide. No weapon to stave off the Salt Sand King and his invincible army. No means of fighting the Master...

"Oh, Ardent," she whispered.

ohardentohardentohardentsohardenedohardent

"Well, the Naysayer poked Serth a couple of times and we think he's done for," Fin announced, slipping up to the rail beside her. "Didn't want to take a pulse, in case his skin would still freeze me. Or burn me. Or whatever."

His voice trailed off as his gaze lingered on what lay

behind them. Fire raged across the dark woods of Meres, and Marrill could just make out the figures of the Rise silhouetted along the coastline, jumping and cheering as they boarded their ships. At least the *Kraken* had too good of a head start for them to catch her. According to Remy, the moment the fire began, the Rise had become way more interested in welcoming their lost king than continuing their pursuit of the *Kraken*.

"I wonder how Vell is doing as the new Crest of the Rise," Fin offered. He smiled, clearly trying to joke about it.

But Marrill didn't feel like laughing. "Everything is awful," she whispered, the words dripping like tears out of her mouth.

everythingisawfulawfulawfulawful

Fin put his arm around her shoulders. "Hey, we've still got some good things! We've got Karny." He dropped a hand down the cat's back. "We've got the *Kraken*. We've got Remy. We've got Fig." Marrill lifted an eyebrow, not recognizing the name. "You know her, she's good people, promise," he said. "We've got the *Naysayer.*"

Marrill groaned. "Okay, that's a negative," she teased. Though she had to admit, just the thought of it did make her *almost* smile.

"We've got each other," Fin offered.

Marrill leaned against him. "Yeah," she said. "We do

have each other. And I guess there's no one else I'd rather watch the world be destroyed in four different ways with than you."

Fin laughed. "Thanks," he said. Marrill couldn't help but smile. They sat in silence for a long moment, watching the ruined heart of the Stream slip farther and farther away.

Finally, Fin cleared his throat. "What do you think happened back there, anyway? With Ardent?"

Marrill bit her lip, trying to keep her warring emotions at bay. If she let them come all at once, it would just be too much—she would be overwhelmed. "I don't know." She shook her head as tears ran down her cheeks.

She couldn't even think of everything that they'd lost in Ardent. Of what he'd meant to her. Of how he'd betrayed them. She couldn't even imagine *why*. She held Karny close, struggling to push the thoughts away.

But there was one thought she couldn't avoid. One truth she knew she had to face. Because all the devastation before them—the Salt Sand King's release, the Iron Tide, maybe even going back to the Meressian Prophecy itself—it all came back to the Master of the Iron Ship. Whatever Ardent had put into motion, they had to stop it.

Marrill sucked in a deep breath, feeling it power her resolve. "But we have to find out," she said sharply.

"Great," Fin said with a snort. "And how do we do that exactly?"

Marrill felt her willpower collapse into a sigh. "Uhm..."

"You follow him," a voice answered from behind them. As one, Fin and Marrill whirled around. Serth stood against the windows of Ardent's cabin. The setting sun shone through from the open door on the other side, backlighting his tall form.

"The whirlpool has taken him back in time." He swept toward them, dark robes flowing out as he moved. White stars sparkled as he drew closer. "Back to the birth of the Stream."

Marrill cringed instinctively as the cruel wizard looked down at her and Fin. Black streaks still marked the trails of the tears he'd cried for centuries. But his eyes were calm, collected, severe.

Marrill looked at Fin. Fin looked at Marrill. Together, they looked into the face of the man who had been the worst enemy either of them had ever known.

"To follow him there, you will need a guide," Serth continued. The once-porcelain skin flushed with the flow of life. "Someone who has been there before." His mouth trembled into a smile.

"Which," he said, "I have."

ACKNOWLEDGMENTS

You would think sailing straight into the sun would make it hard to lose your way, but when the water glows like the sky, pretty soon everything looks the same and you're blind and a bit mad, to boot. Our eternal thanks to our editor, Deirdre Jones, for being the visor that shaded our eyes and showed us the way forward.

Thanks also to Jenny Choy, Sherri Schmidt, Rosanne Lauer, Annie McDonnell, Sasha Illingworth, Angela Taldone, Virginia Lawther, Kristina Pisciotta, Emilie Polster, Kheryn Callender, and everyone else at Little, Brown Books for Young Readers and Orion's Children's Books for keeping the holes plugged and the ship sailing ever forward while we sighted the distant star. And of course, we could never forget chief wizard extraordinaire Victoria Stapleton, who seems to have a quite good relationship with the wind, because she kept it ever at our backs and in our sails.

Also, as always, thanks to Merrilee Heifetz and the good people at Writer's House, for keeping us cool and composed when the light burned brightest. A special thanks to Cecilia de la Campa for rushing to the rudder when the seas picked up unexpectedly and saving us from being swallowed by the whirlpool we didn't even know was right in our path.

Todd Harris's keen eye and unwavering vision managed to sketch the strange shapes revealed by the Lost Sun, no matter how bizarre or terrifying they might be. Without him, the Stream would truly be formless. Red @ 28th and the Flying Biscuit Café gave us a place to lie down in the shade, and Sarah MacLean, Beth Revis, Diana Peterfreund, Ally Carter, Rose Brock, Brendan Reichs, Renee Ahdieh, the folks at Bat Cave, Phillip Lewis, Ross Richardson, and all the folks at FDWNC helped us suss out the meaning in the shadows we saw there.

Our families, as always, were water for our parched lips; without them, the trip would scarcely have been worth making. A very special thanks to Corey Sell for demanding a talking cat—even if we couldn't quite give him a flying one.

More than anyone, however, we want to thank all our readers, for walking into the sun with us. A special shout-out to Rachel Hester, who we have never met, but whose courage and humor is visible from far beyond the horizon. Also to Jacki Altmeyer and her book club at St. Patrick's Elementary in Dilworth for showing us places on the Stream we had never imagined (though Ardent, of course, had been to all of them).

Finally, we can't end this journey without acknowledging the friend we lost along the way. To Heather Heady—for everything you did, for all the support you gave, and most of all, for caring. You are missed. May your light never fade.